DEBORAH

CROMBIE

A SHARE IN DEATH

AVON BOOKS
An Imprint of HarperCollins*Publishers*

This is a work of fiction. Names, characters, places, and incidents are products of the author's imagination or are used fictitiously and are not to be construed as real. Any resemblance to actual events, locales, organizations, or persons, living or dead, is entirely coincidental.

AVON BOOKS
An Imprint of Harper Collins*Publishers*
195 Broadway,
New York, NY 10007.

ISBN: 0-06-053438-9
www.avonmystery.com

Reprinted by arrangement with Scribner, an imprint of Simon & Schuster, Inc.

First Avon Books paperback printing: September 2003

Printed in the U.S.A.

20 19 17 16 15 14 13 12

For Warren Norwood,
who laid the foundation.

*Acknowledgments*

I'd like to say an enormous thanks to Diane Sullivan, Dale Denton, Viqui Litman, Aaron Goldblatt, John Hardie and Jim Evans. They stuck with the manuscript from beginning to end, and their help was invaluable.

Thanks are also due to Susanne Kirk, my editor, and to Nancy Yost, my agent, for their support and encouragement.

A SHARE IN DEATH

1

Duncan Kincaid's holiday began well. As he turned the car into the lane, a shaft of sun broke through the clouds and lit a patch of rolling Yorkshire moor as if someone had thrown the switch on a celestial spotlight.

Drystone walls ran like pale runes across the brilliant green of pasture, where luminous sheep nibbled, unconcerned with their importance in the composition. The scene seemed set off in time as well as space, and gave him the sensation of viewing a living tapestry, a world remote and utterly unattainable. The clouds shifted again, the vision fading as swiftly as it had come, and he felt an odd shiver of loss at its passing.

The last few weeks' grind must be catching up with him, he thought, shrugging away the faint sense of foreboding. New Scotland Yard didn't officially require newly promoted Detective Superintendents to work themselves into early coronaries, but August Bank Holiday had slipped easily into September, and he'd gone right on accumulating his time off. Something always came up, and the last case had been particularly beastly.

A string of bodies in rural Sussex, all women, all similarly mutilated—a policeman's worst nightmare. They'd found him in the end, a real nutter, but there was no guarantee that the evidence they'd so painstakingly gathered would convince a bleeding-heart jury, and the senselessness of it took most of the satisfaction from finishing up the mountain of paperwork.

"Lovely way to spend your Saturday night," Gemma James, Kincaid's sergeant, had said the evening before as they waded through the last of the case files.

"Tell the recruiters that. I doubt it occurred to them." Kincaid grinned at her across his littered desk. Gemma wouldn't grace a poster at the moment, her face white with fatigue, carbon smudge like a bruise along her cheekbone.

She puffed out her cheeks and blew at the wisps of red hair that straggled into her eyes. "You're just as well out of it for a week. Too bad some of us don't have cousins with posh holiday flats, or whatever it is."

"Do I detect a trace of envy?"

"You're off to Yorkshire tomorrow, and I'm off home to do a week's worth of washing and go round the shops? Can't imagine why." Gemma smiled at him with her usual good humor, but when she spoke next her voice held a trace of motherly concern. "You look knackered. It's about time you had a break. It'll do you a world of good, I'm sure."

Such solicitousness from his sergeant, ten years his junior, amused Kincaid, but it was a new experience and he found he didn't really object. He'd pushed for his promotion because it meant getting away from the desk and out into the field again, but he'd begun to think that the best thing about it might be the acquisition of Sergeant Gemma James. In her late twenties, divorced, raising a small son on her own—Gemma's good-natured demeanor, Kincaid was discovering, concealed a quick mind and a fierce ambition.

"I don't think it's exactly my cup of tea," he said, shuffling the last loose sheets of paper into a file folder. "A timeshare."

"Your cousin, is it, who arranged this for you?"

Kincaid nodded. "His wife's expecting and their doctor's decided at the last moment that she shouldn't leave London, so they thought of me, rather than let their week go to waste."

"Fortune," Gemma had countered, teasing him a bit, "has a way of picking on the less deserving."

Too tired even for their customary after work stop at the pub, Gemma had gone off to Leyton, and Kincaid had stumbled home to his Hampstead flat and slept the dreamless sleep of the truly exhausted. And now, deserving or not, he intended to make the most of this unexpected gift.

As he hesitated at the top of the lane, still unsure of his direction, the sun came through fully and beat down upon the roof of the car. Suddenly it was a perfect late September day, warm and golden, full of promise. "A propitious omen for a holiday," he said aloud, and felt some of his weariness drop away. Now, if only he could find Followdale House. The arrow for Woolsey-under-Bank pointed directly across a sheep pasture. Time to consult the map again.

He drove slowly, elbow out the Midget's open window, breathing in the spicy scent of the hedgerows and watching for some indication that he was on the right track. The lane wound past occasional farms, squarely and sturdily built in gray, Yorkshire slate, and above them the moor stretched fingers of woodland enticingly down into the pastures. Crisp nights must have preceded this blaze of Indian summer, as the trees were already turning, the copper and gold interspersed with an occasional splash of green. In the distance, above the patchwork of field and pasture and low moorland, the ground rose steeply away to a high bank.

Rounding a curve, Kincaid found himself at the head of a picture-book village. Stone cottages hugged the lane, and pots and planters filled with geraniums and petunias trailed cascades of color into the road. On his right, a massive stone half-circle bore the legend "Woolsey-under-Bank." The high rise of land, now seeming to hang over the village, must be Sutton Bank.

A few yards further on his left, a gap in the high hedge revealed a stone gate-post inset with a brass plaque. The inscription read "Followdale," and beneath it was engraved a curving, full-blown rose. Kincaid whistled under his breath. Very posh indeed, he thought as he turned the car into the narrow gateway and stopped on the gravel forecourt. He surveyed the house and grounds spread before him with surprise and pleasure. He didn't quite know what he had expected of an English timeshare. Transplanted Costa del Sol, perhaps, or tacky Victorian. Not this Georgian house, certainly—elegant and imposing in its simplicity, honey-gilded in the late-afternoon light. A tangle of ivy softened portions of the ground-floor walls, and bright Virginia creeper splashed the upper part of the house like a scarlet stain.

Closer inspection revealed his initial impression of the house to be deceptive—it was not truly symmetrical. Although a wing extended either side of the pediment-crowned entry, the left side of the house was larger and jutted out into the forecourt. He found the illusion of balance more pleasing, not as severe and demanding as the real thing.

Kincaid stretched and unfolded himself from his battered MG Midget. Only the fact that the springs in the driver's seat had collapsed years ago kept his head from brushing the soft top when he drove. He stood for a moment, looking about him. To the west, a low row of cottages, built of the same golden stone as the house—to the east, the manicured grounds stretched away toward the bulk of Sutton Bank.

Ease seemed to seep into the very pores of his skin, and not until he felt himself taking slow, deep breaths did he realize just how tense he'd been. Pushing the last, niggling thoughts of work to the edge of his mind, he took his grip from the boot and walked toward the house.

The heavy oak-paneled front door was off the latch. It swung open at Kincaid's touch, and he found himself in a typical country-house entry, complete with Wellingtons and umbrella stand. In the hall beyond, a Chinese bowl of bronze chrysanthemums on a side table clashed with the patterned crimson carpeting. The still air smelled of furniture polish.

A woman's voice could be heard clearly through the partly open door on his left, the words bitten off with furious precision. "Listen, you little leech. I'm telling you for the last time to lay off my private affairs. I'm sick of your snooping and prying when you think nobody's watching." Kincaid heard the sharp intake of the woman's breath. "What I do in my off-hours is nobody else's business, least of all yours. You've done well to get as far as you have, considering your background and your attributes." The emphasis on the last word was scathing. "But, by god, I'll see you stopped. You made a mistake when you thought you'd climb over me."

"As if I'd want to!" Kincaid grinned in spite of himself at the intimation, as the second voice continued. "Get off it, Cassie. You're a right cow. Just because you've wormed your way into the manager's job doesn't make you Lord High Executioner. Besides," the speaker added, with what seemed to be a touch of malice, "you wouldn't dare complain about me. I may not give a damn about your doings with the paying guests, but I don't think they would quite fit with the corporate idea of country gentility, unless they're thinking of re-creating an Edwardian house party. I wonder how you're going to manage this week. Musical beds?" The voice was male, Kincaid thought, but light and slightly nasal, with a trace of Yorkshire vowels.

Kincaid stepped softly backwards to the front door, opened it and slammed it forcefully, then strode briskly across the hall and tapped on the partially open door before peering around it.

The woman stood behind a graceful Queen Anne table which apparently served as a reception desk, her back to the window, hands arrested in the gesture of straightening a stack of papers. Her companion leaned against the frame of the opposite door, hands in his pockets, with a slightly amused expression on his face. "Hello. Can I help you?" the woman said, smiling at Kincaid with utter composure, showing no sign of the fury he had so recently overheard.

"Have I got the right place?" Kincaid asked tentatively.

"If you're looking for Followdale House. I'm Cassie Whitlake, the sales manager. And you must be Mr. Kincaid."

He smiled at her as he stepped forward into the room and set down his bag. "How did you guess?"

"Simple elimination, really. Sunday afternoon is our usual check-in time, and all the other guests have either already arrived or don't fit the particulars your cousin gave us."

"There's nothing worse than being preceded by one's reputation. I hope it wasn't too damaging." Kincaid felt surprisingly relieved. She hadn't addressed him by his rank. Maybe his cousin Jack had managed to be discreet for once, and he could enjoy his holiday as an ordinary and anonymous member of the British public.

"On the contrary." Her brows arched as she spoke, lending a flirtatious air to the polite reply, and leaving Kincaid wondering uneasily just what Jack might, after all, have said.

He studied Cassie Whitlake with interest. Hard-pressed, he'd judge her around thirty, but she had the sort of looks that make age difficult to assess. She was tall, as elegant as the curved lines of her desk, and striking in a monochromatic way. Her hair and eyes were the color of fallen oak leaves, her skin a pale cream, her simple wool dress a slightly more intense shade than her hair. It occurred to him that she must have chosen the mums in the hallway—they would complement her perfectly.

Throughout the exchange her companion had kept his casual stance, following the conversation with quick bird-like motions of his head. Now he removed his right hand from his pocket and came toward Kincaid.

"I'm Sebastian Wade, assistant manager, or lackey to Lady Di here, depending on your point of view," he said, offering his hand. He glanced quickly at Cassie, gauging the effect of his barb, then grinned at Kincaid as he shook his hand. There seemed to be genuine warmth in his greeting, and Kincaid found himself more drawn to Wade's engaging maliciousness than to Cassie Whitlake's polished cordiality. A slightly built man in his late twenties, Wade had butter-yellow hair, fashionably cut, and pockmarked skin over thin and rather delicate features. His eyes were unexpectedly dark.

Cassie moved quickly around her desk and disengaged Kincaid with a touch of cool fingers on his arm. "I'll show you to your suite. Then when you've had a chance to settle in, I'll give you a tour and answer any questions you might have." Sebastian Wade lifted a hand to him in mock salute as Cassie led him from the room.

As Kincaid followed her into the hall he admired the way the soft fabric of her dress clung to the outline of her body. A hint of some sharp, musky perfume drifted back to him, not the sort of scent he would have expected from one so elegantly groomed. But he had been right about her height—her head was almost level with his own.

She turned back to him as she started up the stairs. "I think your suite is the best in the house. Such a shame for your cousin and his wife to have to cancel their holiday at the last minute. Fortunate for you, though," she added, and again he heard the hint of archness.

"Yes," Kincaid answered, and wondered for a moment how his kindly, guileless cousin had fared under Cassie Whitlake's sophisticated onslaught.

At the top of the stairs he followed Cassie down a hall that ran toward the rear of the house, ending at a door adorned with a discreet, brass number four. Cassie unlocked the door with her own key and preceded him into the tiny entry. Kincaid couldn't maneuver his bag through the small space without brushing up against her, and the smile she gave him was suggestive.

The entry opened into a sitting room in which Cassie's hand was again evident in the decorating, at least in the choice of colors. The plush sofas and armchairs were a dull gold with rolled arms, buttons and fringes, the curtains were olive green, and the figured carpet combined the two in a fussy, geometric marriage. The whole room, which could have been lifted en masse from any middle-class department store showroom, gave an impression of solid, anonymous respectability.

The room's saving grace was the French door at its far end. Cassie followed Kincaid as he crossed the room, set down his bag, and pulled open the door. They stepped out onto the narrow balcony together. Below them stretched the grounds and gardens of Followdale, leading his eyes up to the bulk of Sutton Bank rising in the distance.

"There's the tennis court." Cassie pointed down to his left. "And the greenhouse. We have croquet and badminton and lawn bowling, as well as riding and walking trails. Oh, and indoor swimming, of course. The pool is one of our star attractions. I think we'll keep you occupied."

"I'm overwhelmed." Kincaid grinned. "I may have a nervous collapse trying to decide what to do."

"In the meantime, I'll let you get settled in. If you want to lay in some supplies, it's only a few steps down the road to the village shop. There's a cocktail party at six in the sitting room, so the guests have a chance to get acquainted."

"I'm afraid I haven't any experience with timesharing. Don't the other guests already know each other, all of them owning the same week?"

"Not really. New people buy in all the time. Owners trade weeks, or use their time somewhere else, so you never really know who's going to turn up. We have several first-timers this week, as a matter of fact."

"Good. I won't be the only novice, then. How many guests are there?"

Cassie leaned back against the balcony rail and

folded her arms, patient with his tourist's curiosity. "Well, there are eight suites in the main house, and three cottage-type accommodations in another building. You may have noticed it to your left as you drove up to the house. I'm using one of the cottages myself right now, the one at the far end." Her spiel of facts and figures came effortlessly, her delivery as smooth as her voice.

She looked steadily and directly into his eyes, and attractive as she was, the calculated and somehow impersonal invitation made him feel uncomfortable. Moved by a perverse desire to ruffle her, to indicate that he was not one to be so easily manipulated, he asked, "Does your assistant live here on the premises as well? He seems a pleasant chap."

Cassie straightened up abruptly. Her voice, as she delivered Sebastian Wade's social condemnation, betrayed a hint of the venom he had heard earlier. "No. In the town with his old mum. She keeps the tobacconist's shop." She brushed her hands together, as if disposing of crumbs. "If you'll excuse me, I've things to do. Let me know if you need anything, otherwise I'll see you later." The smile was brief this time, and held no invitation. Cassie slipped past and left him alone on the balcony.

2

Penelope Mackenzie stole a furtive look into the suite's sitting room, where her sister Emma seemed to be absorbed in checking her life-list against today's notations in her birding notebook. Penny settled herself more comfortably in front of the bedroom window with a quick sigh of relief. She'd have a few more minutes with no demands, a small escape from her sister's solicitous supervision.

Things were different before Father died. Penny hadn't been forgetful then, really; just a little absent-minded sometimes. But after those last, long months of Father's illness some of the tenuous connections between thought and action just seemed to dissolve.

Only last week she'd put a saucepan of water on the cooker and gone into the sitting room for a book. When she remembered the pan, the water had all boiled away and the middle layer of the pan's bottom had melted and run across the cooker's top in a silvery flood. And then there was the leftover Sunday roast she popped into the oven instead of the fridge. Emma had been furious when she discovered it the next day and had to throw it away.

But those were the little things. Penny didn't like to think about the day she went down to the shops in the village, did her errands, and found she couldn't remember how to get home. Instead of the memory of the well-worn path through Dedham village and up the hill to Ivy Cottage, there was only an emptiness in her mind.

She stumbled, terrified, into the familiar warmth of her friend Mary's tea shop. She sat there perspiring, chatting and drinking hot, sweet tea, trying to pretend a gaping hole hadn't opened in her universe, until she saw a neighbor pass. She caught up to him, and asked breathlessly, "Are you going home? I'll walk with you, shall I, George?" As she walked, familiarity with her surroundings returned, filling the vacant space, but the fear settled itself comfortably inside her. She told no one, most particularly not Emma.

Perhaps a holiday was all she needed, a fortnight with no responsibilities. It had taken her long enough to convince Emma that they deserved something after their years with Father. After all, they had his money now and could do what they pleased. She'd seen the timeshare brochure herself, at the travel agent's in the village. And Followdale was lovely, every bit as lovely as she'd imagined.

"Daydreaming as usual, Pen?" Her sister's voice startled her. "Stir yourself, then. We'd best be getting to the shops if we're to return in time to dress for the party." Emma pulled her waterproof jacket out of the wardrobe and began buckling herself into it with her usual no-nonsense briskness.

"Yes, Emma, coming," Penny answered. There was no need to make Emma cross, or even worse, to try her until she spoke with that unaccustomed air of gentle patience. Penny rubbed her forehead with her fingertips, as if the physical smoothing of lines would return the accustomed veneer of placid cheerfulness to her face, and smiled brightly when Emma turned to her.

Twenty-eight . . . twenty-nine . . . thirty . . . Hannah Alcock sat in front of the mirror and counted the smooth, circular motions of the hairbrush. Odd, she thought, how childhood habits stayed with you. She knew of no logical reason why hair should be brushed a hundred strokes a day, but if she closed her eyes for a moment she could see herself sitting at her old dresser in her nightgown, watching the arc of the brush descend through her long, brown hair, and hearing her mother's voice from the hall, "Hannah, darling, remember to brush your hair."

All that was a long time ago—almost thirty years, in fact, since the night she had taken the scissors to her waist-length hair. It had lain like a pall across her back, a rich, shining chestnut brown with glints of auburn, her mother's pride, and she had brutally hacked it off just at the nape of her neck.

Although she'd kept her hair cut short in the years since, she had continued the nightly brushing. A silly ritual, one that should have been discarded with that remote adolescence, but when she was nervous, as she was tonight, she found it oddly comforting. Her stomach muscles relaxed as she breathed with the rhythm of the strokes, and by the time she laid the silver-backed brush neatly beside its matching mirror, she felt a little more capable of getting through the evening.

The cocktail party had already been in progress for a quarter of an hour. If she didn't hurry she would be more than fashionably late. Still, she continued to examine herself in the glass. A good face, she had come to think, once she had outgrown a girl's desire for conventional prettiness. Those round, blond fluffy girls she had so envied were faded now, their skin puffy, hair streaked and tipped to cover the encroaching gray. Her own hair, now carefully and expensively cut, held only a few silvery threads at the temples, and the strong, underlying bone structure she had despised now gave her face an arresting individuality.

It had been years since she had worried about others' opinions. Successful, confident, serene—she thought nothing could disturb her carefully built balance. Nothing, that is, until the strange, slow stirrings of the last year had grown within her, warping the shape of her life, leading her finally to take action that might prove irrevocable folly.

She had planned this face-to-face meeting with all the attention she would have given the most demanding experiment, hiring a private detective to ferret out the details of his life, buying into the timeshare for the exact same week—yet here she was, dithering at the last minute, suffering from stage-fright like the gawky schoolgirl she had once been.

What had she to lose, after all? They might spend a week passing in the halls, a greeting, a casual physical contact, and then he would leave without remembering her name or face. Surely, there could be no harm in that?

Or they might become friends. She wouldn't think beyond that—what she might say to him, how he would react. Tonight, with an easy introduction and polite exchange of trifles sure to follow, was beginning enough.

She rose, picked up her bag from the sitting room, and shut the front door firmly behind her.

Duncan Kincaid leaned on his balcony rail, reluctant to move, reluctant to knot a tie around his throat, to go through the civilized motions required if he were to meet his social obligations. His earlier burst of energy had given way to a creeping lethargy.

It would be easy enough to fix himself some supper, then stretch out on the sofa with the battered paperback copy of *Jane Eyre* he'd found in the drawer of the bedside table. The eggs, bacon, and loaf of fresh-baked whole-meal bread he'd bought at the village shop would be sufficient provision for a quiet evening.

He had been browsing in the shop's biscuit aisle when a girlish voice behind him chirped, "You must be the new guest. We've been so eager to meet you." He turned, and found himself facing a slight woman wrapped in a voluminous, tartan cape. She was, he judged, sixtyish, with a fluffy bird's nest of gray hair surrounding a thin face and a pair of extraordinarily blue eyes. Peeping from the folds of the cape's bottom were a pair of old-fashioned, lace-up ladies' boots.

"Cassie told us your name was Kincaid and we were so thrilled—a Scot, like us, you see—we're MacKenzies. Our granddad had quite a place in Perthshire in his day." The sentences tumbled from her mouth in a breathless flood. "It must have seemed just like this in the old days, I mean how it is at Followdale. I can just imagine—"

Kincaid, amused, interrupted. "You don't live in Scotland now?"

"Oh no. Our father . . . well, you see, there were so many sons that he was forced to find an occupation. He took a position in Essex when he was quite a young man. He was Rector, in Dedham, for forty years before he retired. But all that seems a long time ago, now." She smiled up at him, a little wistfully. "We live there still, Emma and I, though of course somebody else has the old rectory now. We raise goats. Wonderful animals, don't you think? So sanitary, and there's quite a good market for goat's milk and cheese these days. Although Father could never really bring himself to approve. And what about you, Mr. Kincaid? Where did your family come from?"

"I'm a second generation immigrant, like yourself. My father moved from Edinburgh to Cheshire before I was born, and he married an English girl, so I guess my ancestral stock is pretty diluted. And call—"

"I'm Emma MacKenzie," broke in the woman Kincaid had noticed paying at the counter. "My sister Penelope." She took his hand in a firm, dry clasp. "How do you do?"

With her straight, gray, pudding-bowl hair, her mannish, waterproof jacket and her uncompromising expression, she reminded Kincaid of his sixth-form master. Her only ornament was the pair of binoculars slung from her heavy neck. The sisters Prim and Grim, he dubbed them, then felt rather shamefaced.

"I'm sure Mr. Kincaid doesn't want to hear all our family history, Penny. And we must go if we're to change for the party." Emma nodded at him and herded her sister away with all the delicacy of a school chaperon.

"Miss MacKenzie," he called out, as they were almost through the door, "it was nice to meet you. Perhaps I'll see you at the party." He was rewarded by a radiant smile.

A loud knocking on the sitting-room door roused Kincaid and he realized that the air on the balcony had grown chilly. He slipped inside and opened the front door to find Sebastian Wade raising his fist to knock again.

"Sorry," Wade said, "sometimes my enthusiasm gets the better of me. I came to offer myself as escort to the little get-together, and to show you around the house, if Cassie hasn't already done the honors."

"She did promise me a tour, but it never materialized. I'd like to see the house."

"Ah, what a treat you have in store. Manufactured gentility, with all the mod cons. Are you going as is, the weekend gentleman's casual look?" He eyed Kincaid's open-necked shirt and cords.

"No, let me get my jacket," Kincaid answered, and he saw that for all his deliberation his decision had been made for him. He was carried along as easily as a shell in a wave.

"Your suite," said Sebastian in his most facetious tour guide manner, "is called the Sutton Suite, because you have a view of Sutton Bank from your balcony. Clever, yes? They all have the most wonderfully inventive names. So much more personal, the homey touch, like naming one's suburban semi-detached 'Wayside Cottage.' Directly below you is the Thirsk Suite, currently possessed by our rising young M.P., Patrick Rennie, and his wife, Marta, of the perpetual ponytail and black velvet bow. Very county. They own several weeks, spaced out over the year."

Kincaid finished tying his tie in the sitting-room mirror, slipped into his jacket and patted his pockets for wallet and keys.

"Now," continued Sebastian, as they closed the front door and descended the three steps to the main hall, "the suite next to yours on this floor, the Richmond, was taken this morning by Hannah Alcock, a scientist of some sort who looks very professional and efficient. Attractive, too, in a sleek, bony way, if one cares for women who look intelligent." He darted a bright, malicious glance toward Kincaid.

"And you don't?"

"Oh yes, I find a lot of women aesthetically pleasing," answered Sebastian, with the sly ambiguity Kincaid was coming to expect. "Now, the door on your immediate right leads to the pool balcony." He opened it, gesturing Kincaid through first.

Moisture and the odor of chlorine assaulted Kincaid's senses, and his first impression of the small balcony was that he had fallen into a budget Mediterranean fantasy. The floor was covered with glazed red brick, green plants filled every available space, and a black wrought-iron railing overlooked the water below.

"Most ingenious, don't you think? A vantage point

from which we can view our guests cavorting merrily in the pool, that most upmarket of all our assets. Works well in the sales tours, I can tell you. Unless, of course, the guest weighs two hundred pounds and is wearing a string bikini."

Kincaid laughed. "You seem not to consider me a very viable prospect."

Sebastian considered him, his voice for once without its biting edge. "No. I'd say you're not easily seduced by respectability. You have other weaknesses, perhaps? But you wouldn't choose this, would you, if the holiday weren't given to you as a gift?"

Kincaid thought about it. "No, you're right, as pleasant as it is, I probably wouldn't. Too structured. Too cozy. I feel a bit like a child sent to day camp."

"Pudding after supper if you're a good boy. Come on, then. You'd better make the most of the experience if you're not likely to repeat it." Sebastian returned to his professional patter. "There are stairs at the back of this first-floor hall," he noted, gesturing to the side opposite Kincaid's, "that lead down to the rear pool entrance. There is also a spa section of the pool, just beneath us. It's kept heated and you can turn on the jets when you want to use it. I do like it myself; one of the perks of the job."

Kincaid imagined that Sebastian Wade, engaged in a continuous game of one-up-manship with the management, took advantage of any and every perk the job offered as a matter of principle.

They moved across the balcony and through the door into the cooler air of the opposite hall. "The layout's not symmetrical." Sebastian pointed toward the back of the house. "That suite is occupied by the Lyles, from Hertfordshire or somewhere equally dreary. Fussy little man, ex-army, though you wouldn't think it—he looks a perfect twit. He bent my ear this afternoon for what seemed like hours, all about his experiences in Ireland. You'd think he conquered the IRA singlehandedly. For my part, I doubt he tackled anything more dangerous than the Corps of Engineers."

Kincaid grinned at the idea of Sebastian, with his minute and indiscreet attention to detail, describing someone else as fussy.

"This one in the middle is an up-and-down studio affair. That's the Hunsingers, Maureen and John. Retrograde hippies who own a natural foods store in Manchester, arrived last week with their eminently healthy kids." Sebastian looked inquiringly at Kincaid. "You understand that not all the guests arrive and leave at the same time?"

They moved down the hall toward the front landing. "The Frazers, for instance, in the front suite, have been here a week as well. Father and daughter." Kincaid waited for the quip, but none came. Sebastian pushed open the door to the front landing, his face averted.

"What are they like?" asked Kincaid, his curiosity aroused.

"I'll let you form your own opinion," said Sebastian a little shortly. After a moment's awkward silence, he relented. "Nasty divorce. Angela's just fifteen and she's the prize of war. Neither of them really want her and she knows it." The camouflage manner had dropped away, and the light voice was bitter.

Kincaid had the feeling that for the second time that

evening he had glimpsed beneath the brittle shell. A glimpse, however, seemed to be all he was going to get, for Sebastian started down the wide stairs to the entry hall and continued his monologue over his shoulder.

"That leaves the ground floor. The front suite is empty this week. It's called the Herriot, by the way. Just luck we didn't get the Siegfried and Tristan as well. We do like to capitalize on our local celebrities whenever we can. The Rennies we mentioned, and the rear suite on the other side holds the week's treasures, the MacKenzie sisters from Dedham Vale. The dear ladies have enjoyed the first week of their visit immensely—it warms my heart." Seeing Kincaid's smile of recognition, he continued, "I see you've encountered them. But don't let appearances fool you. Emma might be more likely to have been painted by Munnings than Constable, but I don't believe she's quite the battle-ax she'd like you to think, nor the fair Penny quite so dim."

They had reached the entry, and paused. "And the cottages?" asked Kincaid.

"Empty. Except Cassie's." Another closed subject, Kincaid presumed from the abruptness of Sebastian's answer. "The reception room you've seen. Beyond that is the sitting room, which leads into the White Rose Bar. Encourages convivial meetings among the owners. It's supposed to work on an honor system, but you can always tell the ones who don't pay. It's that furtive survey of the room after they've poured a drink, to see if anyone will notice whether they've put money in the bowl."

Sebastian studied himself in the hall mirror, flicked a pale strand of hair into place with his fingertips, then adjusted the fit of his pleated, linen trousers around his narrow waist. "Well, fun and games time. Shall I lead you to the slaughter?" His glance, as conspiratorial as a wink, left Kincaid the uncomfortable impression that he was as transparent to Sebastian Wade as the rest of the world's poor mugs.

The air of the sitting room was pungent with smoke, the throat-catching stuffiness exacerbated by the electric bars glowing red in the fireplace. The guests stood huddled in self-protective groups on the red-and-green patterned carpet, their voices rising in an indistinguishable chorus.

Sebastian led him to the bar and poured him a lager. While he waited, Kincaid noticed a room behind the bar that Sebastian hadn't mentioned. Unlike the polished and uncluttered reception room where Cassie had received him, this was a working office. A gray metal desk and filing cabinet, a sturdy secretarial chair, and a scarred wooden coatrack replaced Queen Anne elegance. Papers partially covered the adding machine and spilled from the desk on to the typewriter. This must be Cassie's domain, the nerve center of the house. No wonder Sebastian had seen fit to ignore it.

Carrying their drinks, they threaded their way back across the sitting room to a vantage point near the door. Sebastian leaned back against the wall with one foot propped behind him and surveyed the room with lively interest. "Now," he said, "Guessing game time. Let's see if you can place the rest of the group." Four people stood bunched in front of the mantel, drinks in hand, attention half on the conversation and half on the room, in the manner of those accustomed to cocktail gatherings. "Scoping things out, aren't they? Making sure they're not missing something more interesting." Sebastian took a sip of his drink, and waited for Kincaid to pin the face to the description.

"Um," said Kincaid, rising to the challenge, "the tall, fair man with the Savile Row tailoring. The M.P.?" Slender, with sleek hair cut to perfection, he had prominent cheekbones that lent distinction to the planes of his face. Even the nails on the hand holding the glass gleamed with careful buffing. When Sebastian nodded, Kincaid continued. "It's not just the looks. He has that air of being on public display, of expecting to be watched. Now, the woman with the frizzy hair and the drooping denim dress. Not his wife, surely? The health store owner. Maureen, wasn't it." Sebastian grinned in approval.

A weedy-looking middle-aged man with thinning hair and spectacles seemed to be monopolizing the conversation. The others' faces expressed varying degrees of disinterest and outright boredom. "Mr. Lyle, from Hertfordshire. Right? And the dark-haired woman with the long-suffering expression must be his wife."

"Bravo. Right so far. Can you polish them off?"

"You make them sound like hors d'oeuvres." Kincaid scanned the room obediently, enjoying the test of his memory for names and descriptions.

At a table near the window sat a bulky man, his thinning hair perhaps compensated for by the great ruff of soft, brown beard covering his chin. He played a game with two small children, and though their faces were intent on a board, he seemed uncomfortable in his jacket and tie. His fingers pulled at his collar and his shoulders moved restively inside the coat. "The rest of the Hunsingers, without a doubt."

Sebastian hadn't heard him. His attention was focused on a girl, standing alone against the wall. She still carried an extra layer of padding, baby fat that softened and blurred her features and made Kincaid think of an unset pudding. The ring of dark shadow surrounding her eyes gave her a nocturnal look, and her spiky, violet-streaked hair seemed a natural extension of her sullen pout. Kincaid nudged Sebastian and spoke softly. "Angela? Maybe you'd better go and see if you can cheer her up. I'm sure I can look after myself."

"Right," said Sebastian. "See you."

Kincaid regretted it almost immediately. Bearing down on him from around the sofa came the woman in the denim dress, armed with a resolute smile. She must have been waiting her chance, he thought, looking around for an escape. A woman standing hesitantly in the doorway caught his eye. She wore a jumpsuit of a silky fabric, cream-colored, splashed with roses, a perfect foil for her striking, angular looks. The missing scientist, he thought, but before he could take a step toward her, Maureen Hunsinger was upon him in a tidal wave of good intention.

Hannah found the party well in progress, and as she entered the lounge, arranged her face in what she hoped was an expression of pleasant anticipation. She made for the bar and fixed herself a whiskey, not able to remember when she had felt the need for Dutch courage.

Next to her, pouring a large cream sherry, stood the fluffier MacKenzie sister, her soft gray hair fanning out in an erratic halo around her face as if she had blown in on a gale. Leaning toward Hannah, Penny lifted her glass and whispered conspiratorially, "A special treat. And what," she continued with an air of innocent confidence, "do you think of our newest addition, Miss Alcock? We met him at the shop this afternoon, a charming young man, so polite. Cassie says he's with the government, something dreadfully dull. You wouldn't think it to look at him."

Hannah followed her gaze across the room, where a tall man leaned against the wall, pinned like a moth by a well-endowed woman in an appalling dress. He didn't look like a civil servant. Nice looking, mid-thirties, or perhaps a bit older, with rumpled, toffee-brown hair and a slightly irregular nose. He listened to Maureen with an expression of amused interest, yet Hannah sensed a watchful quality about him, a stillness that set him apart.

"Kincaid," said Penny. "His name is Duncan Kincaid." Hannah looked away and chided herself for indulging in such a ridiculous flight of fancy when she had more pressing concerns. Then, as though aware of her regard, Kincaid turned and met her eyes, and smiled. A Cheshire Cat grin, equal parts mischief and sweetness, and utterly disarming.

Cassie appeared at Hannah's side with her usual silent efficiency, first heralded by the sharp, crisp scent she wore. It reminded Hannah of burning leaves.

"You and Miss MacKenzie met this morning, I think? Let me introduce you to some of the other guests."

Cassie performed her duties as professional hostess to perfection, as Hannah had known she would. The meeting she desired so fiercely would be accomplished as easily and effortlessly as any chance encounter. She must not, by some slip of the tongue or uncontrolled gesture, give herself away. Her abdominal muscles were clenched so tightly that she was hardly breathing. She forced herself to relax and inhale deeply, forced herself to say, with a smile as brittle as Cassie's own, "Yes, I'd like that."

3

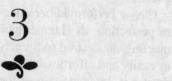

THE TRANQUIL AIR was thick with the smell of wood smoke and cooking. Kincaid sniffed appreciatively as he walked along the short path from the car park of the Carpenter's Arms, and his stomach grumbled in response. Maureen Hunsinger's discourse on the benefits of seaweed and tofu had left him with traitorous visions of steaming steak-and-kidney pie, crisp fried potatoes and apple crumble covered with cream. Cassie had recommended this as the favorite haunt of well-heeled locals, and as Kincaid pushed open the heavy door he could see why. Tarted up the place might be, but the wood fire blazing in the massive stone fireplace at the bar's end beckoned invitingly. He bought a pint of the local ale at the bar and moved to warm his back at the fire, in no hurry now to eat.

Sunday was a slow night for custom and the lounge was quiet. Kincaid sipped his beer and looked around the room with interest. A few regulars chatted with the bartender about the next day's racing at Catterick.

At the far end of the lounge, a woman was seated at

a small table, reading glasses perched on her nose as she studied a menu. He recognized Hannah Alcock, although he hadn't met her at the party. Cassie had managed to introduce him to most of the others, but Hannah slipped away early, and alone. She was intent now upon her menu, and thinking he'd not find a better time to remedy the omission, he made his way across the room toward her.

Hannah Alcock looked up in surprise as he stopped at her table and introduced himself. He thought he saw a brief flicker of disappointment cross her face before she smiled at him, but the impression was so fleeting he put it down to his imagination. She slipped her glasses off her nose and quickly folded them into her bag. "A small vanity," she apologized. "The specs are a necessity of age, and I've not got used to them. Join me?"

"Thanks. They say near vision is the first to go, then before we know it we'll be wearing bifocals. Cheerful thought, isn't it?"

"God forbid." She laughed. "In that case my vanity could become a serious inconvenience. I know who you are, from the party. Penny MacKenzie was quite taken with you."

"The feeling was mutual. Penny's a dear, but I don't seem to have made much progress with her sister. She makes me feel as if I've forgotten my lessons, or my shirttail's untucked."

Hannah laughed. "I know what you mean. Is this your first visit?"

"Yes, and only by my cousin's generosity. And you?"

"Yes. I drove up this morning. It seemed a good

idea," she paused and Kincaid had the feeling she had been about to say something else, "to try a different sort of holiday. I've always—"

"Excuse me, Miss. Your table's ready." The waitress glanced at Kincaid, uncertain. "Will this gent—"

Kincaid stood up, feeling foolishly inane. "Don't let me keep you—"

Hannah reached up to touch his wrist. "No, no. It would be silly for us both to eat alone. Share my table. I'd like the company, really."

"If you're sure . . ." was about all the polite refusal he could muster, suddenly depressed by the thought of his solitary meal.

The steak-and-kidney pie lived up to his every expectation, its crust golden, its interior rich with wine and mushrooms. A surfeit of mushrooms, in fact, for they had begun with the house specialty, mushrooms stuffed with pâté, breaded and deep fried. Maureen Hunsinger, he thought with satisfaction, would be appalled.

Hannah had eaten her trout in parchment with delicate precision and now she aligned her knife and fork in the center of her plate, laying them side by side as neatly as dead soldiers. She contemplated Kincaid over the rim of her wine glass. "Are you married?"

"Divorced."

"Children?"

Mouth still full, he shook his head.

"Are you on good terms, then?"

"Typical." He shrugged and heard the echo of bitterness in his voice. It surprised him that it still bit so sharply. It had been long enough, after all, for time to have worked its healing magic. He'd been doing his Inspector's course at Bramshill then, had accepted an invitation to an Oxford party, and been felled like a sapling under the ax. Victoria. Her name had suited her—fine-boned and blindingly fair (like sunlight on white marble, he'd told her once, in a fit of poetic excess which mortified him to remember), with candy-floss hair and a gravity of expression that intrigued him.

The sweetness lasted less than two years. How could he, trained to read expressions and body language, have been so blind? Lectures missed, dissertation not completed, unexplained absences, and her serious countenance transformed into an impenetrable barrier. When the magnitude of the change finally seeped into his overworked and exhausted consciousness, it had been too late.

"I'm sorry." Hannah's voice recalled him. "I shouldn't have asked."

Kincaid smiled, shaking off the momentary gloom. "It could be worse, I suppose. What about you?"

"I'm a spinster. A good British legal term, that. Very descriptive."

"Not for you, legal or not. Spinster calls to mind little gray-haired grannies, and you certainly don't fit that bill." Kincaid studied her, wondering why such an attractive woman had never married.

As if anticipating him, Hannah said, "I love my work. And I like my independence. It seemed enough." She pulled absent-mindedly at a ring on her right hand as she spoke. Kincaid wondered if the use of the past tense was unconscious.

"Sebastian said you're a scientist."

"A biogeneticist. I'm director of a privately endowed clinic that researches rare viral diseases. Our patron's wife died of CJ and he's devoted himself to finding a cure ever since."

"What's CJ?" asked Kincaid. "Or am I supposed to know?"

"Sorry. It stands for Cruetz-Jakob disease. It causes disorientation, muscle seizures, premature dementia. And it's fatal. It's thought to be caused by a viral particle called a prion." At his questioning look, she elaborated. "Prions are sub-viruses, pure protein with no DNA of their own. They exploit the protein in host cells in order to replicate. Prion seems to be an infectious perversion of a normal human protein called PrP . . . oh dear, never mind. I've lost you. You'd think I'd know better by this time. I've seen that glazed look often enough."

"Is it in London, your clinic?"

"Oxford. We're a small establishment, really, and Miles lives on the top floor of the house."

"Miles?"

"Miles Sterrett. It's called the Julia Sterrett Clinic, after his wife. She was quite young when the disease struck, and he was devastated. His own health has never totally recovered, and just recently it seems to be deteriorating more rapidly. Little strokes, the doctor says." Hannah sipped her wine and Kincaid followed her gaze as she studied a hunting print near the fire. The shadows moving on the elongated forms of the horses reminded him of a cave painting he had seen once.

She set down her glass and smiled at him, changing

the subject. "So, what about you? Penny said you were some sort of civil servant."

Temptation teased Kincaid and he bent before it. "Nondescript government job. Lots of paper work." He felt a million miles from New Scotland Yard, and he was loath to prick the perfect bubble of the evening. The consequences be damned.

"Doesn't suit you. Maybe you're really a spy."

Kincaid laughed. "God, no. That really would be boring, cloak-and-dagger bureaucracy."

Hannah frowned, the skin between her brows forming tiny furrows, and adjusted the position of her cutlery by a millimeter. "That reminds me . . . I mean the cloak-and-dagger part. My flat was broken into about six months ago. Nothing much taken, just my watch, a cheap camera, some small jewelry. But everything was gone through. My desk, all my drawers. It was the most uncomfortable feeling. I was terribly angry, but at the same time it made my skin crawl, thinking about someone looking through my things. Even my underwear. It's stupid, really," she added, sounding slightly embarrassed.

"It's not unusual," Kincaid said. "Most people feel both angry and violated, and it takes a long time to fade." The professional reassurance had been automatic, born from experience. He'd worked burglary in his early days and had calmed his share of the distraught, who almost always found the invasion of their privacy harder to bear than the loss of possessions. Hannah looked at him with interest, breath drawn for a question.

That's queered it, he thought. What a master of deception. A prudent change of subject just might carry him through the evening, if he could keep his foot out of his mouth. "Our waitress looks like she'd like to sweep us out. Let's go, shall we?"

They met in the forecourt of Followdale House, standing awkwardly between Hannah's new Citroën and the Midget. The comparison made Kincaid feel as if he ought to apologize for his old friend. "I like it," he said, in mock defense. "Age and beauty go hand in hand."

Hannah laughed, and the slight clumsiness between them dissolved. "And in this case, beauty is entirely in the beholder's eye."

The night was unusually soft and misty for September, with an almost balmy feel to the air. Kincaid found himself reluctant for the evening to end. "A turn around the garden before we go in?"

"Yes, all right," Hannah answered, and they walked in companionable silence. The light in the garden was diffuse and shadowless, and the white stone lions on the parapets gleamed eerily at them through the mist. Sutton Bank loomed in front of them, a dark hump against the sky. They stopped at the path's end and looked back toward the house. Yellow light spilled from the first-floor windows, and a light flickered in the empty ground-floor suite, so briefly that Kincaid thought it must have been a trick of his eyes.

"We're next to each other, did you know? We'll have to have a competition for the best view. Cassie assured me mine's the best in the house."

"She told me the same thing," said Hannah. "You'll have to recite to me from your balcony, poetry at midnight." She laughed, then stretched her arms above her head and twirled around on the path in an odd gesture of abandon. "It's been a marvelous evening. I had doubts about this holiday. I thought it might have been . . . ill conceived. Oh, I can't explain—it's too complicated. But suddenly I feel as though everything will be all right. You must be a positive influence."

"I'm not sure that's a compliment," he said with a good-natured grin, but he wondered what, or whom, lay behind her burst of exhilaration, as he didn't think the credit was entirely his.

The whistling and piping of birds woke him. The sound drifted in through the open French door on a bar of sunlight, rising and falling on the still air. Kincaid rolled over and pulled the cushion over his head, then stretched and looked at his watch. Seven o'clock.

He had fallen asleep on the sofa, fully dressed, the lamp on, his book open across his chest, after bidding Hannah goodnight at her door. He felt surprisingly refreshed by his unorthodox night. There was just enough time for a swim and a shower before breakfast, and then it promised to be an ideal day for touring the Yorkshire Dales. Leaving his rumpled clothes in a heap on the bed, he slipped into bathing trunks and a terry-cloth dressing gown, and feet bare, let himself out of the suite.

A hushed calm pervaded the house—no odor of coffee or bacon, no hum of conversation from behind closed doors. He paused a moment in the hall, reveling in the peace of the morning and his newly regained sense of physical well-being.

He pushed open the door to the balcony. Perhaps he would have the pool to—

A shrill, keening wail drifted up to him from below. An animal in distress, a puppy or kitten—his first fleeting impression shifted, and with full awareness came the realization that the pitiful cry was human. He leapt down the stairs and shoved through the doors.

The two children stood huddled together on the steps just inside, a few feet from the Jacuzzi end of the pool.

Sebastian Wade's naked body bobbed gently against the side nearest them, caught in the perpetual whirlpool of the bubbling jets.

4

Sebastian floated face down, his skin mouse-colored, his yellow hair waving in anemone spikes which gave it a perverse animation. He wore, contrary to Kincaid's first impression, a pair of bathing trunks patterned with tropical flowers.

A heavy-duty electrical cord snaked over the first-floor balcony, disappearing into the agitated water. Kincaid propelled the now-silent children back through the doors. Their faces were still with shock and he found he couldn't remember their names. He squatted before them and said gently, "Stay here. You mustn't touch the water. Do you understand?" They nodded solemnly and he left them, taking the shallow stairs to the balcony three at a time.

The cord stretched through the railing from the wall outlet near the far door. Kincaid grasped the plug with a fold of his dressing gown and gently pulled it free, then secured it by looping it around one of the balcony struts. Stopping briefly to reassure the children, he returned to the pool, slipped off his dressing gown and began the awkward business of removing the body from the water.

Sebastian's skin felt flaccid and waterlogged. It still startled Kincaid, after all his close habituation with death, that something as intangible as life's presence in the skin could be so positively experienced. Sebastian's body, however, unlike most, was warm, warmer than his own, the flesh butter-slick and evasive.

Kincaid finally managed to heave him out of the pool by grasping him under the armpits, and Sebastian slid onto the brick surround with a small sucking noise. Kincaid rolled him over, checking for vital signs although the rapid decay caused by the body's immersion in hot water made it an obviously futile action.

The pool door swung open and he heard a gasp behind him. He sat back on his knees with an effort and rubbed his hands against his sides, an instinctive gesture.

Emma MacKenzie stood just inside the door, still holding the handle tightly. Thank god, thought Kincaid, that it was Emma and not Penny.

"Dear god. Sebastian. He's dead, isn't he?" Her voice was surprisingly gentle. She came forward and reached out her hand as if to touch him.

Kincaid nodded. "I'm afraid so. Do you think you could go to the office and ring the local police? Then perhaps you could wait and show them the way."

"But . . . what about the children?"

"They've seen the worst, already. I don't think a few more minutes will do any further damage. Someone must stay with the body. If I send them up alone their parents will be down in a flash, and the less disturbance before the police arrive, the better."

Emma considered briefly, absently hugging her folded towel against her body. "All right," she said, her brisk competence once more in evidence. Her bathing sandals flip-flopped against the tiles as she left.

She had accepted his authority without question. Well, Kincaid thought, things would get difficult soon enough. He had made a right fool of himself by pretending not to be what he was, and now he would have to face the music. His policeman's instinct was too ingrained to stifle easily. He could already feel that addictive surge of heightened perception that marked the beginning of a case. Not his case, he reminded himself, with a fierce determination. It wasn't his jurisdiction and the local lads would only consider him a nuisance, Scotland Yard sticking its nose in, uninvited. He didn't know any of these people, except, perhaps, Hannah. He didn't want to have more than a casual connection with them, and he would bloody well not get involved. His conscience pricked. He had liked Sebastian. Suddenly he felt drained and shaken.

It came to him, in the quiet respite between discovery and official action, that he was suffering a degree of emotional shock. He always felt a surge of pity and anger when first confronted with a corpse, but he had learned to distance it, compartmentalize it. Never before had he faced the body of someone he had known, touched, spoken with just a few hours before. He felt a need to differentiate somehow, to make a personal gesture of acknowledgment. He knelt and touched Sebastian's bare shoulder, briefly.

He shivered, his own wet skin chilling now that the first adrenaline rush had passed. No matter what odd kinship he had felt with Sebastian, it didn't alter the fact that his death wasn't his responsibility, he had no more official power here than an innocent bystander. And as there was nothing more he could do for Sebastian Wade, he went in to the children.

The village constable arrived soon after, still buttoning his uniform tunic. He was a large young man, with a round, rubicund face and a slightly bovine expression. "Now then, what's all this about a gentleman being drowned in the swimming pool?"

"He wasn't drowned," said Kincaid. He motioned to Emma, who had followed on the constable's heels, to stay with the children, and opened the pool-area door for the constable. When it had closed behind them, he continued. "He was electrocuted. With some sort of small appliance, I would imagine. I unplugged it from above, before I pulled him out of the water, but I didn't check to see what it was."

"You disturbed the body, sir?" He took the sight of Sebastian, lying like a beached whale on the pool's edge, in his stride, although Kincaid fancied that his face lost some of its rosy color.

"Of course I moved the body, man. I had to make sure he was dead."

Kincaid's exasperation moved the constable to assert his official dignity. He drew himself up to his full, and not inconsiderable, height, pulled out his notebook and pencil, and rocked a little on his heels. He cleared his throat, testing his voice for the proper resonance. "And who might you be, sir?" Unfortunately, he had licked his pencil before putting it to the pad, and that rather detracted from the impression of competence and authority he intended to create.

"My name's Kincaid. I'm a policeman, Detective Superintendent, Scotland Yard. I'm here on holiday and I just happened to be the first one down this morning, except for the children. And, thank god, they didn't touch anything." He had discovered that the children were named Bethany and Brian, and that they had let themselves out of their suite while their parents still slept.

"To go exploring," Brian had explained, a tendency to lisp exaggerated by the gap in his front teeth. "We thought the man was swimming, and he could hold his breath for the longest time. But he didn't come up, and he didn't come up . . ."

"And he looked all wrong, somehow," added Bethany. "We didn't know it was Sebastian—we couldn't see his . . . and then Brian started to cry." She had given her brother a disgusted look, all elder sister superiority now that the horror was away in the next room. "Are we going to be in trouble?"

Brian's small face crumpled, tears imminent again, and Kincaid hastened to reassure them. "I think you both were very brave and very responsible. I'm sure your mum and dad will be proud of you, and as soon as the policemen get here someone will take you upstairs to them."

The constable seemed to have decided that Kincaid could do no more harm. After all, he had already been alone with the body for a considerable time. "Police Constable Rob Trumble, sir. I'll have to telephone Mid-Yorks. If you wouldn't mind—"

"No. Go ahead." Kincaid waved him off and stood irresolutely by Sebastian's body. Just what the hell had been used, he wondered. Taking his dressing gown, he slipped into the warm water. Covering his hand with a fold of fabric, he reached down into the water and carefully pushed the object up from underneath. It was a portable electric heater, about the size of a ladies' handbag, and unless he was very much mistaken, he'd seen it, or one very much like it, under Cassie's gray metal desk.

P.C. Trumble, flushed with excitement and authority, gave Kincaid permission to get dried and dressed, and Emma leave to return the children to their suite. Kincaid had no wish to face the officers of Mid-Yorkshire C.I.D. wet and half-naked, without identification. There was no sense in putting oneself at a definite psychological disadvantage. He had toweled his hair, pulled on jeans and a faded blue cotton sweater. Sneakers on, wallet and keys tucked safely in his pocket, he felt armored enough. Only when he was halfway down the pool stairs again did the hollowness in his stomach remind him that he had not eaten breakfast.

He had been surprised on returning to his room to find it just on eight o'clock, the morning passing at its own measured pace. The calm promise of an hour ago seemed a universe removed. The house was beginning to stir. He heard the soft sounds of doors, sensed movement in the rooms around him. The local lads would have to be quick to contain the guests before they began their daily exodus.

Kincaid joined Trumble in a silent vigil by the pool,

and when Detective Chief Inspector Bill Nash arrived, accompanied by Detective Inspector Peter Raskin, Kincaid felt glad enough of his clothes. Nash was balding, rumpled and portly, a jolly elf of a man with a hearty Yorkshire voice and little black eyes as cold and opaque as tar pits. Nash flicked the proffered warrant card with a finger, and Kincaid had the feeling he'd been assessed and dismissed within the first five seconds.

"Well now," drawled Nash, "one of Scotland Yard's fancy men, with nowt better to do than mess about in other folk's affairs. How convenient for us. Just how did you happen to be so prompt on the scene, laddie?"

Kincaid bit back a retort born of instant antagonism, forced himself to speak reasonably. "Look, Inspector, it was purely coincidence. I've no wish to intrude on your patch, but I would like to watch, if I won't be in the way."

"Aye. Just you make sure of that." Nash seemed to realize that it wasn't politically expedient to order a senior Scotland Yard officer off the premises, but there was no welcome in his voice. He studied the body with ruminative deliberation. "Mr. Sebastian Wade, is it? Assistant manager. Late assistant manager, I should say." He stood in silent contemplation a moment longer, then roused himself. "Peter, take Mr. Kincaid's statement, then he can run along and play."

The emphasis fell on the "mister," and Raskin looked askance at him, then pulled out his notebook and invited Kincaid to a seat on the wooden bench against the wall. He had not spoken since the introductions. Now, with a sideways glance to make sure Nash was occupied, he gave Kincaid a sympathetic lift of his eyebrow. Raskin was a wiry young man, with a thin, dark, saturnine face and a Heathcliff-like lock of dark hair hanging over his brow. Kincaid answered his quiet questions with half his attention and listened to Nash with the other.

Trumble was delegated to see the guests. "Trumble, isn't it? Well now, you round them all up in the sitting room, whether they like it or not, and keep them there 'til I want them. And if any have left, you find out where they've gone and how long ago. Got that?"

"Sir," said Trumble, his enthusiasm subdued. Kincaid felt for him. The most exciting event of his short career, and he was relegated to babysitter and would miss watching the scene-of-crime team. He was too inexperienced to take advantage of the opportunity to watch the guests' reactions to his news, or to listen carefully to what they said to one another when they were all gathered together. Nash didn't enlighten him.

Making, rather than taking, a statement proved a novel experience for Kincaid, and he tried to be as concise about his movements and the sequence of events as possible, all the while keeping an eye on Nash's slow progress around the pool. Nash squatted beside Sebastian's body, forearms resting on his heavy thighs, hands dangling loosely in front of him. He reminded Kincaid, unpleasantly, of a satiated vulture. He repeated the posture before Sebastian's neatly folded pile of clothes, then moved to the pool's edge and craned his neck up at the electrical cord.

"Cut and dried," he pronounced. "Decided to end things. Clever little bugger. Plugged it in up above there, dropped it over, then came down and jumped in. If the shock didn't kill him it would be sure to knock him out long enough for him to drown."

"No." Kincaid said it almost involuntarily. "No, he didn't. Someone came when he was already in the Jacuzzi. He would have had his back to the balcony, that's where the main jets are. Someone very carefully plugged the thing in and dropped it. Even if Sebastian saw it falling he wouldn't have had time to climb out." He didn't add that the heater must have shorted itself out when it entered the water—the jolt of current wouldn't have lasted more than a few seconds.

"And just how do you know so much, laddie? You have the second sight?" Nash turned and gave Kincaid his beady glare. "Looks like a suicide to me. Look at his clothes, neatly folded. Typical."

"No. He was neat. I don't imagine he ever left his clothes in a heap. It was probably part of his routine. He made no secret of the fact that he liked to come here last thing in the evening. I'd swear you won't find his fingerprints on that cord or plug. Suicides don't usually wear gloves. And he wasn't a suicidal type."

He had Nash's full attention now. "You're very sure of your facts all of a sudden, laddie. I thought I heard you tell my inspector just now that you'd only been here a day. Got to know Mr. Wade here awfully well in a short time, seems to me." His voice was soft now, weighted with friendly insinuation.

Kincaid felt his fists clenching. He forced himself to hold his tongue—anything he could say about the time he had spent with Sebastian would sound feeble, ludicrously sentimental. There was nothing for it but to beat Nash at his own game. He smiled at him, and said evenly, "I'm very observant. It's my job, Inspector, in case you'd forgotten."

Whatever Nash might have replied to this not-so-subtle bit of rank-pulling was interrupted by the arrival of the scene-of-crime team from district headquarters. Kincaid was relieved to see that Nash was competent enough to stand back and let them work without interference, although he didn't hold out much hope for the results.

The photographer set up his lights and equipment with practiced ease and began taking shots of the body. The forensic biologist was a fair man with rabbity teeth. He wore shorts, a stained sweatshirt and tennis shoes, and looked thoroughly incongruous pulling on his thin latex gloves. He squatted by Sebastian's clothes, as Nash had done, and began going through them with deft fingers.

There was no sign of a pathologist. Kincaid waited until Peter Raskin was free for a moment and questioned him. "Where's your M.E.?"

"Out on another call, apparently. They've called in a local doctor. Not usually a good idea, but in this case it probably doesn't matter."

"You agree with your chief, then? That it was suicide?"

"No. I didn't say that." Raskin was cagey, and Kincaid saw a gleam of humor in his eyes. "Just that a preliminary examination of the body isn't likely to reveal much, and the district M.E. will do the postmortem when he can get to it. Look," he inclined his head toward the glass doors, "there's your doctor, now."

Only the black medical bag gripped in her right hand identified her. She wore kelly green sweats with trainers and damp wisps of hair curled around her heart-shaped face. Nash, occupied with the photographer, hadn't seen her. Raskin went to greet her and Kincaid followed an unobtrusive pace behind, holding his hand out in turn for her firm clasp.

"I'm Anne Percy." She looked from their faces to Sebastian's still form, and back again. "Are you ready for me? I came straightaway. I was running," she gestured apologetically toward her clothes, "before morning surgery." A small town G.P., Kincaid thought, used to officiating at family deathbeds, not murder scenes—her uneasy small talk served the same function as a police surgeon's black jokes. "What happened here? Who was he?"

She looked at Kincaid as she spoke, and after a barely perceptible nod from Raskin, he answered her. "Sebastian Wade, assistant manager here. Uh, suspicious death." He caught Raskin's quick lift of an eyebrow, a mannerism he was beginning to recognize as a sign of amusement. "Electrocution, or drowning due to electrocution. Sometime late last night, most likely."

"He was found in the spa?"

Peter Raskin took up the story. "Mr. Kincaid found him when he came down for his swim this morning."

"Oh." Anne Percy seemed momentarily nonplussed. "But I had the impression you were a policeman, too."

"I am," Kincaid answered, "but on holiday. A guest."

"Well, I don't know what I'll be able to do for you,

other than certify death." She opened her bag and knelt beside Sebastian's body. "Body temperature will be useless for establishing time of death, as will state of rigor." After gently flexing Sebastian's limp arm, she pulled on her thin latex gloves. "It'll take the post-mortem to give you anything concrete."

Kincaid felt oddly uncomfortable, as if it were indecent for him to watch Sebastian's body violated, and turned away as Dr. Percy got down to business.

Cassie Whitlake stood in the doorway, looking unkempt and disheveled. On her the mild untidiness became shocking disarray. The oak-leaf hair was uncombed, pushed back behind one bare ear. The tail of her blouse hung half out of her skirt and she had shoved her unstockinged feet into a pair of scuffed loafers. The normal pale cream of her complexion would have looked decidedly ruddy next to her present pallor.

Kincaid had turned from contemplating the rear wall of the pool, feeling he'd been squeamish long enough. Besides, the sight of Anne Percy made up for the discomfort of watching what she was doing to Sebastian. He hadn't heard the door swing open.

Cassie held the door's metal handle like an anchor, her dilated eyes fixed on the scene before her. Why the hell hadn't they put a constable on the door, Kincaid thought as he crossed to her, simply to keep things like this from happening. He touched her arm. "Cassie." She hadn't looked at him, all her attention frozen on the little tableau by the pool. Anne Percy carefully slipped off her gloves and closed her bag, speaking a quiet word to Peter Raskin. "Cassie," Kincaid repeated, "let me take you—"

"No. What happened? What happened to him? He had no right. Oh, sod the little bugger." Tears began to slip down her face, more anger and shock, Kincaid thought, than grief.

"Had no right to do what?"

"He's killed himself, hasn't he? Here. He had to do it here, didn't he? Out of spite. Christ, what am I going to say . . . how am I going to explain . . ." The perfect BBC elocution had stretched with shock, the lengthened vowels betraying their South London origins.

"Explain to whom?" asked Kincaid.

"The management. It's my responsibility, to see that things like this don't happen. And you—" she looked at Kincaid for the first time—"you're a bloody cop! That ox of a constable said you were a policeman and were 'assisting them with their inquiries.' You never said. What have you been doing—sneaking about and spying on us?"

"Cassie, I'm sorry. At the time it didn't seem that it was anyone's business what I did for a living."

Her attention drifted away from him, back to Sebastian, and her voice rose alarmingly. "When are they going to take him away? Everyone will see. And why have they shut everyone up together like criminals?"

Anne Percy recognized the sound of imminent hysteria and came toward them, exchanging a glance with Kincaid. "I'm Dr. Percy. Can I—"

"I know who you are." Cassie jerked her arm away from Anne's touch. "I don't need any help. I don't want any sedatives." She seemed visibly to gather herself together, closing her eyes for a moment and taking a breath.

P.C. Trumble, flushed and perspiring, clattered down the tile stairs and skidded to a stop at the glass door. Kincaid had to move Cassie gently aside so that the door would open—this time she didn't flinch from his touch.

Trumble looked anxiously around for Inspector Nash, then gave a quick puff of relief when it seemed he might be spared immediate retribution. "You're all right, Constable." Peter Raskin's quiet voice held a hint of amusement as he joined them. "He's just gone out the back to direct the ambulance crew, now that Dr. Percy's finished."

"Miss," Trumble drew himself up and faced Cassie, "you're not supposed to be here. It's restricted. You have to stay with the others until the Chief Inspector's spoken with everyone." To Raskin he said, by way of apology, "I didn't know about the cottage, sir. The others told me, said somebody should inform Miss Whitlake. So I did, and she said she'd join the others straight away. It was only when she didn't show I discovered she'd come over—"

"It's my right. I'm in charge here. I'm responsible for every . . . all right." Cassie subsided, as she looked at the half-circle of implacable faces. "I'll wait with the others, but it had better not be too long. I've phone calls to make." She was calmer now, and Kincaid thought he detected a certain calculation returning to her manner. Trumble, with frequent mumblings and glances over his shoulder, hustled her off, and Kincaid noticed that Cassie didn't look at Sebastian again.

Well, what had he expected? A grief-stricken farewell scene over Sebastian's prostrate body? Not bloody likely. Not from Cassie, anyway. Any tears shed for Sebastian would have to come from another quarter.

5

PETER RASKIN DREW Kincaid aside, keeping his chief in line of sight and lowering his voice so that it was audible only to Kincaid. "I'll let you know the results of the p.m. And the lab reports, if you're interested. To tell the truth," he looked across the room at Nash, who was telling off one of the ambulance crew in vitriolic tones, "I'm not happy with this suicide business myself. It's too pat. The neat ones usually leave a note, and choose something gradual, pills or injection. In my book, those who opt for the violent end take off, leaving everything in a muddle, and go out and have an accident cleaning the gun. The profile here just doesn't seem to fit."

"Right." It was a shame about Raskin. He had the makings of a good copper—unobtrusive, alert, intelligent, and not so stuck on his opinions that he couldn't see past his own nose—and he had to be saddled with a bugger like Nash. Kincaid wondered what Raskin would make of this disagreement with his chief. If Nash turned out to be wrong, as Kincaid felt sure he would, he'd take it out of somebody's hide, and Raskin would be wise to keep his thoughts to himself until afterwards.

Kincaid took himself off to Thirsk, ignoring the niggling refrain "with his tail between his legs" that kept creeping unbidden into his thoughts. He thought it best to avoid any more confrontation with Nash until he had more ammunition.

A bench on the market square beckoned, along with a warm-from-the-oven pork pie, bought over the counter at a small bakery, some fresh Wensleydale cheese and a crunchy apple from a market stall. He disposed of his impromptu lunch and set off to explore.

By half-past three Kincaid had exhausted the sightseeing possibilities in the little market town. The day turned out to be as glorious as he'd predicted, the autumn air as rich and bright as a plum ready to fall from the tree. He strolled the town, resolute in his determination to be an uncomplicated tourist, shoving away thoughts of the morning's events whenever they threatened his equanimity.

The lovely perpendicular church, with its eighty-foot-high battlemented tower, had been a sight worth seeing. The ground around it rose gently from east to west, while the church itself remained level. As a result, the whole tower end of the church seemed to be sinking gradually into the ground. It made him think of a huge battleship plowing into heavy seas and he felt momentarily unsteady on his feet.

His last stop was the local book shop on the square. He emerged with a paperback copy of James Herriot's

Yorkshire tucked under his arm, assured by the proprietor that it made a wonderful tour guide to the area, much more entertaining than those dry tomes intended for the purpose. Recent years hadn't provided him many opportunities for browsing in small-town book shops, an indulgence that always transported him back to his childhood in rural Cheshire and his parents' small book shop on the town square. One more childhood indulgence would put a fitting period to the afternoon—across the square he saw a tea shop advertising cream teas.

The Blue Plate lived up to its name, with blue plates of various patterns displayed around the room on a plate rail, and cheerful yellow-and-white-checked cloths on the tables. It was not until Kincaid was seated at a small table in the back of the room and had placed his order that he noticed the two women in animated conversation at a window table. Maureen Hunsinger, with her round, cheerful face and frizzy hair, wore a dusty blue garment that looked as if it might have had a previous life as a chenille bedspread.

It took him a moment to place Maureen's companion as Janet Lyle, the ex-army man's wife. Last night she had hardly spoken or smiled and had kept an anxious eye on her husband, glancing at him before she spoke, whether for reassurance or approval Kincaid hadn't been able to tell. Possibly she was shy, or uncomfortable in social gatherings. Now, she was certainly at ease, talking and laughing, leaning forward and gesturing emphatically with her hands, her dark hair swinging against her shoulders every time she moved her head.

Curious, Kincaid thought, after the events of the morning. Was it Sebastian's death they were discussing with such energy? Excitement would be a typical reaction, charged by the relief most people felt at remaining unscathed when death struck so near. But not the good humor they displayed, evident even from a distance.

He listened intently, their voices coming to him in snatches. "Oh god, I remember when mine was that age. It's awful, you don't know how you'll get through it. But you do . . . gets worse." Janet laughed again. She must have an older child, Kincaid thought, not with them on holiday. At boarding school, perhaps? Her voice drifted toward him again. ". . . the best school, Eddie says, then University. I don't see how we can . . ." They leaned closer together, their faces more sober, and he lost the thread of sound. He had no business eavesdropping anyway; their conversation was none of his concern. It was only his cursed cop's habit that made him listen.

The two women had not noticed him, and when his tea and scones arrived he opened his book and buried himself in the pleasures of Yorkshire.

There was no more delaying it. He'd dawdled long enough over scones and strawberry jam, drunk enough weak tea to swamp a horse, and had incited the cheerful waitress to concerned looks in his direction. He paid his bill and retrieved the Midget from the public car park across the square. With the car's soft top folded down to take advantage of the sun, he drove slowly back to Followdale House.

The house seemed hushed and shuttered. Not until he had parked the car and started toward the front door did he notice the small figure huddled at the side of the front step.

Angela Frazer's dark eyes were bare of make-up, the skin around them red and puffy. Even the spiky, violet-streaked hair seemed subdued. She looked at Kincaid without speaking. When he reached the steps, he sat down a few feet away, said "Hullo," and gazed out at the empty drive in what he hoped was a neutral silence. From the corner of his eye he saw her fingers fiddling with the threads hanging from the torn knees of her jeans, and her feet, in dirty, white canvas sneakers, seemed ridiculously small.

After a few moments she spoke, her voice barely a whisper. "You liked him, didn't you?"

"Yes, I did." He waited, careful not to look at her.

"He said you were okay." Her words were clearer now, gaining strength. "Really okay. Not like most of the others."

"Did he? I'm glad."

"They don't care, not any of them. My dad's been beastly. He said, 'Good riddance to the little poof.' They've all been saying . . ." Her voice wavered and he risked a glance at her face, restraining an impulse to touch her. Without meeting his eyes, she folded her arms across her stomach and hunched her shoulders a little lower—a hedgehog posture. "They're saying he killed himself. I don't believe it. Sebastian wouldn't do that." She curled up even further, resting her face against her drawn-up knees.

Jesus, thought Kincaid, what was he to say to this

child that wouldn't make her feel even worse? Had she considered the implications of what she was saying? That if Sebastian hadn't killed himself, someone she knew, and quite possibly loved, might have killed him? Kincaid didn't think so. It was more likely that she hadn't been told enough to realize that Sebastian's death couldn't have been an accident. "Well," he temporized, "I'm not sure anything's definite yet. There will have to be tests and things to find out exactly how Sebastian died."

"Nobody I knew ever died before. Except my grandmother, and I hadn't seen her for a long time." Angela's words were muffled by her knees. "They wouldn't let me see him. My dad said not to be so stupid. But I can't believe he's dead. Gone, you know? Just like that. I feel like I should say good-bye."

"It does help, sometimes, to see someone who's died. A letting go. I think that's why they have open caskets at funerals, except by the time the person's been painted and fixed up at the undertakers they don't bear any resemblance to the person you knew. It makes it worse, in a way."

Angela thought about it for a moment. "Then I don't think I'd want to see Sebastian that way, even if they'd let me. I'd rather remember him the way he was."

"If I were you," said Kincaid, slowly, "I'd have a private farewell. Do something you know he liked. Go somewhere he liked to go, or do something you did together."

Angela lifted her head, her expression brightening. "Yeah. In memoriam. Isn't that what it's called? Maybe I will."

"Angela," Kincaid said, treading carefully, "you saw Sebastian last night, didn't you?"

"At the party. That was when he talked about you. But I didn't get to meet you, because you were so busy with them." Her emphasis fell on the last word, and he guessed that the category included most adults. "Did Sebastian seem any different than usual?"

"You mean depressed? No." Angela's forehead creased in sudden concentration. "Except he left for a few minutes. And when he came back he seemed sort of . . . excited. He had this look he'd get sometimes, like the cat that ate the canary. Pleased with himself. But he didn't say anything. When I asked him, he just said 'Never you mind, little one'—teasing me, you know, the way he did."

"Did you see him later, after the party?"

"No, my dad took me to York, to some fancy restaurant. But he was so cross that it was awful. We had a terrible row on the way back."

"Did your dad go out again?"

"No. Well, I don't think so. I locked myself in the bathroom for hours, I was so mad. I went to sleep on the floor, and when I woke up, he was in bed asleep."

"Must have been a pretty awful row. What was it about?" Kincaid delivered the question lightly, almost jocularly, afraid he'd breach her new-found confidence in him.

"Oh, you know. My mum. Me. He hates my clothes, my hair, my make-up. He said I looked like a slut at the stupid party last night and I embarrassed him. Well, I hope I did. He's embarrassed me enough times, making—" She broke off, dropping her head and twisting her fingers together, suddenly uncomfortable.

Voices came through the closed oak door behind them, followed by a bark of laughter. "That's my dad, now." Angela half stood, listening, like a hare poised for flight. "I'd better—"

"It's all right. I'd better be off myself. Angela," Kincaid said as she started toward the door, and she turned back to him, "Sebastian really cared about you, too. He told me so last night, before the party."

"I know." She smiled at him, and he saw what Sebastian had been astute enough to discover, the kernel of sweetness hidden beneath her usual sullen pose. "Can I call you Duncan? Mr. Kincaid makes you sound ancient." A hint of flirtation, now, in the smile, and in the dark eyes looking at him through the lowered lashes. Kincaid realized he'd have to be careful not to tease her. She was, after all, almost grown.

"Sure. See you."

"Yeah." She slipped through the door and he waited a moment before following. He had the feeling that Angela might like to keep their conversation just between the two of them, and that suited him as well.

Graham Frazer's hearty voice met him as he entered the sitting room. "Well, if it isn't our resident narc." Kincaid was beginning to share some of Sebastian's antipathy for Frazer.

Angela was nowhere to be seen. The circle of faces turned toward him, a parody of last night's innocent social gathering. Hannah was missing, as were Emma and Penny MacKenzie, but the rest seemed to draw together in a hostile shield.

"Mr. Kincaid." Maureen Hunsinger spoke next, reproaching him with all the directness of a child whose feelings have been hurt. "You misled us."

Cassie, who seemed to have temporarily abandoned her managerial distinction and banded with the herd, chimed in. "Oh, he's full of surprises, is our Detective Superintendent Kincaid. All chummy with the local police, johnny-on-the-spot to the rescue. A real hero. Unfortunately, it was too late for poor Sebastian." Her voice was light and mocking. She had recovered her control, all traces of the morning's outburst erased. Her hair and make-up were exquisitely done and she wore rust, a matching skirt and blouse of some dull material with a webbing of fine, brown lines running through the solid color.

"I resent being treated like some common criminal, shut up together and then interrogated. And finger-printed, for God's sake. It's disgraceful." Eddie Lyle sounded aggrieved, as if Sebastian's death had been designed merely to inconvenience him.

"You have no idea what it was like—" began Maureen, then blushed, remembering that Kincaid knew exactly what it was like.

"What have they found out? Your friends told us we were to 'make ourselves available' until cause of death is established. I must say it's a hell of a way to spend one's holiday," said Graham Frazer. His flat, heavy face gave no hints as to what went on in the mind behind it, but his voice sounded somewhat less aggressive.

No one had offered Kincaid a drink, although they clutched theirs like protective talismans, so he answered Frazer over his shoulder as he walked to the bar and made himself a whiskey. "Look, I don't know any more about this than the rest of you. It was purely circumstance that I happened to be the first down this morning."

"That's all very well for you to say," Eddie Lyle said querulously, "but you weren't subjected to—"

"I had to make a statement just as all of you did, signed and sworn," Kincaid interrupted as he rejoined them, then took a sip of his whiskey. No single malt scotch for the honor bar, this was the rawest of blends and it scorched his throat as it went down.

Kincaid noticed that Patrick Rennie hadn't yet spoken, though he followed the conversation with interest. Watching which way the wind blew, thought Kincaid, with a politician's prudence. The man looked more human than he had last night, in a pull-over and rumpled cords, his blond hair a little tousled, but how much was manufactured image and how much the real man Kincaid couldn't tell.

Rennie stepped in now as mediator. "I'm sure Mr. Kincaid has had just as difficult a day as any of us, and has no intention of making this a busman's holiday. I feel we're all being rather unfair."

"Thanks." Kincaid met his eyes and was surprised to see a gleam of knowing humor. A smooth operator, no doubt, but perhaps Rennie didn't take himself too seriously, after all. There was no answering spark in Marta Rennie's eyes. She watched her husband, but unsmilingly, not privy to the brief connection between the two men. Kincaid sensed some tension between the Rennies, but unless his overactive imagination was playing him up again, there were strange little eddies and currents of unease running all through the group, more than he felt could be accounted for by the awkwardness following Sebastian's death.

"How are the children?" Kincaid turned to John Hunsinger, who was hovering on the edge of the group as he had last night.

"More excited than upset, at least for the day. Their dreams may be a different story." Hunsinger's voice was deep and a little gravelly, as if unused to wear. "They said you—"

"You were very kind to them," Maureen broke in, "They've put you right up in the ranks with Doctor Who. What's horrible is that we didn't even realize they were gone. They could have been . . ."

"Where are they now?" Kincaid asked.

"Emma MacKenzie's taken them on a nature walk. Birdwatching. Can you believe it? They seem to have made friends this morning."

The group was breaking up, drifting away in desultory conversation now that their attention was no longer focused on Kincaid. Janet Lyle still stood near them, quietly nursing her drink, while Eddie buttonholed Marta Rennie. "I can't think why provision hadn't been made for an occurrence of this sort. If this were a properly run facility—" a sidelong glance at Cassie "—things like this wouldn't be allowed to happen."

Kincaid resisted the temptation to ask him what on earth he thought might have prevented it, and turned to Janet instead. "Janet, you have children, don't you?"

She flushed, and spoke with a trace of the animation he had seen earlier in the day. "We have a daughter,

Chloe." In response to his slightly questioning look—he supposed he had expected a Cindy or a Jennifer—Janet said, "Eddie named her. He wanted her to be cultured, so he thought she should start off with a name that would suit her later."

"Did it work?" Kincaid asked.

Janet's eyes strayed to Eddie, who had moved off with Marta in the direction of the bar. "Not so you'd notice." She grinned. "She's a typical teenager, only her father'd never believe it. Chloe's just about the same age as Angela Frazer, only she's away at school and Angela's . . . um, between schools, as I understand it." Janet fell silent, her momentary energy dissipated.

Kincaid drained his glass in one swallow. The room felt stuffy and stale. The late afternoon sun beat upon the closed French windows and crumpled cigarette butts overflowed the ashtrays. Even Maureen seemed wilted by the atmosphere, not ready to charge into the gap in the conversation with her usual gusto. The tidying up, thought Kincaid, the airing and ashtray cleaning and magazine straightening, those had been Sebastian's touches, the little bits of grease that made the whole house run smoothly.

Kincaid changed in record time, even for one who was accustomed to being summoned at inopportune moments. Shoving a tie in the pocket of his tweed jacket, he locked the door of the suite behind him and ran down the stairs, escaping into the cool forecourt with a feeling of relief.

As he nosed the Midget through the gate, he spotted Hannah walking down the road from the village. He waited, watching as she came toward him with her purposeful stride. She wore a long Aran cardigan, and the last of the sun lit the dark cap of her hair. When Hannah reached his car she opened the door and got in, without looking at him, without speaking. Kincaid drove on a half mile past the gate and pulled the car onto the verge.

"They interviewed us, Duncan." She spoke into the sudden silence as the engine died, her face still averted. "One by one, in Cassie's office. They asked if we were together last night. Corroborating your statement, they said. They seemed to assume that I knew you were a policeman, and Nash, the fat one, insinuated . . . all sorts of things." She looked at him then, her color rising as she spoke. "Can you imagine what a fool I felt? 'A policeman?' I said, like some fatuous idiot. Why did you lie to me, Duncan?"

Kincaid stalled, gathering his thoughts. "Oh, he's a right sod, our jolly Inspector Nash. I'm sure it's his standard interrogation procedure, making the . . ." he hesitated over his choice of words, "person uncomfortable."

"If you mean 'suspect,' say so. Don't bother to mince terms with me. Besides, I thought Chief Inspector Nash said it was suicide."

"That's the official line," he said slowly. "But he has to go through the motions." Kincaid shifted around in his seat so that he could more easily see her face in the fading light.

"But . . . I would have thought that we alibied each other."

"The high temperature of the water is going to make establishing the exact time of death difficult. But I personally think it likely he was already dead when we were walking in the garden last night. Think about it. He would have gone to the pool between finishing up his duties and going home for the night, not too late, say ten or eleven."

Hannah's face had lost its quick color. "Before he went home for the night? You don't think . . . it was suicide at all, do you?"

"I don't think it likely, no."

"Oh, god. You mean somebody . . . did that to Sebastian while we were talking just outside? And I was acting such a silly fool."

"Quite probably, yes."

"Now it all seems so stupid and inconsequential." She pushed her hair back from her forehead with her fingers and sagged a little in the seat.

"We couldn't have known. And your life isn't trivial or inconsequential. If the things that matter to us every day weren't important, no one's death, Sebastian's included, would be much loss."

"Could we have done anything, helped him, if we'd known?"

Kincaid took her hand and held it in his, palm up, as if reading her fortune. "I doubt it. The shock would have been massive. His heart probably stopped almost instantly. Immediate resuscitation might have saved him, but there's no way to be sure."

She withdrew from him, and her voice came, sharply now, in the near darkness. "Of course, you know about these things. You're the expert. And you still haven't answered my question."

He sighed and looked away, gazing out through the

smeared windscreen at the dim forms of the moors. "I didn't deliberately intend to deceive you. I suppose I just wanted to leave my work behind for a week, to be taken, for once, at face value. You should have seen them in the lounge a few minutes ago. They didn't know whether to spit and snarl at me for putting something over on them, or suck up and pump me for information." He smiled. "They'll never see me as just an ordinary mug again. From now on I'll be a spy in the enemy's camp. I should have known it wouldn't work. My job's not shed so easily."

"I think I see what you mean," Hannah said, examining her fingertips. "And are you a spy in our camp?"

"I don't think so. Neither fish nor fowl, really. I'm certainly a nuisance as far as Nash is concerned, and the fact that I outrank him doesn't help."

"What is it, by the way? Nash never said, only rather sneeringly referred to you as 'your friend Kincaid.' "

"Superintendent." Her eyes widened in surprise. "I know, I know," he said before she could speak. "Newly promoted, however, so it's not quite as bad as it sounds. I went to Bramshill." Seeing her expression of noncomprehension, he added, "Police College, near Reading. Special Course. It accelerates promotion to Inspector by about five years."

What he didn't add was that only "young officers of exceptional promise" were considered for Bramshill, and meteoric rise through the ranks was expected of its graduates. If Nash had checked his credentials he'd be aware of it, however, and would resent him all the more. "All I wanted," he misquoted plaintively, "was a week's holiday, and a little bit of butter for my bread."

It brought a smile. "Weak. But nobody can be all bad who read Milne."

"Truce, then?" he asked, extending his hand.

"Yes. All right." She clasped his hand, briefly. "I feel like a ten-year-old."

"That's the idea." He noted with satisfaction that some of the strain had left her face. "I'm running away." He gestured toward his jacket. "Come to York with me for dinner, where no one knows either of us."

She shook her head. "No. It's been a shocking day. I think I'd rather be alone. Just drop me at the house as you go."

Kincaid turned the car in the narrow lane and delivered Hannah as she asked, reaching across the Midget's narrow passenger space to open her door and let her out. The lights glowed softly in the windows of Followdale House, as welcoming as death.

6

Sergeant Gemma James eased her Ford Escort into a space no bigger than a motorbike. Even her deft maneuvering couldn't quite overcome the limitations of space—when she cut the engine and jerked up the handbrake, the car's rear end stuck out into the street at an angle. Home early, an unusual feat, and still no place to park, because her neighbor's teenage sons had cluttered every inch of the curbside with their clunkers. Even the baby had left his tricycle overturned in the middle of the path.

She unbuckled Toby from his carseat and lifted him from the car. Balancing the squirming toddler on one hip and her shopping on the other, she kicked the Escort's door shut with unnecessary spite. She negotiated the path well enough until she caught her toe on the tricycle wheel, stumbled and swore.

An alliterative name and the mortgage on the semidetached house in Leyton were about the only things Rob had left her, and the house's attributes were dubious—a view of Lea Bridge Road, red brick, peeling paint, a shriveled patch of front garden and next-door neighbors who seemed to be running a scrap yard.

Toby wriggled and shrieked, "Down, down," kicking his feet against her thigh.

"Shhh. In a minute, love, in a minute." Gemma bounced him on her hip and jingled her keys while she hunted for the right one. As she deposited Toby on the hall floor, she felt a large damp patch on the hip of her linen jacket. "Bloody hell. That's torn it, now," she muttered under her breath. Toby was soaking wet, and when she scooped him up again the odor of stale urine burned her nostrils. "Bloody day care," she said. One of Toby's blond eyebrows lifted in such a comical expression of surprise that she had to laugh.

"Bloody," he repeated seriously, nodding his head.

"Oh, lovey." Hugging him to her fiercely, sopping nappy and all, she whispered in his ear. "Mummy's teaching you such bad habits. But it is bloody, it really is." She carried him upstairs to his cot and stripped him off, then sponged his damp bottom with a wipe. "You're too big a boy to be wearing nappies. Two already, aren't you, love? A big boy."

"Me two," Toby repeated, grinning at her.

Gemma sighed. She'd taken her holiday earlier in the summer, and she didn't see how she could possibly train him unless she could stay home with him for a few days.

She pressed her lips against his stomach and blew hard. Toby squealed and giggled with delight as she swung him down and slapped his bottom. He took off around the house, roaring like a freight train, chubby legs pumping, and Gemma followed him more slowly.

Fortified with a glass of Spanish plonk from the fridge, she put away her shopping and picked up the sitting room, tossing Toby's toys and books in baskets. She had tried to brighten the place up. White, rice-paper globes from Habitat to cover the bare lightbulbs, rice-paper shades on the windows, printed cotton cushions on the dull three-piece suite, colorful travel posters on the walls—but the damp still seeped through the wallpaper and the cracks in the ceiling spread like ivy.

The dull thud of heavy metal rock started up next door and the walls began to vibrate. Gemma fetched a broom from the kitchen and banged the handle smartly against the connecting wall. The noise abated a fraction of a decibel. "If you don't turn down that bloody racket I'll phone in a complaint," she shouted at the wall, even though she knew they couldn't hear a word.

Then the absurdity of it struck her and she started to laugh. Just look at her—standing there screeching like a fishwife, red hair flying, broom in hand—a proper witch. Still smiling, she rescued her wine from the kitchen, sat down on the sofa and propped her feet on the trunk that served as a coffee table. Toby, unperturbed by the noise, pushed a plush teddy bear along the floor and made zooming noises.

She should be as tolerant, Gemma thought wryly. Ten years ago she would have been right in there with the kids next door—but then again, maybe she wouldn't. At eighteen she'd been much more concerned with making a different life for herself than in having a good time. She'd stayed at school and done her A levels, watching her friends drift away to take sales clerk's and cashier's jobs, or get married. On her nineteenth birthday she applied to the Metropolitan Police. Two years later she opted into the C.I.D., her career advancement laid out in her mind like a map.

She hadn't counted on ending up in a neighborhood like the one she'd left. But then she hadn't counted on Rob James, either.

Toby climbed up beside her and opened a picture book. "Ball," he said, jabbing his finger at the page. "Car."

"Yes, you're a clever boy, love." Gemma stroked his straight, fair hair. She really couldn't complain. She'd done well enough for herself so far, in spite of the obstacles. And tomorrow she had a half-day off, free to spend with Toby.

Perhaps some of her bad temper, she admitted grudgingly, was due to the fact that she'd become very quickly accustomed to working with Duncan Kincaid, and the day had soured a bit without his presence.

And that, Gemma told herself firmly, was a tendency to be kept very well in hand.

Kincaid woke late on Tuesday morning, with that sense of malaise that results from oversleeping. The bedclothes were rumpled and askew. His tongue felt furry—the residue of too much wine the night before.

An unpleasant dream lingered on the edge of his consciousness, teasing him with tattered scraps of images. A child in a well—the small voice calling to him . . . he couldn't find a rope . . . descending into the well, moss coating the palms of his hands like gelatinous glue . . . to find only bones, small bones that crumbled to dust as he touched them. Ugh! He shook himself and groped his way to the shower, hoping the hot water would clear his head.

Kincaid emerged feeling ravenously hungry. He carried his makeshift breakfast of buttered bread, cheese and a cup of tea out to the balcony, and leaned on the rail as he chewed and thought about his day. He found he'd lost his enthusiasm for playing the tourist. All his plans seemed uninspired, deflated, a reflection of the dull, overcast day. Even the thought of walking the Dales alone, a prospect which had seemed glorious two days ago, failed to please him.

His conscience was nagging him. All these dreams of things left undone, or not done soon enough. His subconscious was throwing little poisoned darts at him, and some appeasement would have to be offered. Official action was difficult, but he felt a need to take some assertive step.

He'd visit Sebastian's mum. A condolence call. An old-fashioned custom, traditional, respectable, and often mere empty etiquette, but it would at least give him the sense that Sebastian's death had not passed unmarked.

Cassie would have the address.

As Kincaid turned from locking his suite door behind him, he found Penny MacKenzie hovering uncertainly in the hall. She was dressed this morning in slacks, sweater and sensible lace-up walking shoes, and seemed in some way diminished, as if she had shed some dimension of her personality along with her eccentricities. A lady, past middle age, a little frail perhaps, but ordinary. Her enthusiasm was missing, Kincaid realized, her bubbling manner replaced by hesitancy.

"Morning, Miss MacKenzie."

"Oh, Mr. Kincaid. I was hoping . . . I mean, I thought if you were . . . I'd just wait . . ." The words ran down and she stood silent, looking at him helplessly.

"Did you want to talk to me about something?"

"I didn't want to speak to that man, Inspector Nash, because if it weren't important, I'd feel such a fool. And Emma said you were a policeman, too, so I thought you might be able . . . I didn't want Emma to know, you see . . . I told Inspector Nash I'd been asleep, but it wasn't quite true, really. Emma gets so upset when I forget things, so I waited until she'd gone to sleep . . ."

"Did you forget something, then?" Kincaid leaned against the wall, patient and relaxed, his professional manner slipping over him. He took care not to hurry her.

"My handbag. In the lounge. I had such a good time at the party. I had a sherry. I don't usually, it must have made me forgetful . . ."

Penny's voice trailed off again, and Kincaid dared to prompt her. "Did you go out to look for it, after Emma fell asleep?"

"I waited until she started snoring. She never wakes after that." A faint trace of her impish grin appeared. "The house was so quiet. I felt a little . . . skittish. An unfamiliar place, and dark. I didn't expect—" She broke off, the momentary ease vanishing as swiftly as it had come. "It probably didn't mean anything. I couldn't stand to cause anyone distress. To be fair, I think perhaps I ought to speak—"

"Penny, there you are. I've been looking everywhere for you." Emma MacKenzie's head appeared at the top of the stairwell, followed by her body as she puffed her way up the last few steps. "What are you doing skulking up here?"

"I just wanted a word with Mr. Kincaid, Emma."

Penny was apologetic and flustered, and, Kincaid thought, a tiny bit relieved. He cursed under his breath. He'd get nothing more now, whatever she'd steeled herself to say would have to wait.

"Miss MacKenzie's just been telling me what I should see—"

"Well, for goodness sake, let Mr. Kincaid get on with it, then, and come along or we'll miss the best birding of the day. It's already late." Emma turned, and muttered "A whole morning wasted . . ." as she stomped back down the stairs.

Kincaid winked at Penny behind Emma's back as they followed obediently behind.

Cassie, as far as Kincaid could see, had not been one to suffer an uncomfortable night. He found her in her office, serene among the clutter, looking rested, sleek and so self-satisfied he almost expected her to purr. She smiled brightly at him, and gave him his rank—letting him know, thought Kincaid, that they weren't going to get too chummy.

"What can I do for you, Superintendent?"

"Sleep well, Cassie?" She only smiled and waited,

as if expecting greater things from him. "I thought you might be able to give me Sebastian's address."

"Playing the good Samaritan?" Cassie mocked him.

"I thought someone should. You said he lived with his mum. What about his dad?" Kincaid propped himself on the edge of her desk, riffling his fingers through the loose papers scattered on its top. He leaned toward her, encroaching on the deliberate distance she had placed between them.

"Died years ago, or at least that's what he always said. Mummy raised her boy alone." Cassie crossed her arms under her breasts and tilted her head to look up at him.

"Cassie, did you see Sebastian after the party that night? He seemed perfectly all right earlier."

"I went over to my cottage about ten. He was tidying up in the lounge. He said he'd lock up—he usually did. Liked to play lord of the manor, padding around the house at night arranging everything just so. Then, last thing, he'd use the Jacuzzi. If I were awake I'd hear his motorbike start up when he left—he parked it right alongside the cottages." Cassie seemed to be talking as much to herself as to Kincaid, her voice quiet and touched with what might almost have been a trace of regret. "I don't remember hearing it that night, though I wasn't conscious of missing anything at the time."

"And did you see or hear anything else after you'd turned in that night?"

"Don't cross-examine me, Superintendent," Cassie said nastily. "Your Inspector Nash has already done enough for the two of you." She flipped through a Rolodex on her desk and scribbled something on a scrap of paper. "Here's your address. Now if you don't mind, I've got work to do."

He'd blown it. All Cassie's armor had fallen back into place with a clang.

Eddie Lyle sat in the sitting room armchair, a newspaper spread open on his lap.

Kincaid, retreating from Cassie's office, paused in the doorway. Could he escape with a nod and a greeting? His hesitation proved his undoing.

Lyle looked up and spoke. "Mr. Kincaid." He rattled the paper. "We've made the local rag this morning. I do hope the nationals don't pick it up. I don't want my daughter distressed by reading some sensational account."

Caught between going and staying and not wanting to commit himself to a prolonged conversation, Kincaid wandered over to the sofa opposite Lyle and leaned against its rolled, velvet back. The tufted buttons dug into his thigh. "Your daughter's the same age as Angela Frazer?"

"Yes, she's fifteen, but—"

"Most fifteen-year-olds don't read the papers, Mr. Lyle. I wouldn't worry."

"Chloe's not a bit like Angela Frazer, Mr. Kincaid. She's a very good student, and I've always encouraged her to keep up with world affairs."

"She's away at school, then?"

"Yes, but close enough that we can have her home most weekends." Lyle took off his spectacles and pinched the bridge of his nose between his thumb and forefinger. "My daughter's going to have all the advantages, Mr. Kincaid. She won't need to scrape and struggle for things the way I did."

Finding Lyle almost bearable now that he wasn't spouting pompous grievances, Kincaid refrained from saying that few children seemed to appreciate being given advantages their parents lacked—they saw such benefits as their due.

Lyle must have done well enough for himself, though—a daughter away at school, clothes which looked expensive even if ill-fitting, and timeshare holidays didn't come cheaply. "I understand you were in the army?"

"They educated me, but I got no free ride, if that's what you're thinking. I paid my dues, Mr. Kincaid, I paid my dues." Lyle looked back at his paper, folding it and snapping the crease in sharply.

Having a conversation with Eddie Lyle was a bit like treading on eggshells, thought Kincaid, no matter how carefully you stepped, you made a mess of it.

The address was a narrow, terraced house in one of the winding alleys behind Thirsk's market square. A brass knocker shone and a few defiant petunias still brightened the window boxes. Before he could ring, the door opened and he faced a middle-aged woman with faded, fair hair.

"Mrs. Wade?" The woman nodded. "May I come in? My name's Kincaid." He handed her his I.D. card and she examined it carefully, then stepped back in silent acquiescence. She wore what appeared to be her Sunday best, a navy, serge shirtwaist with white cuffs and collar. The pale hair was carefully combed, but her eyes were red and swollen with weeping and her face sagged as if gravity had become an unbearable burden. Even her lipstick seemed to be slipping from her lips, a slow, red avalanche of grief.

"I knew he was dead." Her voice, when it came, was flat, uninflected, and directed somewhere beyond him.

"Mrs. Wade." Kincaid's gentle tone recalled her, and her eyes focused on his face for the first time. "I don't want to mislead you. I'm not really here on police business. The local C.I.D. is officially investigating your son's death. I had met Sebastian at Followdale, where I'm staying as a guest, and I wanted to offer my condolences."

"She said, that nice policewoman who came yesterday, that a policeman staying in the house had found him. Was that you?"

"Yes, more or less," Kincaid said, afraid the knowledge that the children had actually discovered her son's body would only add to her distress.

"Did you . . . how . . ." She abandoned whatever she had been going to ask, finding, Kincaid felt, that hearing a physical description of the circumstances of her son's death was beyond her present level of endurance. Instead she looked at him again, and asked, "Did you like him?"

"Yes, I did. He was kind to me, and very amusing."

She nodded, and some tension in her relaxed. "I'm glad it was you. No one's come. Not even that Cassie." She turned from him abruptly and led the way into the sitting room. "Would you like some tea? I'll just put the kettle on."

The room in which she left him was cold, clean,

well-kept and utterly devoid of charm or comfort. The air had the stale odor of an old steamer trunk. The wallpaper had once been rose. The furniture might have belonged to Mrs. Wade's parents, new and dubiously respectable fifty years ago. There were no books, no television or radio. She must live in the kitchen, Kincaid thought, or a back parlour. This room had surely not been used since the last death in the family.

The tea things were carefully arranged on an old tin tray, with mismatched, faded china cups and saucers. "Mrs. Wade," Kincaid began when she had settled herself in one of the horsehair chairs and was occupied pouring the tea, "how did you know, yesterday, that your son was dead? Did someone tell you?"

"He did." She answered flatly, glancing quickly at him and then back at her tea. She held the cup close to her chest, both hands wrapped around it as if its warmth could revive her. "I woke in the night, early morning really, and I felt him there, in my room. He didn't speak to me, not out loud like, but somehow I knew that he wanted me to know that he was all right, not to worry about him. And I knew he was dead. That's all. But I knew."

And so she had risen, and dressed, and waited all those hours for someone to come and tell her, to make death official. Ten years ago Kincaid would have scoffed at her story, put it down to overwrought imagination charged by grief, convenient hindsight. But he had heard too many similar accounts not to have some respect for the lingering power of the spirit.

Kincaid set his cup down gingerly in its saucer, the violets on the cup meeting the saucer's roses in delicate profusion. Mrs. Wade's attention had wandered from him again. She sat with her eyes fixed on the opposite wall, the forgotten teacup still clasped in her hands. "Mrs. Wade," he said quietly, "who were Sebastian's particular friends?"

Her eyes came back to him, startled. "I can't say as he had any, not really. He was at work all day and into the evening, most days. He liked to use the . . ." she faltered for a moment, "pool, after work. One of the perks of having a cushy job, he called it. I know he didn't get on with that Cassie. Said she lorded it over everybody, and her no better than she should be. A construction foreman's daughter from Clapham. Liked them to think she came from landed gentry, or some such. He used to tell me about the folk who came to stay, what they wore, how they talked. Sometimes he could make it seem like they were right there in the room with you." She smiled, remembering, and Kincaid could hear Sebastian's light voice, wickedly mimicking the pompous utterances of his unsuspecting victims. "But no one ever came back here with him. Mostly when he wasn't working he stayed in his room."

"Would you mind if I had a look at Sebastian's room, Mrs. Wade?"

He didn't know what he'd expected. But whatever preconceptions had hovered on the fringe of his imagination—posters of rock stars, perhaps, remnants of adolescence—they had been nothing like this.

This, it seemed, was where Sebastian had spent his money, apart from the payments on his motorbike, and what he spent on his clothes. The room was fitted with a pale gray Berber wool carpet, a flat commercial weave, very expensive looking. Lustrous green plants filled strategic corners. The dresser and side chairs looked like antiques, or good reproductions. The bed had high, matching curved ends. Kincaid believed it was called a sleigh bed, and again, probably a reproduction. Hanging on the pale gray walls were museum-quality framed prints, some Modernists, one or two Kincaid thought he recognized as American Impressionists.

Sebastian's reading matter was equally eclectic, housed in a simple pine bookcase which was the only visible holdover from his boyhood years. Childhood classics propped up stacks of magazines detailing the art of motorcycle maintenance. Stephen King mingled with espionage and the latest techno-thrillers—Sebastian's taste had apparently run to the complicated and the devious. On the top shelf Kincaid discovered an old edition of the Complete Sherlock Holmes, and a worn set of Jane Austen.

Clothes hung neatly in the wardrobe, organized by type as well as color. The sight of those garments, waiting for their owner to pick and choose, match and discard them, struck Kincaid as almost unbearably sad.

He found the files in the back of the wardrobe, stowed carefully in a cardboard box marked "Insurance."

7

KINCAID THANKED MRS. Wade as kindly as he could, taking her small hand in his for a moment. She had drifted away again while he was upstairs, and her eyes focused on him with difficulty. She smelled faintly, he noticed, of chewing gum and fresh-cut tobacco, the aromas of the tobacconist's shop.

"What about the shop, Mrs. Wade? Have you got someone to take over for you?"

"I've shut it just now. Didn't seem right. I meant to leave it to Sebastian, you know. Not for him to serve behind the counter, not with his advantages, but he could have hired someone and still had a nice little income. I put all the insurance money from his dad into it. It should have been his."

Kincaid patted the limp hand, searching for some words of comfort. "I'm sure he would have appreciated it, Mrs. Wade. I'm sorry."

The brass knocker winked brightly at him as he closed the door. The morning had turned fair and blowy while he'd been inside. A piece of yellow paper fluttered under the Midget's wiper like a butterfly trapped in the sun. He'd collected a parking ticket for his trouble—the local traffic constable, at least, was vigilant.

Kincaid retrieved the ticket and stuck it into his wallet. He folded the Midget's top down, lowered himself into the driver's seat and sat in the silent street, thinking. What to do, now, with this unexpected information? He couldn't ignore it. Why, in the name of all that was competent, hadn't Nash's men searched the room already? It had been nearly thirty-six hours since Sebastian's body had been discovered, and Nash had only sent a W.P.C. to break the news—he hadn't even interviewed the mother, for Christ's sake. Actually, he amended, "thank god" might be a better qualification, as he couldn't imagine that Nash would have done anything to ease her distress.

Nash would have to be told, there was no help for it. And help, decided Kincaid, was just what he needed. He turned the key in the ignition and lifted the car phone from its cradle.

Kincaid counted himself extremely fortunate in his immediate superior. Chief Superintendent Denis Childs was an intelligent man whom Kincaid liked personally and respected professionally—and Kincaid knew that the luck of the draw could have just as easily given him a chief like Nash, although he liked to think that a copper of Nash's caliber would never make it past Detective Constable at the Yard.

Denis Childs was a massive man, dwarfing Kincaid's rangy six feet, and with his olive skin and bland inscrutability of feature, he sometimes made Kincaid think of an Eastern potentate—one finger on the political pulse and the other on his harem.

"Sir," Kincaid said, when they were finished with the standard greetings, "I've run into a little problem."

"Oh, you have, have you?" Childs said equably, with his usual disinclination to be ruffled. "And just how little is it?"

"Um," Kincaid hesitated, "the situation's a bit tricky. Yesterday morning I found the house's assistant manager electrocuted in the swimming pool. The local D.C.I. is of the opinion that it was suicide, but I think he'll find it's not when the lab reports come back. At any rate, I'm not too happy about the whole thing. I just . . . um . . . happened across some files of the victim's that contain some fairly damaging information on some of the timeshare owners."

"Just happened, my ass. You've been snooping, Kincaid, where you'd no right to stick your nose." Childs' voice contained a note of approval. "Blackmail, eh?"

"Funnily enough, I don't really think so. Not directly, anyway. I wondered if you could smooth the way for me to make a few discreet inquiries. Don't want to step on any toes—" Kincaid paused. "Actually, I'd like to stomp the bastard's shins, but in the interest of departmental good will . . ."

"I imagine you've already stepped on plenty, if you've been looking about. The A.C. will appreciate your restraint," Childs added sarcastically. "But I'll see what I can do. I believe the Chief Constable up there is an old friend of the A.C. Perhaps the A.C. would be willing to have a word with him on your behalf. Offer the Squad's assistance if the business does turn nasty. I'll have a word in his ear. In the meantime, try to keep out of trouble."

"I'll tread like an angel," Kincaid said. "All right if I call Sergeant James?"

"On your head be it," Childs answered, and Kincaid hung up, satisfied.

Gemma James shoved two combs into her ginger curls, one more attempt on her part to bulldoze them into professionalism. She frowned at herself in the mirror, pulled the combs free and quickly brushed her hair into a pony-tail at the nape of her neck. "I give up," she said aloud. If God had seen fit to give her red hair and freckles, she might as well accept them gracefully and stop harboring secret desires to be an icy blond or a sultry brunette. A little make-up toned the freckles down to a barely noticeable dusting, and that would have to do.

The phone rang just as she scooped up a rambunctious Toby, ready to take him to the sitter's. The morning off had improved her outlook, and she reached for the receiver with a return of her usual energy. "No, no, love. Let Mummy get it." She gripped Toby's clutching fingers with one hand and picked up the phone with the other, shifting her handbag and balancing the toddler on her hip. Gemma rested her cheek for a moment against his flaxen hair. It was straight as a die, thank god, a genetic wild card, unlike either her own or his dad's dark mop.

"Gemma?"

"Sir. How's your holiday?" Gemma grinned into the

phone, both surprised and pleased to hear Kincaid's voice. She toed the uneasy line between Christian name and title.

"Sorry to interrupt your morning, Gemma. Are you working on anything in particular?"

It was business, then, and she'd called it right. "Not really. Why?"

"I'd like you to do some checking for me, and I'd like you to do it as unofficially as possible. I've cleared it with the Guv'nor, but I don't really have any official jurisdiction."

"Gossip with the old biddies?" Gemma knew Kincaid's indirect methods.

"Right. Although in some cases you may have to speak directly to relatives. The problem is that I don't really know what I'm looking for. Anything in these people's lives that doesn't mesh, doesn't seem quite right. Let me fill you in."

Gemma listened, and wrote, having long since set the squirming Toby down. With half her mind she heard him pulling pots and pans out of the cupboard, his favorite pastime, but her attention was concentrated on Kincaid, and when she finally hung up she wore a small, satisfied smile.

As Kincaid locked the Midget and started across the gravel toward Followdale House, Inspector Peter Raskin came out the door and ran nimbly down the steps to meet him.

"Sir, I'd just about given up on you," said Raskin, by way of greeting. "Thought you might like to know what the scene of crime lab came up with."

Kincaid glanced up at the blank faces of the windows above them. "We do need to talk. Let's move away a bit." They strolled down to the bench at the end of the garden—the same spot where he and Hannah had stood two nights before and thought how gay and welcoming the house looked with the light spilling from its windows. "You first," said Kincaid, when they had settled themselves on the bench.

"You were right about the heater and the plug. There's not a smudge of a print anywhere on it that doesn't belong to Cassie Whitlake. So, either Cassie plugged it in, and in that case why would she implicate herself, or the person who did wore gloves. Now, if it were Sebastian—and I never heard of a suicide wearing gloves—what did he do with them? His clothes, his shoes, his wallet, even his handkerchief and comb were folded in a neat stack by the bench. Did he plug the heater in, go dispose of the gloves somewhere, then come back and undress and hop in? I don't buy it." Raskin paused. "The heater might have shorted itself out before he could get in the pool. And I never knew a neat suicide not to leave a note."

"I didn't buy it, either," said Kincaid. "What about the p.m.?"

"The best the doc can give us from the stomach contents is between ten and midnight."

"Not much help, but then I didn't expect it would be. None of the guests have a definite alibi?"

"Not to speak of." Raskin ticked them off his fingers. "Cassie says she went to her cottage, alone, around ten, and didn't come out again. The Hunsingers had gone to bed and to sleep, after tucking in the children and having some herbal tea. Marta and Patrick Rennie say they were in their suite all the time, but she doesn't look too comfortable about it. The MacKenzie ladies retired around ten, were both asleep by eleven. Janet Lyle had a headache, and her husband fixed her a cup of tea. She then went to sleep and he did, too. Um, let's see, who's left?"

"The Frazers?" Kincaid prompted.

"The Frazers, father and daughter, arrived back from dinner in York about ten-thirty, whereupon they both went to bed."

"And Hannah and I," Kincaid continued for him, "were walking in this garden around eleven o'clock—"

"After which you each went, alone, to your separate suites," finished Raskin, and stretched his fingers until the knuckles popped.

"Pretty bloody useless, the whole lot," said Kincaid in disgust. "Any of them could be lying and we'd never be the wiser. For starters, I don't think Angela Frazer has a clue whether her dad was in the suite or not. They had a terrible row on the way home and she locked herself in the bathroom. Went to sleep on the tiles."

Raskin grinned. "Your interrogation technique must be a sight better than my chief's—he didn't get more than sullen 'yeses' and 'noes' out of her."

"I don't doubt it. Peter," said Kincaid, feeling his way cautiously. "I paid a call on Sebastian's mum." Raskin merely raised his eyebrows. "I had a look at his room. He kept files on the timeshare owners, some of them potentially damaging."

Both Raskin's eyebrows shot up this time. "Nash'll have you on a platter, sir. Since the lab work came back he's sent a team round there—he'll likely have a stroke when he finds out you've been there before him."

Kincaid grinned a little guiltily. "It wasn't premeditated. I've since repented and pulled a few strings to smooth your chief's ruffled feathers. But it might be wise on my part to stay out of his way until things have had a chance to percolate down from the top. If Nash chews me out and then has to eat his words, it'll make him even more difficult to deal with."

Raskin gave him a considering look. "Scotland Yard going to be 'helping us with our inquiries'?"

"Could be. All very politely and politically done, of course."

"Of course," Raskin responded, and they grinned at each other in complete understanding. "All right," prompted Raskin, "could you tell me, sir? Just what sort of dirt did the ever-curious Mr. Wade dig up?"

Kincaid stretched out his legs and contemplated the toes of his trainers meditatively. "There were files on a number of guests who must own other weeks, but I think it would be practical to assume that we should concentrate on those who are here this week. Somehow Sebastian came across a rumor circulating in Dedham village that Emma and Penny MacKenzie helped their dear old dad to a speedier end than nature intended." Raskin looked startled but didn't interrupt. "He was diabetic and they administered his insulin themselves—they could have increased his dosage a bit."

"I suppose it's possible. I've heard more unlikely stories. Next prospect?"

"Graham Frazer. It seems that he's been carrying on

a very torrid affair with Cassie Whitlake—a situation that doesn't appear to be too damaging to either of them, except that Frazer is involved in a bitter custody battle over Angela and any misconduct might provide ammunition to be used against him. Those are Sebastian's assumptions, by the way. He was very thorough.

"He also noted a growing sense of marital discord between the Rennies. That's all on this lot—except a note of an old drug conviction against Maureen Hunsinger."

Raskin spluttered. "Our Lady of the Earth? I thought nothing unnatural ever passed her lips."

Kincaid grinned at his reaction. "It's really not too unlikely. The natural foods movement is in some ways an outgrowth of the hippie culture of the sixties and seventies, and this conviction was twenty years old. How Sebastian found out about it I can't imagine."

"What about the others?" Raskin asked.

"This is the first visit for Hannah Alcock and the Lyles. Maybe he hadn't come up with anything."

"The same is true of the MacKenzies," Raskin reminded him.

Kincaid frowned. "That's something to consider. I wonder how he got hold of that little story."

"Nothing on your cousin?" Raskin's eyebrow tilted at a wicked angle.

"No, thank god," Kincaid said with relief. "Jack was clean as a whistle. That would have put me in a spot."

"And who," said Raskin deliberately, "would you put your money on as the blackmail victim?"

Kincaid didn't answer for a moment. He gazed at the silent bulk of the house, and when he spoke it was almost inaudibly. "Oddly enough, no one. I'm not sure Sebastian was blackmailing anyone. At least not for money. It looked like he kept a file on almost every owner. Mostly harmless stuff—almost like character studies. Maybe he only wanted emotional leverage." Kincaid rubbed his face with his palms. "I don't know . . . I'm riding completely on gut reaction. I just can't see him as an extortionist."

"I can imagine what my chief would have to say about that. He doesn't go in much for gut reaction. Uses his for putting away beer."

"I'll bet." Kincaid laughed, feeling restored by Raskin's easy humor. "And speaking of your chief, I think I'll make myself scarce for the afternoon, until my Guv'nor has had a chance to drop a few stones in the pond. Otherwise Nash might just run me in. Think I'll do a bit of hiking. I am, after all," Kincaid said ruefully, "supposed to be on holiday."

The sight of Emma MacKenzie on the bench above the tennis court made Kincaid detour from his course toward the back of the garden. She peered intently at the tree tops through her binoculars, her concentration undisturbed even when Kincaid sat down beside her. He waited silently, following her gaze, and after a moment he saw a flash of red. "Blast. Lost it," said Emma, lowering the binoculars.

"What was it?"

"A male bullfinch. Common enough but don't often see them. They're very shy."

"I've never watched birds," Kincaid offered. "Must be interesting."

Emma gave him a pitying look, as if at a loss to explain a lifetime passion to one who could make such an innocuous remark. "Hmmmf." She looked away from him, her gaze drawn to the trees. "An art. You should try it." She thrust the binoculars at him. "Take them. I'm going in for the afternoon, worst time of day."

"I will." Kincaid took the binoculars and lowered the strap carefully over his head. "Thanks. I thought I might climb Sutton Bank." He hesitated, then said as neutrally as he could, "Miss MacKenzie, did you talk much with Sebastian?"

Emma had been making gathering motions, as if to rise. She paused, then settled herself more comfortably on the bench. "He seemed an intelligent boy, but difficult. Quick to take things as slights, I'd say, under all that quick, sly patter." She was silent for a moment, considering. "He could be kind, though. He was kind to Angela Frazer. I think he saw her as some sort of fellow outcast, always on the fringe of her father's doings. And he seemed to despise Graham Frazer. I don't know why. He was kind to the younger children as well, thought up activities for them, things that would amuse them. He seemed comfortable with them."

"Kind to children and animals," Kincaid muttered, more to himself than Emma. Her spine tensed and she inhaled sharply. He could see all her barriers going up and he cursed himself for his tactlessness. "No, no, I'm not ridiculing you," he said quickly. "I found I liked him, too, even on such short acquaintance, and rather in spite of myself. And," he added, with an easy smile, "you're very perceptive."

Emma had relaxed again, but he sensed that the flow

had stopped. To press her would only activate her conscience, and she would censor any inclination to indulge in "idle gossip."

"What should I look for?" he asked, gesturing with the binoculars.

"You wouldn't know a robin from a magpie, I imagine. You'd better borrow this"—she handed him a small, well-worn guidebook—"so that you will have a reference. Just be observant. I shouldn't think that watching birds would be all that different from watching people. Oh, yes," she said, noting his surprised glance. "You're very practiced. A talent partly learned and partly natural, I should think. You inspire confidence in others with that air of sincere attention to every word, a little well-judged flattery. And I had better go before I say something I shouldn't." With that, she pushed herself off the bench and strode toward the house without a backward glance.

8

The footpath crossed a small stream at the back of the grounds, then turned abruptly right to follow the stream toward Sutton Bank. It was easy walking at first, cool under the overhanging branches, the ground padded with leaf litter and crunching acorns. Boughs heavy with horse-chestnuts drooped overhead, and twice Kincaid saw crimson toadstools among the fallen leaves, bright as drops of blood. There were no birds. The wood remained eerily still and silent.

He eventually came out into the sunlight and began to climb. The binoculars thumped regularly against his chest with each step, a second heartbeat. Blackberry brambles growing into the path scratched his hands and snagged his clothes. He paused every so often to extricate himself. As he neared the summit, Kincaid felt almost overcome by drowsiness, the sun and the dusty, pollen-laden air affecting his senses like a drug. He came across a patch of brown brake fern to the side of the path, trampled and flattened as though someone else had lain there. It was irresistible.

Kincaid stretched out among the dying fronds and went instantly to sleep.

A shadow across his face woke him. It took his confused brain a second to sort out the images his eyes sent it—huge red and yellow barred wings hovered above him, and a human face suspended between them peered down at him. A hang glider. Bloody hell. Sutton Bank, he remembered reading in the brochures provided by the timeshare, was a popular spot for hang gliders, but the damn thing had nearly scared him out of his wits.

Kincaid sat up and watched the glider descend toward Followdale House, then raised Emma's binoculars and focused them on the car park. Hannah's metallic Citroën turned in the gate and stopped on the gravel, and her small form, distant and unrecognizable except for some quality of posture, made its way to the door. He lowered the glasses and stretched, then rested his elbows on his propped-up knees. The combination of deep sleep and sudden awakening had cleared his head like a tonic, leaving his mind remarkably sharp and focused.

The whole bloody business didn't make sense, not from what he knew so far. He couldn't for a minute see either of the MacKenzie sisters committing premeditated murder. Reluctant euthanasia, possibly, but killing someone to cover their deed up, never. He could, however, easily imagine them shielding someone else in a mistaken sense of duty or obligation.

Had Sebastian threatened to expose Cassie's affair with Graham? That would certainly explain the conversation he had overheard. But if that were the case, why would either of them care enough to kill him to prevent it? The timeshare management might not approve of Cassie sleeping with the owners, but surely her behavior wouldn't be that damaging.

And Graham? Kincaid didn't believe custody judges expected divorced fathers to remain celibate. Besides, he'd wager Angela knew exactly what was going on, if not all the intimate details. She was a good bit sharper than her dad credited. So if Cassie and Graham were together the night of Sebastian's death, why hadn't they alibied one another?

Kincaid sighed. He didn't have enough information for even these vague suppositions. Gemma might turn up something, but he couldn't depend on it. There was no alternative he could see but to stretch his already untenable position a little farther. He couldn't go back to his holiday resolution, blithely ignoring the whole matter. He had an unhealthy tendency, probably necessary to his job, of worrying at a thing like someone putting a tongue to a sore tooth—the more it hurt, the harder it was to leave it alone.

But there was something more, a sense that the script played on untended, heedless of his puny actions.

Enough. Kincaid stood up abruptly. He'd be reading Camus and crying in his beer if he went on like this. It was time he did some more digging of his own.

The cocktail hour drew Followdale's guests like the curious at the scene of an accident. They came, Kincaid thought, overcoming their distaste, their self-preserving instinct for gossip stronger than their discomfort in one another's company.

Discomfort wasn't exactly the noun Kincaid would have chosen to describe the tableau presented by the M.P., Patrick Rennie, and Hannah. They stood before the mantelpiece in animated conversation, seemingly unaware of the bodies milling about them. Rennie looked elegantly casual, his gleaming pale hair accentuated by the teal blue of his pullover. Cashmere, thought Kincaid, it had to be cashmere. Nothing else would do. Hannah laughed, her face turned up to Rennie's, her expression almost jubilant.

Kincaid stood still in the doorway, feeling childishly, ridiculously, slighted. How absurd. They had enjoyed each other's company, nothing more. He had no claim on Hannah's attention, or affections.

He made for the bar, turning a bland smile on Maureen as he passed, determined to reach the bar before she could buttonhole him. Beer tonight, he thought. The bar's whiskey was best kept for medicinal purposes. He poured a pint of dark ale and conscientiously clinked his money into the bowl.

Marta Rennie sat alone at one of the small, round tables in the bar area, its glossy faux-wood surface marred by moisture rings and cigarette ashes. She took a fierce drag on a cigarette. Under the table her foot tapped with a convulsive rhythm. Suffering a few pangs of jealousy of her own, thought Kincaid. Nothing made a better prospect for damaging slips of the tongue than the proverbial woman scorned, and Kincaid set out to take full advantage.

"Mind if I join you?" Kincaid gave her a smile.

"Suit yourself." Her nasal vowels were as flat and disinterested as the look she gave him. Kincaid slid a stool back and eased onto it before drinking off some of his beer. Marta continued to smoke, her eyes fixed on some invisible point in the distance, and Kincaid took his time, studying her. In coloring and feature she might have been her husband's sister rather than his wife, and Kincaid always suspected more than a hint of narcissism in those who chose physical mirror images of themselves as mates. But at close quarters Malta's well-bred polish was marred by the stench of stale tobacco.

"I was surprised to see such a crowd tonight. You'd have thought the circumstances would have been a bit dampening." Kincaid's weak conversational gambit elicited no response at all. This night wouldn't make records for boosting his ego. Marta ground her cigarette out in the cheap tin ashtray and sipped her drink with a not-quite-steady hand. It looked like pure gin, or vodka, and Kincaid realized Marta Rennie was well on her way to tying one on.

When she did speak it surprised him. "Fifteen years. Must have at least fifteen years on him." Kincaid could hear the slight slur in her voice now, the exaggerated sibilants.

"Who does?"

"That scientist . . ." She lapsed into silence again. A pale yellow silk scarf had replaced the black velvet bow at the nape of her neck. The scarf's soft bow had come half undone and hung, bedraggled, down her back.

"You mean Hannah?"

"He's so bloody impressed. With her 'accomplishments.' " Marta sneered the word. "But he didn't want a professional wife. Oh, no, charity work . . . somebody to sit next to him at banquets and look nice. A wife to trot out on speaking platforms like a prize pony at a gymkhana. Bloody useless." She held her drink up and squinted into its depths as if it, crystal ball-like, contained some redemption.

"I'm sure your husband appreciates what you do for him."

"Like hell." Marta lit another cigarette. "Though I dare say," she continued through a cloud of smoke, "he does appreciate Mummy and Daddy pouring money into his campaign fund."

Kincaid decided subtlety would be wasted on Marta in her present condition. "I hear," he leaned toward her and lowered his voice conspiratorially, "that Inspector Nash isn't happy with the suicide verdict on Sebastian. It's a good thing you and Patrick were together that night. Now there's a thing that could really cause him image problems with those conservative constituents."

Marta focused on him, puzzled. "What could?"

"A murder investigation." Kincaid dropped it gently, like a pebble in a pool.

Marta gave him a sly, sideways look. "I was asleep, wasn't I? Very convenient. He was, too. Asleep, I mean. Aspiring politicians," she stumbled a bit over the syllables, "shouldn't run around at night when the wife's asleep. Very stupid. Patrick," she enunciated his name very clearly, "is never stupid." Marta drained her glass and set it down with a thump. "Buy me a drink?"

"Sure. What are you having?"

"G and T. No T."

Kincaid refilled her drink and took it back to the table. Angry as she might be, Marta Rennie was sly with a drunk's cleverness. She hadn't lost sight of the side on which her political bread was buttered.

Kincaid wandered back into the sitting room, half-drunk, beer in hand, in search of more sober prospects. Enjoyment, it seemed, was contagious. The guests had gathered around Hannah and Patrick as if hoping some of the spontaneous pleasure would rub off. Eddie and Janet Lyle, Maureen Hunsinger and Graham Frazer. And Penny. Penny sipped her sweet sherry, her face flushed with excitement. Only Emma, John Hunsinger, and the children were missing.

Kincaid joined the fringe of the group. Hannah smiled at him and he returned her smile, infected by her apparent delight in spite of himself.

"What's the joke?" Kincaid asked Hannah. "Have I missed something?"

"Patrick's just been telling the most amusing story about one of his constituents—"

Rennie demurred. "Oh, it's nothing really. My most loyal campaigner, but she can't remember my name. She's an old dear, active on every committee in the county, raises oodles of money. I wouldn't dare suggest she let someone else introduce me. But I've got a very important by-election coming up, and I imagine she'll stand up to introduce me at the final rally, open her mouth and stop, utterly without a clue."

Rennie told his anecdote with charm and practiced ease, and Kincaid could imagine the ladies "of a certain age" cooing over him, and fighting for his attention with the ferocity of ferrets.

"I forget things, too, sometimes," said Penny, into

the pause that followed. "Just the other night I couldn't find my bag. I looked everywhere for it, and then I came downstairs and I'd left it right here on the table!"

"Those things happen to me all the time, too," Maureen put in good-naturedly. "Sometimes I think I'd forget my children if they didn't remind me."

"Eddie's mother forgot things." Janet Lyle spoke quietly, with a diffident glance at her husband. "We were desperately concerned about her. We didn't think it safe for her to live alone, but she wouldn't agree to go in a home."

"Very proud. Very independent to the last," Eddie agreed.

Maureen responded with ready sympathy. "Oh, dear. What happened?"

"An accident. In the car." Eddie shook his head. "We'd spoken to her over and over again about her driving. She wouldn't listen. Our Chloe was heartbroken." Kincaid fancied he heard a touch of satisfaction in Lyle's voice, an "I told you so" not quite conquered.

Patrick spoke into the chorus of concerned tut-tuts. "It's very difficult, caring for an aging parent. I hear it from my constituents all the time."

Now, thought Kincaid, are we going to hear the stock conservative solution, or is he genuinely concerned? His eyes swept the circle of faces, expecting expressions of kindly interest.

The response seemed quite out of proportion. Penny MacKenzie's eyes had filled and tears hung quivering on her lower lashes. "Excuse me." The whisper was almost inaudible. She thrust her sherry glass into Maureen's hand and fled the room.

"What on earth?" Patrick spoke into the silence that followed the banging of the reception room door. "Did I put my foot in it, somehow?"

"I don't know," Maureen answered. "I believe Penny and Emma cared for their ailing father for a long time. Maybe the reminder upset her."

"How difficult for her," said Janet Lyle, and they nodded sympathetically. All except Hannah, who, Kincaid noticed, had gone very pale, and looked, for the first time since they had met, her age.

"I'd better be off, myself." Hannah gave a brittle smile and left the room without so much as a glance at Patrick.

"Dear god, it's catching," Cassie spoke for the first time. "Poor Patrick. Let's hope you haven't the same effect on the voters." Until then she had stood at the back of the group and left them, for once, to their own devices. Her tone was caustic.

Before Rennie could respond, his wife appeared in the doorway of the bar. She walked as if she were treading on egg shells, with the exquisite care of the very drunk. The yellow scarf trailed over her shoulder like a banner. "What's the matter," she said with great deliberation, "has someone got their feelings hurt?"

The croquet mallet hit the ball with a satisfying smack. Brian Hunsinger whooped with delight as his ball slammed his sister's well away from the wicket. "I got you. I got you," he shrieked and swung his mallet again in pantomime.

"Baby!" yelled Bethany. "I won't play with you. You cheat. It was my turn."

"Was not."

"It'll be too dark to play soon." Angela broke into the squabble. "Come on, Beth. It's your turn now. I'll bet you can knock Brian's ball halfway to the drive."

Angela as peacemaker. Quite a change, Kincaid thought, from the sullen child who sat in corners and spoke to no one. He stood on the steps and watched the three children. At the other end of the garden Emma MacKenzie and John Hunsinger sat together companionably on the stone bench. Certainly they seemed in better accord than the group that had just broken up inside.

Patrick Rennie had hustled his wife out of the room, his face flushed with embarrassment. "Too bad. Poor Patrick," Marta Rennie said over her shoulder as her husband maneuvered her through the doorway. The last thing they heard was an echo of her spiteful giggle from the entrance hall.

Cassie turned on her heel and left the room without a word. Graham, who had been as silent as Cassie all evening, said, "Shit. Maybe she's got the right idea," and disappeared into the bar.

Maureen looked around as if surprised to find her husband and children not attached to her. "Oh dear, the kiddies haven't had their tea," she said and hurried from the room.

"Well, it was a nice party. I mean, until . . ." Janet ducked her head, her eyes straying in her husband's direction.

"Appalling. Absolutely appalling. How the man has the nerve to stand for public office with a wife like that, I can't imagine." Eddie stalked from the room, and Janet followed with a last apologetic glance at Kincaid.

Cassie pulled her sweater over her head in irritation. The angora fiber woven into the sweater's wool had rubbed her skin until it felt as if it had been scrubbed with a wire brush. But the color, a dull olive, flattered her, and she had dressed with special care. Not that it had mattered. She could have worn a flour sack for all the difference it had made.

Nothing had gone right for her since the minute she walked into the sitting room for cocktails.

Nothing had gone right for her, in fact, since that dreadful row with Sebastian on Sunday afternoon. Cassie dropped her sweater where she stood, kicked off her linen slacks in the direction of the bedroom and shrugged herself into an old satin dressing gown left lying across the armchair the night before. She'd made little effort to imprint her personality on the bland chintz-and-oak atmosphere of the cottage. She even preferred to make love in the big house, when she could manage it.

The brief flicker of pleasure on her face at the thought vanished as she remembered the last time she had met a lover there. She'd known exactly what she must say, must do, and it had slipped out of her control, somehow, all her intentions retaining no more force than a trickle of water. All the carefully gathered strands of her life seemed to be falling from her hands, one by one.

The gentle tapping on the cottage door jerked Cassie out of her reverie. Anger rushed through her. She yanked open the door. "I told you never to—"

Duncan Kincaid stood there, with his infuriating cat-that-ate-the-canary grin. "Expecting someone else? I'll go away again."

After a moment Cassie pulled the door wide and stepped back, not speaking until she had closed it behind him. "What are you doing here?" She drew the dressing gown more tightly around her body.

Kincaid gazed around the room, hands in his pockets, and Cassie suddenly remembered the clothes discarded on the floor. She bent and picked them up, threw them into the bedroom and shut the door.

"Nice." Kincaid indicated the cottage. "Do much entertaining here?"

Cassie held herself in check, refusing to be baited. Just what in hell did he know? "Just you." She smiled at him with a trace of her former poise. "Like a drink?"

Kincaid shook his head. "No, thanks. We've just had an object lesson in the evils of alcohol, don't you think?" His smile invited her to share his amusement at the debacle of the cocktail party, but Cassie wasn't to be drawn.

"Cassie." He perched himself on the arm of one of the overstuffed chintz armchairs and regarded her with an open, friendly look that she found even more alarming than the smile. "If you and Graham Frazer were together the night Sebastian died, why didn't you say so? It'd be so much easier on both of you."

Turning away from him, she walked around the counter into the kitchen. "Coffee, then?" She filled the coffeepot, the ritual movements buying her time to think. How much did he know? What could she gain by denial?

"Look, Duncan. Don't give me that sympathetic tone, as if my welfare were tops on your list of priorities. I'm not stupid. And just what makes you think I was with Graham that night?" She kept her voice level, bantering.

"You've been having an affair with him for quite some time. It seemed likely." Kincaid rose from the chair and pulled up a stool across the counter from her, making her feel trapped in the tiny kitchen. The electric kettle sang and she poured the boiling water into the drip pot. Mugs hung on a rack next to the pot. She plunked two on the counter and stared at them, biting her lip. Pansies and roses intertwined gaily around their surfaces. They were cottage property, not her own.

"What makes you think I've been having an affair with Graham?" Some coffee missed the mug and splashed onto the counter as Cassie poured.

Kincaid accepted the mug. Cassie pulled her hand back quickly, hoping he hadn't noticed its slight trembling. "What puzzles me," he said, ignoring her question, "is why you've made such a point to keep it secret. You're both single, consenting adults. And I don't think for a minute that Angela would be shocked."

Cassie wrapped her long fingers around the mug until it grew too hot to bear, as if pain might sharpen her wits. Honest entreaty, she decided, was the way to play it. "It's Graham. It's this custody thing. Right now he only has extended visitation. The hearing's coming up soon and he's petitioning for complete custody. He feels he won't be considered a responsible parent. The whole thing's stupid, really, if you ask me. He's only doing it to spite Marjorie." She took a sip of the hot coffee and winced as it scalded her tongue. "I'll have to own up to your Chief Inspector Nash, of course. I didn't realize it was going to be so important." Kincaid sat silently, watching her across the rim of his cup as he sipped, and Cassie heard herself sounding as fatuous as she felt.

"Of course," Cassie continued, digging herself in deeper by the minute, "I'd rather it not become general knowledge about Graham and me. To tell you the truth, it's just about finished between us, and it wouldn't do my professional standing much good if it were to get about. So I thought . . ."

"So you thought," Kincaid finished for her when she trailed off, "you'd just conveniently not mention it. I can't say I blame you. I'm sure it all seemed a great fuss about nothing. What did it matter where anyone was when Sebastian decided to plug himself into the swimming pool? There's only one little problem. I think Chief Inspector Nash is very shortly going to come to the conclusion that Sebastian had a little unsolicited help getting himself killed. And then it matters very much what everyone was up to on Sunday night."

Kincaid gave her a brief, encouraging smile, as if he had uttered nothing out of the ordinary, and he spoke as quietly and casually as he had begun. A tremor of fear ran through Cassie's body. A moment passed before she trusted herself to speak. "I thought . . . I wasn't here. We weren't here. Graham and I."

Kincaid's eyes widened. "Surely not with Angela—"

"No. In the empty suite. We always met in the empty

suites, when we could. We were together all the time. It was after midnight when I came back here."

"And you didn't think, didn't wonder why Sebastian's bike was still parked outside?"

"No." The word hung between them, charged, and Cassie felt she had been judged and found wanting.

"You didn't see or hear anything else, anything not as it should be?"

"No." She couldn't tell him about the note. Quickly scribbled, wedged into her door, it proved someone else had been abroad in the late hours of that Sunday evening. And it had driven all thought of Sebastian, or anything else, from her mind.

"Thanks, Cassie. For the coffee." Kincaid stood up and Cassie came around the bar and followed him to the door.

As he opened it she touched his arm and he paused. "Will it . . . Do you think it will all have to come out? About Graham and me?"

"I don't know. Maybe not. But I wouldn't count too much on Nash's discretion."

She nodded. "What made you change your mind? About Sebastian committing suicide?"

"I didn't. I never thought for a moment that he had." The door clicked softly shut as he left her.

Hannah stood just inside the open French door of her suite, the room unlit in the gathering dusk. The children's voices came easily to her, but she couldn't see them without stepping out onto the balcony and she didn't want to be seen. Her emotions were so raw she felt she might be transparent even from a distance.

The reality of what she had done, what she still contemplated doing, seized her with cold fingers. She'd been living in some fairy-tale never-never land, where all stories had happy endings, and she was the fairy godmother, coming to right a lifetime of wrongs. Dear god, what a fool she had made of herself!

Her oft-played scenario had never included sexual attraction, so when the whirl of feelings caught her up so swiftly she hadn't realized at first what was happening. The knowledge crept in insidiously, and some feral part of her mind toyed with the idea of riding with it, letting it take her where it would. She could just not tell him the truth, and there was no other way he would ever know.

The sudden vision of herself brought on by the cocktail party conversation had shocked her to her senses, terrified that she could have contemplated such utter folly. She had never, when she built detailed pictures in her mind of what their relationship would be, imagined herself as . . . old. Never imagined growing older, never imagined being pitied and dependent. Whether she told him the truth or not, she would still have to face the ultimate fact. Or simply walk away, returning to the sterility of her life as if nothing had happened. And what about Duncan? What must he think of her, flitting about from man to man like some middle-aged butterfly. She felt she owed him some explanation, but she couldn't tell him all of it, not until she had come to some resolution. A sense of urgency clutched her. It would have to be soon.

Penny knew how the rabbit felt, trapped by hounds, spurred by cunning. If she went out the front door she'd run right smack into her sister, and Emma was the last person she wanted to face. She didn't want to see anyone—any attempt to explain her behavior would humiliate her even further.

In the end she'd gone upstairs and down the long corridor to the rear stairs and the pool exit. From there it had been easy enough to make her way along the path to the tennis court, screened by trees and heavy shrubbery. She sat huddled on her favorite bench above the court, her small figure almost indistinguishable in the dim light.

Emma and the children must still be out in the garden, for she could hear the little boy's high-pitched voice above her, fading in and out on the breeze. It was quite funny the way Emma got on with Brian and Bethany. They'd never really known any children—no nieces and nephews to care for, no close neighbors running in and out begging milk and biscuits—and Penny was never quite sure what to say to them. Emma, however, just bossed the small pair about in her usual gruff way. The children seemed to accept it without question and they all got on remarkably well together.

Is that, Penny wondered, the way Emma would treat her, with that same gruff kindness, but in her case stained by pity? Would people speak about her the way they had spoken about poor Mrs. Lyle, and commiserate with Emma behind her back? Would she reach the point where Emma didn't dare leave her alone, a danger to herself and others? It was an unbearable thought. The tears came again, unbidden, and Penny sat helplessly as they ran down her face and leaked salt into the corners of her mouth. Emma would tell her to stop wallowing and buck herself up, but Penny had never been much good at maintaining what Emma called an even keel.

Penny sniffed and searched in her pocket for a handkerchief. She'd have to try to pull herself together, for Emma's sake as well as her own. Besides, she had a moral obligation that needed her attention. She had made up her mind at the cocktail party. It would never do to cast false suspicion on someone. What she had seen must have another, logical explanation, and the only fair way to find out was to ask.

9

KINCAID BROKE TWO eggs into the skillet next to the bacon and congratulated himself on mastering an unfamiliar cooker. It had taken some adjusting and a grease burn on his thumb to get the temperature just right, but the bacon had come out perfectly. He turned the eggs as the toast sprang up in the toaster, and by the time he'd transferred the bacon and toast to his plate the eggs were ready as well.

The knock came as he was pouring his coffee.

Hannah Alcock leaned against the wall outside his front door, hugging herself in her long, Aran cardigan. She wore no make-up, her lips pale in contrast to the bruised hollows beneath her eyes.

"Hannah. Come in." Kincaid led the way into the suite and pulled out a chair at the tiny table for her. "Are you all right? You don't look at all well this morning."

"Didn't sleep." She slumped down in the chair as if it had taken all her effort to stand up.

"Can I get you anything? Toast? Coffee?"

"Coffee would be nice, thanks."

Kincaid poured another cup and sat down opposite her, pushing the milk and sugar across the table. She stirred her coffee for a moment before meeting his eyes, then tried a wan smile. "I feel an idiot coming here like this. I thought I'd say 'we need to talk,' but I realized it's not true, really. It's I who needs to talk." Hannah paused and looked away for a moment, moving her shoulders in a little self-deprecating shrug. "I feel I owe you some explanation for the way I've behaved. It's not—"

"Why should you feel that?" Kincaid asked, puzzled. "I've no reason to pass judgment on you."

"Oh god, Duncan, don't protest. It only makes this more humiliating for me. Then I start to think I was only imagining that there was . . . I don't know . . . some feeling, some rapport . . . between us. It's happened to me once or twice before. You meet someone, spend an evening together, find yourselves talking as if you'd known each other for years, saying things you wouldn't say to people you *had* known for years." Her smile was rueful. "It's a rare gift, an evening like that, and one I hadn't planned on."

At least, thought Kincaid, she was more honest than he. There had been some spark of affinity, of possibility, between them and he had felt hurt to find her sharing the same sudden intimacy with Patrick Rennie. Not merely sexual jealousy, although there was a bit of that as well, but more a sense of confidence betrayed. "All right, Hannah. I'll grant you that." He looked at her carefully, noted the unaltered porcelain complexion and fine bone structure, noted also the drawn look around the shadowed eyes. "But it's more than that, isn't it? You're not just worrying about my sensitive feelings."

Hannah was shaking her head before he'd finished the sentence. "No. I mean yes. I don't know." Her hand jerked as she spoke, and her undrunk coffee slopped a milky pool on the table's surface. "About Patrick. It's not what you think." The lift of Kincaid's eyebrows would have done Peter Raskin credit. "I know how it must look." She met Kincaid's eyes. "That I've gone middle-aged gaga over any man who looks at me twice. It's not like that at all. Oh, Jesus, I wish it were that simple." She dropped her face into her hands, fingers splayed across her eyes.

"Hannah . . ." Kincaid reached out a hand to touch her, drew it back.

Through her fingers she said, "You have to understand. I thought I'd made a perfect life for myself. I was smart, capable, respected. I'd been lucky enough to find work that I loved." Hannah raised her head. "People usually think I didn't have a chance to marry. The old sexually deprived spinster stereotype. God!" she said bitterly. "You'd think we'd grown past that, but we haven't. Women are still judged first as a commodity, a man's appendage. If you don't have a man you don't measure up. Simple. As for sex"—she gave a harsh laugh—"sex is easy. It's marriage that terrified me. Losing control." Hannah pushed her cup forward with her fingertips and looked out the French door. "My parents ordered every aspect of my life, what I ate, what I wore, how I cut my hair, who I saw, even what I thought. The one step I might have taken for myself they . . . took out of my hands. So I swore I would never let anybody else do that to me. Can you understand that?"

"Yes," Kincaid said softly, "I think so."

"So I went along for years, captain of my own ship and all that, and then suddenly this last year it all began to seem so empty. Oh, I had lovers all right, but no one with hooks in my life. Maybe," she sighed, and Kincaid felt some of her tension relax, "I am suffering from menopausal dementia, some hormonal imbalance. But it doesn't feel that way." She spoke now more to herself than to Kincaid, her gaze unfocused. "There's no wholeness, no connection. It feels . . ." The flow of words stopped. Hannah fell silent for a moment, then focused clearly on Kincaid. "I've done it again, haven't I? Just like that first night, and you thought I'd bored you with my life story then. I'm sorry."

"Hannah, what does this have to do with Patrick Rennie?"

She chewed her lip, then took a deep breath before she spoke. "I can't tell you. Not yet. But I will—" She cut off the beginning of his protest. "No, I want you to know. But first I have to explain some things to Patrick. Then you can tell me whether I need a shrink or a solicitor." She smiled at him with a touch of the humorous directness he'd first found so appealing. "I promise I will tell you. Afterwards."

"All right." Kincaid leaned back in his chair and pushed away his plate with its congealing egg.

Hannah's eyes strayed to his plate. "Oh, god, I've spoiled your breakfast. You haven't touched it." Her thighs bumped the table as she stood and more coffee joined the drying puddle on the table. "I'd better go. I really am sorry about all this, Duncan."

"Stop apologizing, for god's sake. You've nothing to be sorry for, and besides, it's out of character." He followed her to the door. "And I don't mind about the bloody breakfast."

"My whole life is out of character right now." She laughed, the first sound of spontaneous pleasure he'd heard from her that morning. "Thanks. Just be patient with me. Please. I know I've no right to ask."

"Sure." Kincaid stood with his hand on the door and spoke to her back as she walked away from him down the hall. "I'm good at that."

"Sir," Gemma's voice practically vibrated with early morning efficiency, "I've got some news on those inquiries you wanted."

Kincaid swallowed a mouthful of makeshift bacon sandwich. His short absence had not improved the eggs, and the cold toast and bacon he'd rescued as an afterthought as he dumped his plate in the sink.

"Gemma. God, I hate people to sound so bloody cheerful in the morning."

"Sir?"

"Sorry. Never mind. Any trouble getting clearance?"

"No, sir. The Guv'nor oiled the machinery pretty well, I think."

Kincaid smiled at the thought of his chief having a few discreet words in a few shell-like ears—Gemma's previous assignments had probably vanished in an eddy of paper in the secretarial pool. "Spill away, then.

No, hold on"—he scrambled for a pen and notebook he'd left on the sofa, pulled the phone over to the small table and took a sip of his cold coffee—"okay."

"I've been to Dedham Vale. Dull as dishwater, in my opinion." Gemma, with the ingrained prejudice of the North Londoner, didn't find much to recommend in rural villages.

"That doesn't surprise me. What else?"

"I wandered around for a bit until I found the local G.P.'s office. It seems he took care of the Reverend MacKenzie in his last illness. Knows everyone, of course, even with the National Health sending a lot of his old patients to the new clinic at Ipswich."

Kincaid couldn't resist teasing her a bit. "Got quite chatty with him, did we?" He could imagine Gemma's freckled face turning pink with annoyance. She would probably accuse him of being patronizing if she weren't on her best professional behavior, but he wasn't, really. It was just that Gemma was blind to her own assets—the frank openness of her face encouraged people's confidence in a way that a more sophisticated beauty never would.

Gemma remained silent for a moment, her usual response. When she couldn't tell whether or not he was joking, Kincaid thought, she ignored him.

"Sir, about the doctor."

"Sorry, Gemma. Go ahead."

"Well, it seems he looked after old Mr. MacKenzie for years. And the daughters. The old man was diabetic, very infirm. Lost his eyesight, kidneys failing. The doctor says he just slipped away in his sleep one night, no reason to think there was anything funny about it. But," Gemma allowed a tinge of satisfaction to creep into her voice, "I found out from the travel agent in the village where your rumor may have originated. Someone else from the village owns time at Followdale House—a retired major who, according to the receptionist at the travel agent's, is as big a gossip as any malicious old biddy you could find."

Kincaid considered a moment. "That might explain it. What else?"

"Cassie Whitlake's parents, in Clapham. The father's a building contractor's foreman. They're very proud of her. Wonderful job, clothes right out of *Vogue*, her mum says, that smart."

"I can imagine," Kincaid said drily.

"But I got the impression she doesn't visit them often. Tells her mum she can't take a holiday when other people do, it's her busiest time. She calls them, though, and her mum says she's sounded over the moon lately. Says she has a real good prospect, one that would really make people sit up and take notice of her. 'A job?' I asked, not sure what she meant. 'No, a man,' her mum says, 'an important man.' "

"Doesn't sound much like Graham Frazer. I wonder what she's playing at."

"There's a sister still at home, Evie. Taking a secretarial course. Evie says she's just as glad Cassie doesn't come home—all she does is act like Lady Muck." Kincaid heard a hint of laughter in Gemma's voice, some of the formality dropping away in the telling of her story.

"How'd you manage to get her alone? Cup of tea?" Kincaid knew Gemma's adroitness with the forgotten handbag, the helping out in the kitchen—and her ability to dig out the minutiae of people's lives.

"Uh huh. Evie says Cassie told her that if she, I mean Evie, played her cards right, she just might do half as well. A bitch, Evie called her. Not exactly what I'd call strong on family loyalty."

"Um," Kincaid said, "I can see where Cassie might merit that description. That it?"

"Just about, sir. I've written it up."

"Well, keep at it, Gemma. You never now what you might turn up. What's next?"

"The Sterrett Clinic, where Hannah Alcock works."

"Call in when you can. I've got to go. There's someone banging on the bloody door."

Kincaid yanked the door open, annoyed before he saw who it was, resigned to a thoroughly unpleasant few minutes afterwards. Chief Inspector Nash stood there, a messenger not sent by the gods. His retribution, thought Kincaid, had arrived.

"Well, laddie. Quite the lay-about, aren't we. Just got up?"

"Chief Inspector Nash. Do come in. What a pleasant surprise."

"I'm sure it is, laddie." Nash traded sarcasm for sarcasm, and sat deliberately down on one of the suite's dining room chairs, uninvited. Kincaid grimaced, repelled by the sight of the few greasy strands of hair stretched across Nash's shiny scalp.

"What can I do for you, Inspector?" Kincaid asked, not wanting to give Nash the advantage of opening the conversation.

"Pretty fancy accommodation. Must be nice on a superintendent's salary." He minced the title.

"Chief Inspector," Kincaid said slowly. "Come off it." He propped himself against the arm of the sofa. "What's up. You didn't come here to compliment me on my taste."

Nash considered him, the black eyes glinting with what might have been humor in someone else. "The lab report's in. No evidence of fingerprints on plug, cord or heater. It seems," Nash paused for effect, "that you were right. Coroner's refused to give a verdict of suicide." Nash settled himself more comfortably on the chair and appeared to change the subject.

"The Chief Constable's had a word in my ear. How fortunate it is that Superintendent Kincaid just happened to be on the scene and offered to assist us with our inquiries. You're considered quite the wonder boy with the higher ups, according to him. But you listen to me, laddie," Nash straightened up in the chair, all the malice in evidence now, "I don't appreciate wonder boys on my patch. I don't appreciate you going around with your trumped up condolences to Mrs. Wade so you could poke around where you had no right. Your rank and your fancy opinions," he jabbed a finger at Kincaid, "don't mean shit to me, laddie. And if you don't stay out of my business I'll see you're sorry for it.

"As far as I'm concerned, if the little bugger didn't kill himself, he was blackmailing somebody and got what he deserved. And I don't need any help from you to find out who."

Nash put his hands on his knees and leaned forward, poised, Kincaid thought, for his spring at the jugular, when a frantic pounding sounded at the front door. Kincaid pushed himself off the edge of the sofa and went quickly to open it. Three times a charm, he thought hopefully.

Inspector Raskin stood panting at the door, his tie askew, his hair falling almost over one eye in a rakish comma. "Chief Inspector Nash?" he said, in between gasps for breath, and when Kincaid nodded, followed him into the suite. Raskin looked from Nash to Kincaid and spoke, finally, into the distance between them.

"It's Penny MacKenzie. Down at the tennis court. She's dead."

10

KINCAID CLUNG TO his disbelief until they reached the tennis court. Hannah sat against the court's wire wall, her knees drawn up and her hands clasped together above her breasts, her face slack with shock. Penny's small body lay beneath the net, touched with some quality of stillness that was utterly, inarguably final, Kincaid felt his breath rush out as if he'd been punched in the chest.

"Miss Alcock came pelting across the garden into the drive just as I got out of my car." Inspector Raskin nodded his head toward Hannah as he spoke quietly to Kincaid. "She said she thought Miss MacKenzie was dead and I came down with her at once."

Kincaid hesitated for a moment, then went to Hannah and sank down on his knees beside her. "Hannah. Are you all right?"

"I don't know. I felt as though I couldn't breathe." She looked about her with a puzzled expression. "I told Inspector Raskin I'd stay while he fetched you. I don't remember sitting down."

"Can you tell me what happened?"

"There's not much. I'd gone for a walk after I left you this morning, thinking, not paying much attention to things. I saw her as I came down the path."

"What happened then?"

"I went to her. At first I thought she might have been taken ill, fainted or something. Then I saw her head." Hannah stopped and swallowed. "But still, I thought she might be breathing, so I felt her chest, then her throat for a pulse. Her skin felt cool." Hannah began to shiver. "I didn't know what else to do."

Kincaid reached over and tucked the lapels of her heavy cardigan more tightly together. "I'm sure you did everything you could for her. The important thing now is to look after you. You've had quite a shock." He looked around. Raskin knelt over Penny's body, not touching her, and Nash, having stopped to phone divisional headquarters, had not yet appeared. "But I'm afraid you'd better stay at least until Chief Inspector Nash arrives. He'll want a statement from you. Why don't I take you up there?" He nodded toward the bench on the path above the court and helped Hannah to her feet.

"Duncan." Hannah turned to him as he pushed aside the gate for her. "It couldn't have been an accident, could it? She couldn't have fallen and hit her head?"

"I don't know yet, love, but I doubt it very much."

"But why?" Hannah's fingers tightened convulsively on his arm. "Why would somebody want to hurt Penny?"

Why, indeed, thought Kincaid as he made his way back to the court. Because Penny had seen or heard something that threatened someone's security, and if he hadn't been so dense, he'd have found out what it was.

Kincaid squatted reluctantly beside Raskin.

Penny lay on her right side, her fist curled beneath her cheek, her bright blue eyes closed. Only the awkward angle of her legs indicated something amiss, until one saw the back of her head. The indentation, though small, had bled freely, and a little blood had puddled beneath her. A tennis racquet lay a few inches from her outstretched left hand, as if she had fallen in the midst of a leaping volley at the net. A smear of blood showed rust-colored on the racquet's edge. Penny's binoculars lay partially beneath her side, and Kincaid fought the sudden urge to move them, as if it mattered whether or not she were comfortable. "Oh, Christ," he said, his eyes stinging and his throat suddenly contracting. He pressed his fingers underneath his cheekbones until the pressure eased.

"Hmmm." Raskin didn't look up, his gaze focused intently on the injury to Penny's skull. "Not nice. Not nice at all, I don't think. I'd say she was standing at the net, possibly looking at something through her binoculars, when chummy snuck up behind."

"And I'd say," added Kincaid, when he could trust himself to speak again, "that chummy has had a run of bloody good luck. Acts on impulse, grabs the first thing to hand and what do you know, it works. But it might not have. That portable heater might have blown every fuse in the house and shorted itself out without frying Sebastian. And Penny . . ." He looked away. ". . . It wasn't that hard a blow. I've seen people walk to hospital with head injuries worse than that."

"I thought the same," Peter said thoughtfully. "But in either case he didn't have much to lose. Sebastian wouldn't have seen him. He could have hit Penny again if she hadn't fallen unconscious. Do you suppose he waited?" Peter looked at Kincaid from under his raised brow. "I don't think she died right away. She bled quite a bit."

"Bloody bastard." The dam Kincaid had clamped on his anger cracked and he drew a deep breath, fighting it back. "I doubt it. Too chancy, even for our chummy. Now we're both saying 'he.' There's no indication."

"Merely generic," Peter answered. "No, there's nothing in either case to rule out a woman. If it is the same person."

"Oh, I think so. I'd even bet on it. The same person, both times for the same reason. Penny saw something connected with Sebastian's death, I'm sure of it. She started to tell me, but we were interrupted and I never found out what it was. But Sebastian . . . what did Sebastian see? Or find out? That's the question. What runs behind all this? And," Kincaid stood up and straightened his stiff knees as he looked toward the gate, "just where the hell is your chief? He's taking his own sweet time about it."

"Well, you know Chief Inspector Nash, sir," said Raskin, sardonically, "he likes to delegate."

"Then he can delegate someone to take Miss Alcock's statement later. I'm going to take her up to the house. He can erupt as much as he likes." But Kincaid stood a moment longer, staring at the tennis racquet. Most of the varnish had long since disappeared from its wooden perimeter, some of the webbing had sprung and the grip was stained and frayed. Not, thought Kincaid, exactly state of the art. "Where did he—chummy—get the racquet? He couldn't have carried it with him just on the off-chance he might find someone to bash with it."

"There," Raskin pointed, "behind the gate." The wooden box blended into the shrubbery outside the fence, its faded green paint acting almost as camouflage. About the size of a child's coffin, the box was secured with a simple metal hasp. "For guests' use, I imagine."

"Okay," Kincaid thought aloud, "say he sees Penny going off alone and follows her . . . she stands so conveniently with her back to him, concentrating on a bird . . . he knows where the racquets are kept . . . but he won't have picked it up bare handed, not our chummy. What did he use? A glove? A plastic bag? He will have gotten rid of it, most likely. I'd tell scene-of-crime to have a look for it."

"I'll pass the suggestion along." Peter Raskin grinned. "Strictly as my own, of course."

Hannah sat with her eyes closed, her cheek resting against her drawn-up knees. As Kincaid bent over her she opened her eyes and then smiled sleepily at him. "Do you know, I think I actually went to sleep. How extraordinary. I feel weak as a kitten."

"It's the shock." Kincaid held out a hand to her. "It does strange things to the system sometimes. What you need is a cup of the good old British restorative—hot, sweet tea. I'm going to take you up to the house. Nash can send someone to take your statement later."

"All right. Duncan," Hannah looked down at the court, where Peter Raskin stood quietly waiting, "someone will have to tell Emma. What if—"

"No, no, don't even think about it. If we pass anyone, say you don't feel well. I think," Kincaid added, his voice grim, "I should tell Emma myself."

Kincaid's knock on the door of the MacKenzies' suite echoed hollowly. He had taken Hannah in through the rear entrance; the sound of the children shrieking in the swimming pool came clearly to them through the pool's glass door. The rest of the house seemed deserted, and he had turned away from Emma's door when he heard it open behind him.

"Sorry," Emma said, "I was dripping. Been swimming with the children, the little monsters." She continued rubbing her hair with a towel and it stuck up in dark spikes, making her look oddly young and reminding him for a moment of Angela. The bathing suit, however, was vintage post-war, black, with a skirt in the front that discreetly hid the tops of the thighs. Emma gave him one of her rare, surprising smiles. "If it's Penny you want, you're out of luck. Went out to do some early birding. Don't know what got into her, usually she's a lazy duck."

"No, Emma, actually it's you I wanted. Could we sit down?" Kincaid wondered what universal formula required that a person should sit down to receive bad news. Was it merely a precaution against fainting or falling, or had it become a kind of foreshadowing, effective in easing the shock?

"Of course." Emma looked puzzled, but led him to

the sofa without protest. She sat carefully in the armchair, spreading the towel under her damp suit, and Kincaid leaned toward her.

"Emma, I'm afraid I've got some very bad news." She didn't speak, but he saw the fear spread across her face. "It's Penny."

Emma's hand went to her chest, fingers clenching into a ball. "Dead?" The word came out in a whisper.

"Yes, I'm afraid so."

Emma closed her eyes and leaned her head against the chair's back, only the gentle rise and fall of her chest assuring Kincaid that she was breathing. After a moment he began to wonder if she had fainted, but then she spoke to him, without opening her eyes. "What happened?"

"We don't know yet, exactly. Hannah found her in the tennis court. Her head had been injured."

"Could she . . . could she have fallen? Hit her head?"

"It's . . . possible."

Emma heard the hesitation in his voice. She opened her eyes and transfixed Kincaid with her stare. "You don't think so." Kincaid didn't answer. It had been a statement, not a question. Emma pulled herself upright in the chair and spoke again, her voice regaining some of its gruff strength. "I want to see her."

"Um . . . I'll see what I can do. You'll have to wait until the doctor and the police team are finished. If you'd like to get dressed, and collect yourself a bit, I'll wait for you outside the front door. Emma," Kincaid hesitated. Expressing condolences never became any easier, even with years of practice on strangers. "I'm sorry."

"I know," Emma answered, and Kincaid thought he had never seen an expression so bleak.

Inspector Raskin breasted the tennis court path and raised a hand to Kincaid, who stood irresolute in the gravel forecourt. They met on the lawn, Raskin puffing a bit from his quick climb. "Have to take up jogging again. Getting warm, too." He ran a finger under his collar and moved his shoulders as if he'd like to shrug out of his jacket. "Mission accomplished?"

"Yes. And Peter, I've been to see Miss MacKenzie."

Raskin's habitual expression of sardonic amusement softened. "Thanks. You saved me that one. How did she take it?"

"Quietly. You didn't expect her to have hysterics, did you?" Kincaid paused. "But very hard, I think. She wants to see her sister. I told her I'd try to arrange it."

Raskin thought for a moment. "Dr. Percy's here, you'll be pleased to know." He grinned slyly at Kincaid. "Scene-of-crime unit's here as well."

"I gathered that." Kincaid nodded toward several strange cars parked haphazardly on the gravel.

"The Home Office pathologist is on his way, and the undertaker's van. If Miss MacKenzie could see her before they load her up, it would save her having to make a formal identification at the undertakers. Don't see why not. I'll take statements as soon as they're finished down below. You want to tag along? Or are you still neither fish nor fowl?"

"Fowl, I think, by this time. But I told Miss MacKenzie I'd wait for her."

Kincaid left him and walked down the path until he

could see the activity in the court. A uniformed constable stood sentinel at the gate and an area around Penny's body had been marked off with white tape. Anne Percy knelt at Penny's side, and Nash stood silently nearby, surveying the scene like a malevolent idol.

Dr. Percy closed her bag, rose, and went to speak to Chief Inspector Nash. She looked up, saw Kincaid on the path and flashed him a brief smile. Kincaid thought she looked more professional today and even more attractive than before dressed in a heather-colored sweater and trousers.

She came up the path toward him, swinging her black bag. "I may get used to standing in for the police surgeon," she said by way of greeting. "I've certified death, that's about all I can do here."

"Will you wait for the pathologist?" Kincaid asked.

"Yes. I understand Miss MacKenzie has a sister. Do you think I should see her?"

"Would you?" Kincaid asked. "Although I'm not sure she'll welcome it."

Anne Percy smiled. "That's all right. I'm used to these situations."

The undertaker's van stood with its rear doors open, waiting, and Kincaid stood waiting as well. He found it odd not to be directing the swirl of activity around him, or even performing an assigned task, as he had done often enough.

The front door opened softly behind him and he turned to see Emma MacKenzie hesitating in its sheltered arch. She seemed to have shrunk, her take-charge briskness evaporated. The lines between nose and mouth cut sharply into her face.

"Are you all right?" Kincaid asked.

"Your Dr. Percy's been to see me. Kind, but unnecessary."

It relieved Kincaid to find her voice as scratchy and acerbic as ever, although he thought she, in her gruff way, was acknowledging his concern. She looked past him at the waiting van, started to speak, then lifted her hand in a supplicating gesture. "Not long now," he said gently. "I believe they're almost finished."

Emma fixed her eyes on Kincaid's face. "She seemed so resolute this morning. Purposeful. You know how Penny always flits . . . flitted from one thing to the next. Quiet, too. When I questioned her she just smiled. Silly goose, I thought, keeping secrets . . ." Her voice faltered.

"Miss MacKenzie, don't. We're both guilty of not taking her seriously."

A shuffling sound came from the garden. The undertaker's attendants maneuvered the stretcher over the crest of the path and started across the lawn, followed closely by Inspector Raskin. Penny lay wrapped and taped in black polythene, as neat as a Christmas package.

Kincaid took Emma's arm. "Are you sure you want to do this?" Emma's head jerked once in assent, but she didn't brush away Kincaid's hand as they started down the steps. The polythene's final closure had been left undone, and Raskin carefully turned back the fold to reveal Penny's face. Emma stared for a long moment, then nodded once again. Raskin refolded the polythene and sealed it with a roll of tape he carried in his hand. The attendants slid the stretcher into the van and closed the doors with the swift, fluid movements of long experience, and as the driver climbed into his seat Kincaid heard him say, "C'mon mate. We'll miss our dinner if we're not careful." The van's brake lights flashed as it turned into the road, and Kincaid realized that the day had grown overcast.

"She did say something this morning," Emma broke into his thoughts. "While she was collecting her things. It was almost . . . you'll think I'm foolish."

"No, I won't. Go on."

"It seemed almost like a litany she was repeating to herself. 'One or t'other, one or t'other . . .' It was something our father used to say to us when we were children. Whenever we had to make a difficult choice. One or the other."

11

Gemma stuck her head out the Escort's window and called to the petrol station attendant. "Can you tell me how to find Grove House?"

"Next left, miss, just round the corner. It's the old manor house. You can't miss it." He was young, and nice looking, and his amiable response cheered her, even though she must have missed the damned house. Three times she'd driven around the village, and she couldn't tell by this time where she'd been and where she hadn't.

Villages gave her the pip, anyway, and this one made no exception. Deep in Wiltshire, surrounded on all sides by old gravel quarries, it was almost an island. No storybook high street here, with rows of neat shops—this one looked all higgledy-piggledy, with clusters of new houses that seemed to turn in on one another, and an occasional old place tucked in between.

None of them the right one, though. Number Two, Grove House. No street name or number. How was anyone expected to find it?

Gemma turned left at the pub, and before she knew it she found herself dead-ended in a cul-de-sac of newish homes. Working herself into a temper of frustration wouldn't do a bit of good, she thought. She took a deep breath, carefully reversed the car, and crawled back along the curb.

Ten feet from the corner pub, she found a gap in the hedge. A small metal plaque had been set into the open wrought-iron gate. Grove House, Gemma read. The Escort's tires crunched on the gravel as she pulled the car into the drive and stopped. The clatter from the road came only faintly through the high hedges, and the smell of newly turned earth drifted in through the car's open window. A wheelbarrow and spade stood near a heap of compost on the lawn. At least, she thought, it must be compost—her expertise in gardening consisted of cutting the six-foot-square patch of grass the advertisement for her house had called "a spacious back garden."

The house itself gave a swift impression of gray stucco and slate and trailing green creeper, with a tangled hedge jutting out at a right angle from its center—the division between Number One and Number Two. She wondered how the house had looked new, and for a moment she imagined that the house had walled itself in, unchanging, as the village grew up around it. "A bit fanciful for you, love," she said aloud, then shook herself and got out of the car.

Number Two turned out to be the left-hand side, half hidden behind the central hedge. Gemma smoothed her hair with her hands and adjusted her shoulder bag before she rang the bell. Quick footsteps sounded on tile and a woman opened the door. She was slender, with a fair, faded prettiness and a tentative smile. "Mrs. Rennie?" asked Gemma. "My name's Gemma James." She handed the woman her warrant card. "With London C.I.D. I'd like to speak with you for a few moments if I could."

"Yes, of course." Mrs. Rennie looked puzzled. "What can I do for you?" Her expression became slightly apprehensive. "It's not about that awful business up in Yorkshire, is it? Patrick telephoned and told us—" Gemma saw apprehension spring to alarm in the woman's eyes. "It's not Patrick? Something's happened to Patrick?"

"No, no." Gemma hastened to reassure her. "Your son's fine, Mrs. Rennie. We're just making some routine inquiries of all the guests at Followdale House." She smiled her best encouraging smile.

"Silly of me. Just for a moment—" Mrs. Rennie collected herself and her manners, ushering Gemma into the foyer. "Do come in. I shouldn't have kept you standing on the step." An enormous bowl of meticulously arranged flowers stood on a narrow table—that, and the softly lit oil portraits running along the hall and up the stair, were all she glimpsed before Mrs. Rennie led her into the drawing room.

"Sit down, please. Would you like some tea?"

"That would be lovely. I had quite a drive getting here," Gemma answered, thinking that in this house she would not invite herself into the kitchen to help. Left alone, she examined the room. Like the rest of the house, it had an air of worn elegance—expensive things well used; the oriental rug under her feet had threadbare spots, the chintz-covered chairs and sofa sagged where most sat upon. There were books, and maps, and objects that she thought might have come from the Far East. And the room, with its shabby gentility redolent of good wools and sensible shoes, raised in Gemma a deep discomfort.

She smelled the mingled scents of flowers and furniture polish and dusty book bindings, and thought of her own semidetached, where the smell of grease and cooked cabbage from next door seemed to seep through her walls, and no matter how much she threw open her windows and aired things it never quite went away. She thought of the matching beige suite in her sitting room, with its rough, cheap fabric, and her fingers stroked the smooth chintz. Well, she did the best she could, what with her salary, and Toby's day care, and Rob's not being too dependable with his child support.

Clinking sounds from the direction of the kitchen broke into her reverie. She sighed, then straightened her spine against the chair's soft back. Mrs. Rennie pushed open the swinging door with her shoulder and maneuvered the tea tray through it. When Gemma rose to help, Mrs. Rennie stopped her with a quick shake of her head. "No, don't get up. I can manage."

Gemma took the cup offered her and balanced it carefully on her knees. "Mrs. Rennie," she asked as she stirred her tea, "have your son and his wife been visiting Followdale House long?"

"About two or three years, I'd say. Marta was quite keen on it at first, and they really looked forward to their visits."

"And they don't, now?" Gemma sipped her tea. It was Earl Grey, which she didn't like, but its flowery perfume seemed appropriate to the room.

"Well, I suppose it's become a bit old hat, as most things do. And Patrick's so busy these days, with all his political commitments. But come to think of it," Mrs. Rennie drew her brows together in a small frown, "it's Marta who's suggested they trade their time or spend it somewhere else."

"But they didn't?"

"No. No, Patrick wasn't enthusiastic."

"You must be proud of your son, Mrs. Rennie. I understand he's doing very well."

"Yes. Better even than we might have expected. They speak of his rise in the party as 'meteoric.' " She smiled fondly, but Gemma heard in her voice some reserve, some hint that Patrick Rennie's life might not be all it was cracked up to be.

"Have your son or daughter-in-law ever mentioned noticing anything odd at Followdale House? Sometimes," Gemma continued confidentially, "people comment on things and then forget all about it."

Mrs. Rennie considered for a moment. "Not that I can remember. Patrick is not one to say unkind things about people, or to repeat gossip." Although the tone had been mild enough, Gemma felt she'd been rather subtly put in her place.

Gemma finished her tea and carefully set her cup and saucer down on the polished wood tray. "Thank you, Mrs. Rennie. You've been very kind and I mustn't take up any more of your time." They rose, and Gemma hesitated as they started toward the door. "Um,

I wondered if I might wash my hands and freshen up a bit before I go?"

"Of course." Mrs. Rennie led her into the foyer. "Up the stairs to your left."

"Thanks." Gemma stopped before the first portrait. The boy gazed inquiringly back at her. His fair hair seemed just about to break free of its neat brushing, and the blue eyes in the slender face seemed friendly and interested. About twelve or thirteen, Gemma guessed, with the top of a school tie peeping from the neck of the blue pullover he wore. She wondered if her Toby would ever be that good-looking. "What a wonderful portrait. Your son, Mrs. Rennie?"

"Yes, that's Patrick. We had it commissioned. It is very good of him."

"The resemblance between you is quite striking."

Mrs. Rennie laughed. "Oh, yes. That's our best family joke." Gemma's face must have registered her incomprehension, for Mrs. Rennie said quickly, "I'm sorry, I see you don't know."

"Know what, Mrs. Rennie?"

"That Patrick is adopted." Her expression softened. "He was three days old when he came to us. It was all very quietly and discreetly done, none of the fuss of going through a national agency. My husband's solicitor arranged it all. Of course, we explained it all to Patrick as soon as he was old enough to understand."

"No, I didn't know." Gemma studied the portrait. "The resemblance is quite remarkable."

"A little divine intervention, perhaps," Mrs. Rennie answered, and Gemma saw a quirk of humor in her smile.

Gemma looked down into the drive from the toilet

window. She'd heard the sound of a car as she dried her hands, and as she watched, a tan estate car disappeared into a carport around the side of the house. She didn't dare snoop—the old wooden floorboards creaked and she felt sure the progress of every footstep would be audible downstairs.

The voices came clearly to her as she descended the stairs. "Louise, they have no right. It's completely—" Their heads turned as she reached the last landing. The man was tall and thin, with the small bristly mustache that was almost a badge of the retired military.

"My husband, Major Rennie." His wife rested her fingers lightly on his arm, a restraining gesture.

"I don't know how we can help you." His face had flushed pink—no wonder, thought Gemma, that his wife tried to soothe him. "I'm sure this sordid business has nothing to do with us, or our son. If you have any further questions you can put them to our solicitor—"

"John, I'm sure that's not necessary—"

"As I told your wife, Mr. Rennie, it's nothing to be concerned about. These sort of questions are routine in a murder investigation."

Even softly spoken, the power of the word "murder" silenced them both, and in their faces Gemma read the beginnings of fear.

"I've commandeered Cassie Whitlake's office." Peter Raskin grinned. "I wouldn't say it was graciously lent. Pick an inconspicuous spot and make yourself comfortable." He surveyed the room from the door. "Only one chair this side of the desk." He turned back into the bar and swept up a barstool with one hand. "This do?"

"Admirably," answered Kincaid, and settled in a corner of the small office. "Suits my precarious position." He watched as Raskin tested the swivel of Cassie's chair and gave it an approving pat. Raskin's deft fingers shoved and patted the tumbling pyramid of Cassie's papers until he'd made a neat stack in one corner of her desk. "She won't be too pleased." Kincaid nodded toward the desk's now clear and orderly surface.

"She won't be the only one. All the guests are present and accounted for now, and I've had the P.C. round them up in the sitting room. They're going to be tired and fretful and wanting their tea, so the sooner we get this over with, the better.

"Let's have the Hunsingers first and get them out of the way. I understand from Emma Mackenzie that they were in the pool with the children all morning." Raskin slid around Cassie's desk and went into the bar, returning a moment later with a very subdued Maureen Hunsinger.

Maureen gave Kincaid a tremulous smile as Raskin offered her the chair. She perched stiff-backed on its edge, her white, crinkled-cotton dress ballooning about her. Kincaid thought she should have looked ridiculous—her hair even more frizzy than usual from her hours in the pool, her face red and puffy from weeping, but he found a certain dignity in her posture and in her obvious grief. A voluptuous and rather erratic madonna, he thought, and suppressed a smile.

"John's with the children. Will you be wanting him, too?"

"Probably just to sign your statement," Raskin answered diplomatically.

"It's been terrible for the children. First Sebastian,

now this. What are we to tell them that makes any sense? We thought this morning that if they had fun in the pool they would forget what had happened there, but now—" Maureen sounded near to tears again. "I wish we'd never come here."

"I understand how you must feel, but I'm afraid we'll have to ask you to stay on a bit longer, at least until we complete the formalities." Raskin's voice was gentle and sympathetic, and Kincaid saw Maureen relax a little in her chair. "Now, if you wouldn't mind telling me what you did this morning?"

"The children woke us. We had breakfast, then after a bit we all went down to the pool. Emma joined us—"

"For how long?"

"Oh, about an hour, I suppose. She said she'd had enough, then not too long afterwards the children began to get hungry again, so we came up ourselves. We were just changing when Janet Lyle came and said something was happening—she didn't know what." Maureen leaned forward in entreaty. "Please tell me exactly what's happened. I know Penny's . . . dead, the constable told us. But what happened to her? Is it like . . . Sebastian?"

Raskin spoke formally, the policeman's best emotional defense, Kincaid thought wryly. "Miss MacKenzie suffered a severe blow to the back of the head. I'm afraid that's all we can tell you just now."

Maureen sank back in her chair, and it seemed to Kincaid that with the confirmation of her worst fears, all the emotional tension drained from her. She took her leave quietly, but when she reached the door she turned and spoke. "I'm going to see about Emma.

Someone must. She shouldn't just be left on her own like this." The set of her mouth brooked no argument.

They came and went in quick succession, with varying degrees of cooperativeness.

Cassie slid into the visitor's chair, slipped off her pumps and tucked her feet up under her. It was as deliberate a demonstration of ownership, thought Kincaid, as he'd ever seen. She glared balefully at the neat stack of papers on her desk. "You do realize how long it will take me to put that right again?"

Peter Raskin allowed himself a hint of a smile. "And I thought I'd done you a favor."

"Where's Chief Inspector Nash?" Cassie's eyes went quickly to Kincaid.

"Attending the autopsy," Raskin said. "Rank hath its privileges. Now, if you wouldn't mind—"

"I was here all morning. Working."

"Did—"

"Oh, I used the downstairs loo once or twice, if that's the sort of thing you want to know. I straightened the sitting room and the bar. Patrick Rennie was working at the sitting room desk. And Eddie Lyle came through for something or other. I saw no one else."

"Admirably succinct, Miss Whitlake," said Raskin, unruffled by her assumption of the interview.

"Call me Cassie. Please." Cassie switched the seductiveness on full power, and Kincaid watched with interest to see how Raskin would respond. She stood suddenly and leaned over her desk, forcing Raskin to move back as she opened the center drawer. "Sorry." After rummaging for a moment, she produced a crumpled pack of cigarettes and a book of matches. "Secret vice. Doesn't impress the customers." Her hand trembled as she struck the match, and Kincaid thought that for all her aplomb, her nerves betrayed her.

"The Superintendent here," again that swift glance at Kincaid, "thinks I ought to fess up. And I'd much rather confess to you, Inspector, than Chief Inspector Nash." Cassie awarded Raskin a floodlit smile.

"Do go on."

"I said that I spent Sunday night alone in my cottage. Well, it's not true. I wasn't alone, and I wasn't in my cottage. I'd met Graham Frazer in the empty suite . . . oh, around ten, I guess, and we were there until nearly midnight." Kincaid marveled at her ability to turn a potentially embarrassing revelation into an almost flirtatious challenge.

"Did you do that often?" Raskin asked, then colored slightly as he realized how it sounded. "I mean, the two of you." Not much better, thought Kincaid, amused to see a crack in the imperturbable Raskin's composure.

"Well, we've had a thing, you might say, for the last year or so." Cassie drew on her cigarette and leaned forward confidentially. "Graham didn't want anyone to know. Custody problems. Of course, I would have said something right away if I'd known it would be important. I hope," her voice became intense, "it won't have to go any farther."

Raskin stood and moved toward the door. "I can't make any promises, of course." He sounded ingratiatingly smitten. "Thank you for being so cooperative, Miss Whitlake." Raskin's emphasis fell on the formal address. He'd had the last word, after all.

"How'd you manage to worm that tidy bit of information out of her?" Raskin asked Kincaid when he had shut the door.

"My irresistible charm." Kincaid grinned. "That, and a bull's-eye guess. I told her I knew they'd been together, but I didn't understand why they wouldn't admit it. Figured I had nothing to lose."

"Apparently not. Let's have Mr. Frazer in next and see what he has to say about it all."

Graham Frazer began as intractably as he meant to end, with a bulldog glare at Kincaid. "Stopped sitting on the fence, then? Give you a sore bum, I should think." Angela, following in his wake, looked mortified.

"Daddy—" Frazer ignored her and sat in the chair, leaving his daughter to stand, awkward and hesitant. Kincaid stood and offered her his barstool with a flourish. He won a small smile.

"I was working in the suite all morning. Catching up on some paperwork," Frazer said in response to Raskin's question. "Angie was sleeping. That's what teenagers do, isn't it?"

Angela bristled on cue. "Daddy, that's not—"

"Fair," Raskin finished for her, and smiled. "What is your business, Mr. Frazer?"

"I'm in assurance. A bloody bore, but there it is. It pays the bills."

"I see." Raskin carefully straightened his notes. "And you didn't leave your suite for any reason before ten o'clock this morning?"

"I did not." Even the bullying humor had left

Frazer's voice, and he offered nothing further. "Now if you're quite—"

"Angie," Kincaid interrupted, "what time did you wake up this morning?"

She looked at her father before she met Kincaid's eyes. "About ten, I think."

"Angie," said Raskin, "you can go now, if you've nothing to add to your father's statement." Frazer started to rise. "Mr. Frazer, if you don't mind, I've a few more questions to ask."

"I do mind. Do I have a choice?"

Raskin waited until Angela had gone out and closed the door behind her. "You can have a solicitor present if you wish, of course, but these are very informal inquiries, Mr. Frazer. We are not accusing you of anything." Frazer deliberated, then nodded once. He's decided he's better off not to make a fuss at this point, thought Kincaid.

"Mr. Frazer, Miss Whitlake has informed us that the two of you were together on Sunday evening, from around ten o'clock until midnight. You had both previously made statements to the contrary. According to Miss Whitlake you urged her not to mention this as you were concerned about your child-custody hearing."

Graham Frazer's flat, heavy face didn't register emotions easily, but Kincaid thought his utter stillness indicated the extent of his shock. After a long moment, he spluttered, "She told you that? Cassie? She was the one who insisted—" He fell silent, then said softly, "Bitch. I knew she was trying something on."

"Are you saying that you were not the one to suggest

lying about your activities that evening?" Some of Raskin's polite formality had dropped away.

"Yes. I mean no. It wasn't my idea. Why should it make any difference to the damned custody hearing? And even if it did, I'm not sure I'd care—I'm beginning to think Marjorie's welcome to her. No, Cassie was the one worried about her *reputation.* Begged me not to embarrass her." Frazer gave a mirthless snort. "She's the one who's made *me* look a fool."

Edward Lyle entered ahead of his wife, and only remembered to offer her the chair when Raskin greeted her. Kincaid quietly fetched another stool and resumed his unobtrusive seat. Lyle seemed subdued, less bristly with righteous indignation than Kincaid had seen him before. "I don't know what I can tell you, Inspector." Lyle ran a hand through his thinning hair. "Most unfortunate, most unfortunate about poor Miss MacKenzie."

Unfortunate? Kincaid thought it an odd word choice. The morning had been rather more than unfortunate. Raskin let the comment fade into silence before he spoke. "If you would just tell me what you and your wife were doing this morning, I'm sure that will be sufficient, Mr. Lyle."

"Well, we breakfasted as usual—I like a proper breakfast, you know. Then I walked down to the village for a paper, left Janet writing some letters in the suite. After I returned I had a look at the paper, and we had begun going over some maps, planning the afternoon's outing, when all the commotion began. That's all, Inspector. I must say—" he began, his voice sliding into the querulous range, when Raskin broke in.

"Is that correct, Mrs. Lyle?" Lyle drew breath to protest, but his wife began to speak.

"Yes . . . of course. I was writing to Chloe, our daughter. She's at boarding school. It's such a shame we weren't able to acquire time that coincided with Chloe's holidays. She would have—" She glimpsed her husband's disapproving expression. "Sorry. How stupid of me. I'm glad she's not here." Her brow furrowed and she took a breath, as though nerving herself to speak. "Inspector, this is terrible, what's happened, but I don't understand what it has to do with us." She turned toward Kincaid as she spoke, including him in her appeal, the severity of her thick, dark hair softened by the lightest dusting of gray, her skin clear, her dark eyes expressive.

Kincaid thought suddenly what an attractive woman she was—or would be, if she didn't wear that constant air of anxious diffidence. He remembered the burst of animation he'd seen as she sat in the tea shop with Maureen, and he wondered what she would have been like if she had not married Edward Lyle. And why had she married him? That, Kincaid considered, was the real question. Fifteen, twenty years ago, had she seen some promise, now dissipated, in this weedy, self-important man?

"Mrs. Lyle," Raskin answered, interrupting Kincaid's musing, "we must ask everyone the same questions, just in case they might have seen or heard something helpful. I'm sure you must understand that."

"We've seen nothing out of the ordinary at all, Inspector," said Lyle. "Nothing at all."

* * *

Patrick Rennie, always the gentleman, solicitously seated his wife in the chair. Marta looked as if she needed all the support she could get—she was obviously not one of those lucky few who escaped hangovers. The flaxen hair hung limply, pulled back from her face with a plain elastic band.

"Marta," Patrick explained, "spent the morning in bed, as she didn't feel well." His expression earnest and pleasant, he didn't look at his wife as he spoke. He had gone down to the sitting room to work on a speech, he told them, so as not to disturb her.

"Did you stay there all morning, Mr. Rennie?" asked Raskin.

"Oh, I popped in and out. You know how it is. Said 'hallo' to Cassie. Ran upstairs for a book—quotations come in handy when you're writing a speech. Lyle came in and waffled about for a bit. Ruined my concentration, just when I was getting to the good bit. Didn't see anyone else. Oh, and Inspector," there was just a hint of playfulness in his voice, "I did see you and your chief come through. Saw the car pull up through the sitting-room window." Cocky bastard, thought Kincaid.

"Mrs. Rennie?" asked Raskin.

She hadn't been able to keep her hands still, fretting for something more than her tea, Kincaid imagined. She licked her lips before she spoke. "I slept all morning, just as Patrick says. Felt bloody awful. Flu or something. I'd just got up and started coffee when Patrick came in and said there was a lot of running up and down stairs, slamming doors, something going on." She fumbled in her bag for a cigarette. "I'm sorry about Miss MacKenzie. She seemed a nice person." An inadequate eulogy if he'd ever heard one, thought Kincaid, but at least Marta Rennie had spared a thought for Penny.

"Miss MacKenzie seemed rather upset when she left us last night. She couldn't have—"

"No, Mr. Rennie," Raskin answered his unspoken question, "I'm afraid there's no possibility the injuries could have been self-inflicted."

12

"THAT'S THE LOT, then." Peter Raskin yawned and stretched.

"And just as damned useless as the last time," Kincaid said in disgust. "Five minutes, that's all it would have taken. Any one of them could have nipped down to the tennis court and back up again. Except the Hunsingers, of course," he corrected himself, "and I never considered them very seriously anyway."

Raskin sat up in the swivel chair and studied Kincaid for a moment. "What about Miss Emma MacKenzie? And Hannah Alcock?"

"Oh, I suppose it's within the realm of possibility. Emma could have followed her sister down to the tennis court—"

"A true domestic," Raskin interrupted. "You know that sometimes it's those years of togetherness that blow up—"

"Over what? The goats? And you know as well as I do that most domestic violence is precipitated by alcohol and occurs on the spur of the moment." Kincaid's words came more sharply than he intended. "Anyway, I don't believe it. Emma was devoted to Penny. She'll be lost without Penny to look after and worry over," he raised his hand as Raskin started to speak, "and don't give me that mercy-killing line, either. Not with a tennis racquet."

"All right," Raskin conceded. "I'll admit it's pretty unlikely. What about Miss Alcock?"

Kincaid shifted uncomfortably on the barstool. "I don't like it, Peter. I doubt we'll get a more exact time of death from the pathologist than the circumstances provide. According to Emma, Penny left the suite about half past eight. Miss Alcock came to see me about the same time, stayed for . . ." he trailed off, thinking, "maybe half an hour. My sergeant called very shortly after she'd left, and I looked at my watch then. It was five past nine. You bumped into Miss Alcock in the car park, coming to fetch us, at—"

"Nine-thirty. Half-hour news had just finished on the car radio."

"So . . ."

"She would have had time," Raskin said quietly. "Just. And I saw her coming across the lawn from the tennis court path. The sensible thing for her to do would be to tell me she'd just found Penny's body."

"But I don't believe it." Kincaid stood and began to pace restlessly around the cramped office. "It's too pat. And what possible motive could she have?"

"What motive could any of them have? None of it makes any damned sense," Raskin said in exasperation. "And Chief Inspector Nash is not going to leave the issue, you know," he added.

"I know." Despite his opinion of Nash, Kincaid had a hard time defending his certainties even to himself. He just couldn't swallow the idea that Hannah had sat confiding in him over coffee and then had gone down and cold-bloodedly murdered Penny. Was it his pride at stake, his judgment, or simply his belief in her basic human decency? Could he be depended upon to do his job thoroughly, if it were his show to run? He didn't fancy explaining his reservations to Chief Inspector Nash. "Where's your Super, anyway, Peter? A Chief Inspector in charge of a murder investigation isn't normal procedure."

"In hospital recovering from viral pneumonia." He pulled a face.

"Poor you. That calls for some sort of commiseration." Kincaid stepped into the bar and returned with two glasses and two bottles of beer.

"Thanks. I guess we've done about all we can here tonight," Raskin looked at his watch, "and I'd best be off home." But he sat watching the foam subside on his beer.

"I just realized I don't know a thing about you, Peter. Married? Kids?"

"Yes. Two. A boy and a girl. And I'm missing my son's football practice right now." He glanced again at his watch. "Not that he's not used to it." Raskin sighed. "I'm sure it's good for him—disappointment builds character, right?" Sardonic amusement flickered in his face again. "And I know all about you. The Chief Inspector ran a thorough check, hoping he'd dig up some skeletons to rattle. What he did find gave him terrible indigestion. One of the Met's wonder boys, darling of the A.C."

They laughed, then sat drinking in companionable silence. It came to Kincaid that he dreaded spending the evening alone, and any contact with those in this house remained charged with doubts he couldn't resolve. "Peter, you don't by any chance have Dr. Percy's address?"

Raskin choked a little on his beer. "She's married, you know."

"I'd rather assumed she was," Kincaid said, but his heart sank a little, and he hastened to assure himself that his interest was strictly professional. "There are some questions I wanted to ask her, not being invited to attend the postmortem . . ." He kept his expression bland, standing on his dignity.

"Okay, I'll buy that. And the Great Wall of China," Raskin said, and Kincaid grinned in spite of himself.

"Mr. Kincaid." The voice came softly from the darkened garden. "Or is Superintendent the correct address?" Kincaid recognized the speaker now. Edward Lyle moved from the shadow of a decorative urn, gesturing toward Kincaid's car. "I'm sorry to disturb you if you've an appointment to keep, but I wondered if I might have a word."

Lyle's manner was more ingratiating than usual, and Kincaid sighed. He had been expecting this from some quarter. "No, no. What can I do for you?"

"I realize this is all very distressing, Superintendent, but I feel Chief Inspector Nash is overstepping his rights. This holiday was to be a special treat for my wife, to rest her nerves, and she's been upset enough by all this without the Chief Inspector's bullying. And any rest I might have expected has been quite shattered. I certainly didn't come here to be—"

"Mr. Lyle," Kincaid said patiently, "I have no jurisdiction over Chief Inspector Nash, as I've explained before. I'm strictly on sufferance myself. I'm sure he's just doing his job." Kincaid heard himself uttering clichés and grimaced—Lyle seemed to inspire them.

"My work, Superintendent, is quite taxing, and no one seems to take into account—"

"Just what is it you do, Mr. Lyle?" Kincaid attempted to stem the flow of grievances. "I don't believe you've ever said."

"Civil engineering. Firm's doing quite well." Lyle puffed up a bit. "Good opportunity for investment just now, if you're in—"

Kincaid cut him off. "Thanks, but coppers don't usually have enough to float a fiver. Now, if you don't mind, I'd better be off. I'm afraid I can't help you with Inspector Nash—a word from me wouldn't predispose him in your favor." Pompous self-serving little bugger, he thought as he got in his car and waved at Lyle. He and Nash deserved one another.

The single-track road wound back toward the very base of the hills. Kincaid had left the Midget's top down and turned the heater up full blast, hoping the crisp evening air would clear the cobwebs from his brain. The sky looked faintly luminous against the opaque shapes of the trees.

Presently he saw the lights of the bungalow through the trees on his left and pulled the car carefully into the leaf-covered drive. It was a low house of rose-colored brick, with light streaming from the large French-paned windows either side of an arched front door.

He rang the bell, and the door swung open, revealing two small girls with dark hair surrounding heart-shaped faces. They gazed at him solemnly, then before he could speak they burst into a fit of giggles and ran toward the back of the house, shouting, "Mummy, Mummy!" Kincaid thought he'd better have a look in a mirror before long, if the mere sight of him reduced children to hysteria.

The room stretched the width of the house, with dining furniture to his left and the sitting room to his right. What he could see of a worn rug was liberally covered with doll-hospital casualties. Books flowed off the tables, a fire burned steadily in the sitting-room grate, and the temptation to sit down and go to sleep became almost unbearable.

Anne Percy appeared, wiping her hands on her white cotton apron, and saved him from embarrassment. She smiled with pleasure when she saw who it was, then looked at him more critically. "You look exhausted. What can I do for you?" The little girls were peeking out from behind her like Chinese acrobats, only slightly subdued by their mother's presence. "Molly, Caroline, this is Mr. Kincaid."

"Hallo," he said, gravely. They giggled again, and swung out of sight behind her back in unison.

"Come into the kitchen, if you don't mind my cooking while we talk." She led him through the swinging door in the back of the sitting room into a large, cheerful room full of the aroma of roasting chicken and garlic.

Anne shooed the children out with a reminder that

supper wouldn't be ready for a half hour yet, pulled up a tall stool for Kincaid, and went back to stirring something on the cooktop, all with a graceful economy of movement. "Drink? I'm having Vermouth, since it went in the chicken, but you look as though you could use a whiskey. Off-duty and all that. Is it really true that policemen don't drink on duty, or is it just a myth perpetrated by the telly?"

"Thanks." Kincaid gratefully accepted the whiskey she splashed into a glass, and after the first sip warmth began to radiate from the pit of his stomach. "And no, it's not true. I've known quite a few who do. Chronic alcoholism is just as likely to turn up on a police force as anywhere else, I guess. Maybe more so, considering the stress level. But I don't, if that's what you're wondering. Don't like to feel muddled."

"I know your rank but not your given name. I can't go on calling you Mister or Superintendent. Doesn't seem appropriate in the kitchen."

"It's Duncan." He grinned at her surprised expression. "Scots forebears. And my parents had an inordinate fondness for Macbeth. It could have been worse. They could have saddled me with Prospero or Oberon."

"Lucky you. My family still calls me Annie Rose. It makes me feel three years old, not a grown woman with children of my own and a fairly respectable profession. My patients call me Dr. Anne. It makes them feel more comfortable."

"I'd settle for just plain Anne." He sat and sipped his drink while she moved from cabinet to cooktop and back, feeling the warmth of the room and the whiskey move through him like a tide. He felt as though he had been sitting on this stool, in this kitchen, for years, and could go on sitting there for as many more. Concentration became Anne Percy, he thought, watching her tuck her hair behind one ear as she stirred. She had the same heart-shaped face as her daughters, but the soft, fine hair was lighter, the color of demerara sugar.

She checked a casserole in the oven, then dusted her hands off and turned to face him, leaning against the counter. "Now. Everything should take care of itself for a few minutes."

Kincaid found himself at a loss, distracted by a floury smudge on her eyebrow. What he wanted from her was so formless, so nebulous, that he couldn't think where to begin. "I'm finding myself in a very awkward position. I've no official sanction to investigate either Sebastian's or Penny's death—not yet, anyway. And yet I'm involved, even more so than I would be under ordinary circumstances, because I was acquainted with them both."

Anne Percy studied him with the same serious regard she had given her casserole, and Kincaid felt suddenly uncomfortable, as if his face might reveal secrets he hadn't intended. "I've been known to lose my professional detachment upon occasion, too." Her apparent non sequitur, thought Kincaid, went right to the heart of the matter. "I checked on Emma this morning, to see if she wanted a sedative or—"

"She didn't," Kincaid interrupted, smiling at the thought.

"Damn right, she didn't. She gave me hell. But she talked to me. People do, sometimes, when they're in shock. They tell you things that ordinarily they wouldn't dream of revealing. Emma had been worried about Penny's behavior for months, and it seemed to be getting progressively worse. Episodes of forgetfulness, confusion. It sounds as if it might have been the onset of Alzheimer's, or some form of premature senility. I don't know if it's any comfort to you, but the quality of her life probably would have deteriorated rapidly."

"No," Kincaid said angrily, "no, it bloody well isn't. Whatever the quality of her life, no one had the right to take it from her. And I'm an utter fool. It might have been prevented. She tried to talk to me and I wouldn't take time to listen, because it wasn't my case, because I didn't want to take responsibility, because I judged her as foolish and ineffectual. I should have known better—it's my job, for god's sake. Now we'll never be sure just what she saw. The night Sebastian died, Penny waited until Emma fell asleep and then went downstairs. She'd forgotten her handbag and didn't want Emma to know. A silly little thing, but if she knew Emma was worried about her forgetfulness—"

"You think that Penny was killed because she saw something that would lead to Sebastian's murderer? That just one person is responsible for both deaths?"

"I think, from something Emma overheard Penny say, that Penny saw two people that night—two people not where they were supposed to be. Did she remember where she had left her bag, and slip into the sitting room in the dark? Did she see someone coming out of Cassie's office?"

"Did they see her?" Anne asked, caught up in his reconstruction.

"Well, we don't know, do we?" Kincaid asked softly. "But I think not. Either the plan would have changed, or Penny would have died then and there. This . . . person . . . is a remarkable opportunist. It seems to me that neither killing was premeditated, not in the usual sense, but they were both done with great ruthlessness and a willingness to take almost insane risks. It was sheer, tremendous luck to have managed both these killings without being observed—"

"Except, perhaps, by Penny," Anne interrupted.

"Yes. But it's rather an odd profile. People who kill on the spur of the moment usually do it in anger and regret it afterwards. Those who premeditate like to plan it carefully and execute it from a distance, with as little risk of discovery as possible. Poisoners are the perfect example."

"Maybe this person has an inflated idea of his own invincibility."

"Could be, but I don't think these are random killings by a psycho, violence for violence's sake. There's an objective in this, a sort of single-minded cunning." Kincaid laughed abruptly, then shrugged. "Sounds fanciful, doesn't it?"

"Possibly. But back up a minute, Duncan." Anne frowned, the smooth skin between her brows crinkling with her intensity. "If the murderer didn't see Penny, how did he know she'd seen him?"

"I think," Kincaid measured his words carefully, "that she told him." Seeing Anne's incredulous expression, he shook his head before she could interrupt him. "I know it sounds crazy, but Penny . . ." He searched for words that would make Anne see Penny the way he had seen her, hoping the whiskey hadn't made him maudlin. "Penny lived with scrupulous honesty—except perhaps in protecting Emma. She wouldn't have wanted to falsely accuse someone."

"You think she just walked up to this murderer and said 'I saw you. What are you going to do about it?' But that's—" Anne's voice rose with righteous indignation, and Kincaid thought he'd hate to be a patient who'd disobeyed a reasonable doctor's order.

"Foolish. And if Penny saw two people, she picked the wrong one to speak to first." Kincaid stretched and looked at his watch, took another swallow of the whiskey. "I should be getting back, just in case something turns up. Peter Raskin's taken some pity on me—if he hears the p.m. results tonight he might let me know. Thanks for letting me sound off." In spite of his words, he stayed slumped on his stool, swirling the remains of the whiskey in his glass.

"Stay for dinner. There's plenty. Tim's out on call so we won't wait for him. We never know how long he'll be."

"What does he do, your husband?"

"He's an obstetrician." She spluttered a laugh at the sight of his face. "Close your mouth. That's most people's reaction. But who could be more sympathetic to a doctor's schedule than another doctor, or a vet? Or a policeman," she added thoughtfully.

"Now I know where I went wrong. I should have married a doctor. My ex-wife wasn't sympathetic to my schedule at all." He finished his drink and stood, finding it a great effort. "I'd love to stay, but I'd better not. Maybe some other time." They stood, suspended in a brief awkward silence, then Kincaid reached over and rubbed the smudge from her eyebrow with his thumb. Anne caught his wrist and held it for a moment, then turned away.

"I'll show you out, then."

The children were arguing intensely over whose turn it was to bandage the doll, their faces rosy in the firelight.

"Goodbye, Molly and Caroline."

"Are you going to visit us again?" said Molly, curiously.

"I hope so."

"Come any time." Anne's fingers brushed his arm, light as down.

As the door closed behind him Kincaid saw that all the light had gone from the sky behind the hills.

13

“I’M THE QUEEN,” Bethany said imperiously, adjusting the white square of cloth on her head, “and this is my crown. You be the baby prince.”

“Don’t wanna be the baby prince.” Brian stuck out his lower lip.

“You be the baby prince or I won’t play.”

Brian shuffled his feet, hands in pockets, defeated but not about to give in gracefully. “Why? Why do I always have to be the baby?”

“Because.” Bethany spoke with the certainty of a seven-year-old’s power over a younger brother, the wisps of brown hair escaping from her braid detracting not a whit from her command. Kincaid stood in the hall outside his door and watched in amusement as Bethany draped a small blanket over her brother’s unwilling shoulders. The children were camped on the broad first-floor landing, illuminated by shafts of early morning sun from the three windows overlooking the drive.

“Once upon a time,” began Bethany, “there was a

queen who lived in a castle with her darling baby, the prince."

"Yuck!" said Brian vehemently. Bethany ignored him.

"One day an evil wizard came to the castle and stole the prince away to his cave. The queen didn't know what to do." Kincaid wondered how the queen had so conveniently rid herself of the king, and wondered at the thoroughly modern Maureen exposing her children to old-fashioned fairy tales. Maybe it was a modern fairy tale, with a liberated queen.

"Hullo," he said, walking down the hall to join them. "You two are up early." His own night had been so unsatisfactory that he'd been glad to see the first faint light at the windows, and had waited impatiently, action constrained, until the house began to stir. "Is this the castle?" Kincaid indicated the landing with his hand.

Bethany nodded seriously. "You're stepping in the moat."

"Oh. Sorry." Kincaid stepped back a pace and squatted on his heels. "Better?" A ghost of a smile accompanied the nod this time. "If I were the prince," he continued, looking at Brian, "I'd think of some really super way to escape from the wizard. Put his dragon to sleep, or steal the wizard's spells. The queen wouldn't have to rescue you at all."

The balance of the children's expressions changed, Brian's more cheerful, Bethany's sliding toward belligerence. Brian wouldn't keep the upper hand for long. Kincaid spoke to Bethany, a forestalling tactic. "I like your crown, Beth." The children looked at one another and drew closer together, squabbles forgotten in sudden discomfort.

Kincaid's attention sharpened. He looked more closely at the white cloth. A handkerchief, slightly frayed at the edges, most likely a man's since it lacked any lace or embroidery. A small spot of rust marred one corner. Kincaid's heart jumped. "Where did you get the crown, Beth?" He kept his voice calm.

The children only stood silently, their eyes widening. Kincaid tried again. "Is it your daddy's?" Negative head shakes greeted this—an improvement over no response at all. "Did you find it somewhere?"

Brian looked at Bethany in mute appeal, and after Kincaid waited another patient moment, she spoke. "We were playing in the front hall. Mummy and Daddy said we could play anywhere in the house except the pool, but we weren't to go outside."

"Quite right, too, I should think," Kincaid prompted, when she paused. "What were you playing?"

Bethany cast a quick glance at her brother and decided he wasn't going to speak for himself. "Brian was playing with his Matchbox cars. He was driving one on the edge of the umbrella stand and it fell in."

"And when you reached in for it, you found the handkerchief?"

Brian found his tongue, perhaps encouraged by Kincaid's friendly tone. "Right at the bottom. All wadded up. Like this." He made a fist. "Squashed."

"Do you mind if I take it for a bit? I think Chief Inspector Nash might like to see it." The children nodded vigorously. Kincaid imagined that their brief encounters with the Chief Inspector had not made them anxious to repeat the experience. He thought for a moment, decided two polythene bags from the kitchen might just do the trick. "Leave it just where it is for a minute, okay? I'll be right back." Next time he went on holiday, if ever there was a next time, he'd pack his murder kit.

Voices came clearly through the open door of the untenanted ground-floor suite. Kincaid stood in the hall, his prize held gingerly between his fingers, and listened. "If God had given you sense enough to wipe your ass, laddie, you'd do as you're told and not stand there gawking like a halfwit." There was no mistaking Chief Inspector Nash's dulcet tones. The indistinguishable reply must be Raskin, not off to a jolly start with his superior.

"Damn." Kincaid swore under his breath. He'd seen Raskin's battered Austin from the first-floor landing and had hoped to catch him alone, hoped to let Raskin take credit for the find. Bearing such a gift himself would do nothing to improve his working relationship with Nash, but getting it to the lab was too urgent to wait for a better moment. He stuck his head around the corner and peered in.

Nash sat at the small dining table, surrounded by files. The telephone cable stretched dangerously across the room from the sofa table so that the instrument could rest at Nash's elbow. Probably Raskin's point of contention, thought Kincaid. "Temporary incident room?" he asked pleasantly.

"And what's it to you, laddie?" Nash replied, his black-currant eyes sweeping over Kincaid with displeasure.

"Such as it is, sir." Peter Raskin spoke into the pause. "It seemed the best option. Couldn't take over Miss Whitlake's office indefinitely. And it was a bit cramped." Raskin seemed to hear himself chattering, opened his mouth and closed it again.

Kincaid crossed the room and carefully placed the polythene bag on the table before Nash. "The children found this in the umbrella stand this morning."

Nash picked up the bag and held it to the light. "A handkerchief? Well, well, it quite takes my breath away." He smiled derisively. "What will the wonder boy think of next?"

"Look, Inspector," Kincaid said as patiently as he could, asking himself just how much his own instinctive dislike fueled Nash's hostility. "The handkerchief has what looks to be a bloodstain in one corner. It could have been used to protect the tennis racquet from fingerprints. It's certainly worth sending to the lab."

"If there had been anything worth finding my scene-of-crime people would have found it." Even the sarcastic pretense of civility vanished from Nash's voice, as did the heavy Yorkshire accent. "You have no jur—"

Kincaid's temper erupted. "If your scene-of-crime team had been doing its job properly they would never have missed this. I'm sick and tired of your deliberate opposition, Chief Inspector. The only reason you're in charge of this investigation is that your Superintendent is laid up in hospital flat on his back. If you won't co-operate and aren't able to keep your feelings about me from obscuring your judgement in this case, I'll see you never have this much authority again." Nash's face flushed such an unhealthy shade of purple that Kincaid felt suddenly afraid he'd gone too far—the man might have a stroke on the spot.

"You'll do no—" The phone rang, its insistent burr startling them all. Nash grabbed the receiver. "Nash here. What—" Whatever diatribe he had been about to utter died on his lips. "Sir. Yes, sir, he's here now." His eyes darted to Kincaid. "Yes, sir. I think that's clear. Every courtesy." Nash replaced the receiver in the cradle with great deliberation, looked first at Raskin, then Kincaid before he could bring himself to speak. "It seems that the Chief Constable has had a chat with the Assistant Commissioner, Crime. The Chief Constable thinks you might be of some help to us in this investigation, and the A.C. has given his approval. Could it be," the heavy sarcasm was directed at Kincaid, "that the A.C. was the one did the calling, not the other way around?"

"Could be," Kincaid answered noncommittally. "Chief Inspector, I don't want to tell you how to do your job. I'd just like to have access to the investigation."

"You mean you'd like to interfere whenever and wherever it bloody well suits you?"

"Something like that." Kincaid smiled.

"I may have to let you stick your toffee-nosed face into my business, but that doesn't mean I have to like it," Nash responded, his heavy face set implacably. "You." He turned toward Peter Raskin, whose studied neutrality wouldn't save him from becoming next in line as whipping boy.

"Chief Inspector," Kincaid interrupted before Nash could vent his temper on Raskin's undeserving head. "What about last night's autopsy report?"

Nash shuffled the papers on the table until he found the manila folder, then scanned the contents. "According to the pathologist, she died sometime between the time she was last seen and the time she was found." Kincaid saw a flash of humor in Nash's eyes, evidence, he hoped, of a tiny thawing.

Kincaid snorted. "Very hopeful, that. What else?"

"Penny MacKenzie's skull seems to have been unusually thin. Great physical strength would not have been required to strike the blow. He estimates the assailant to have been of average height, male or female. If a woman struck the blow she probably used both hands." Nash leaned back and the fragile dining chair creaked alarmingly. "It occurs to me, Superintendent," he said conversationally, a smile stretching the corners of his mouth, "that your lady friend, Miss Hannah Alcock, found herself very conveniently placed to discover poor Miss MacKenzie's body." Nash's détente had been brief.

The phone rang again before Kincaid could reply. He appreciated the reprieve. Wandering absently about the room as Nash spoke, Kincaid stopped at the bedroom door, where Cassie and Graham said they had met the night Sebastian died. He remembered the flash of light he and Hannah saw through the window. Ten to midnight, Cassie had said. A long time for what Cassie had portrayed as a hurried sexual encounter. What else had gone on between them? Had they argued?

The names ran through Kincaid's head—Cassie and Graham, Hannah and Patrick, Cassie and Patrick . . . The idea that came to him seemed plausible. Might

Hannah, like Penny, have found out something that cast suspicion on someone else? And might Hannah, like Penny, be withholding it out of some sense of honor or fair play?

Nash finished his call, and Raskin took advantage of the opportunity to speak. "I'll just get this off to the lab, sir." He swept the plastic bag off the table. Kincaid met his quizzical glance and thought they might call themselves even in favors rendered.

"Thanks," Kincaid said, then turned to Nash. "I'll be off, then, Chief Inspector, if there's nothing else? I'll be around the house if you should want my advice." He lifted a hand and left the room before the idea of taking his advice could give Nash apoplexy.

As he crossed the hall his eye fell on the umbrella stand in the entry, a brass bucket with a red-and-green paper print of a hunting scene wrapped around it. Gay red-jacketed riders jumped elongated horses over fences. Before them the hounds ran, then clustered on their quarry. The fox lay dying.

Hannah answered her door quickly, with the air of someone expecting bad tidings. She had taken more pains with her appearance than yesterday, yet the skillfully applied make-up didn't hide the unnatural pallor of her skin or the shadows under her eyes.

"Duncan." She spoke his name in a breathless rush. Kincaid caught the same flicker of disappointment in her eyes that he imagined he'd seen that first night, as he stood at her table and introduced himself. "What . . . Is there . . ."

"No," he said softly, answering her unspoken question. "There's no news. I only came to see about you." And what he could see made him distinctly uneasy.

"Come in, come in. Let me make you some coffee. I was just having some." Hannah turned abruptly and went into the kitchen, bumping her arm against the counter as she rounded it.

Hannah's suite, as Kincaid had discovered yesterday, was not the mirror image of his own. The size and placement of the rooms differed slightly, as did the color scheme—dusty pinks rather than dusty greens. Nor had it acquired, as had his, the lived-in look of a near-week's worth of occupancy. No books or clothes scattered absentmindedly about the sitting room, no dishes left drying on the draining-board.

Kincaid stood awkwardly in the doorway of the galley kitchen, watching Hannah's jerky movements, so different from her usual self-contained gestures. Whatever had been troubling her, Kincaid guessed, she had resolved on a course of action and was working herself up to it. "Can I help?" he asked, as Hannah spilled coffee grounds across the counter.

"No. I can manage. Thanks." She swept the spilled coffee into the filter and put together the small drip pot. "There. Won't be a sec now." Hannah's gaze drifted across Kincaid's face and away, not meeting his eyes. The coffee pot had not quite finished dripping when she yanked the filter out and splashed coffee into a cup.

"Come on. Let's go sit down." He placed a hand between her shoulders and guided her into the sitting room, wondering all the while how he could ease into what he wanted to say. Sitting down didn't seem to calm Hannah—she sat hunched on the sofa's edge and her hands trembled as she lifted her cup.

"Cold?" Kincaid asked.

"Me or the coffee?"

"Weak. Your humor, not the coffee." Kincaid smiled and she seemed to relax a bit. "Hannah," he said slowly, "has Patrick Rennie ever said anything to you about Cassie Whitlake?"

"No," she answered, puzzled, her eyes meeting his directly for the first time, "why should he? I mean," her response grew more forceful, "why should he speak to me about Cassie, and why should he know anything to speak of? You don't think that Cassie . . . had anything to do with . . ."

"I think that Patrick might know quite a bit about what Cassie has or hasn't had anything to do with—might know, in fact, far more about Cassie Whitlake than he'd like anyone to guess, especially his wife."

"Patrick . . . and Cassie?" The patches of rouge on Hannah's cheekbones flared scarlet against the sudden chalkiness of her skin.

"Oh, I think so." Kincaid spoke conversationally, sipping his coffee. "You see, Cassie's been having an affair with Graham Frazer for some time, but I gather there's been a change recently. A new lover, someone with real prospects, a rising star. And Cassie has become desperately anxious that no one find out she's still seeing Graham."

He paused, gauging Hannah's reaction. She sat very still, the coffee cup sagging, forgotten, in her fingers. "In fact, I wouldn't be surprised if she's tried to end it with Graham, and he's being stubborn about it. He strikes me as the stubborn type.

"Now," Kincaid continued, "give the situation a half-degree twist and look at it again. Cassie doesn't want Patrick to find out about Graham, right? End of romance, end of prospects, real or imagined. But what about Patrick? What would it mean to Patrick if anyone, especially his wife, found out about Cassie? Marital squabble? Messy divorce? Scandal in the gutter press?"

He tilted his head questioningly, as if Hannah had expressed some skepticism. "Old-fashioned, you think? Not scandal enough to ruin a budding political career? Maybe not. But consider this—Marta Rennie's parents are very politically active in the constituency where Patrick is standing his by-election. In fact, they're Patrick's biggest financial supporters. I'd say it's not the best time for them to find out he's been cheating on their darling daughter. Wouldn't you?"

"No." The word was barely a whisper. Hannah seemed to gather herself, then spoke again. "No. I don't believe it. I won't believe it. Patrick would never—" Her voice rose, edging toward hysteria. "How could you say such things? Why are you doing this to me?"

"Hannah, listen to me." Kincaid leaned forward, reached out a hand toward her. She jerked away from his touch as if she'd been stung. "Hannah, if you know something about Patrick Rennie, something you saw or heard, something he told you, you mustn't keep it to yourself. It could be dangerous. I don't want to see you end up like—"

"No! That's absurd. I won't even listen to it." She stood up, her breath coming in short gasps. "Just get out."

Kincaid stood and they faced one another. He could see her body trembling, feel her breath against his face. "Why, Hannah? What loyalty do you owe him? What has Patrick Rennie ever done for you?"

For a long moment he held her gaze, then the fury seemed to drain from her. She half turned from him, her head drooping as if her slender neck no longer had the strength to support it. "Patrick Rennie," she said simply, "is my son."

14

THE SMALL ENTRANCE building of Rievaulx Abbey sold tickets and souvenirs as well as serving as a sort of mini-museum. A glass-covered scale model of the complete abbey invited scrutiny. The walls were covered with drawings and photographs detailing the abbey's history, but Hannah passed them by with only a glance. She'd done her homework last night, after Patrick mentioned he intended coming here.

Then it had simply seemed an opportunity to talk with him alone, skirting the dangerous edge of revelation. She'd meant to wait until their relationship had progressed a bit from its first spontaneous warmth—she'd meant to build trust and confidence between them, lead into it gently, ask him, perhaps, how he felt about his real mother.

Now her mind shied away from all her rehearsed scenarios, unable to fasten on anything coherent. But tell him she must. Somehow hearing Kincaid's suspicions had forced her hand, made it impossible for her to continue the relationship under false pretenses. How could she expect Patrick to be honest with her if she hadn't been honest with him? And she must hear his own account, judge for herself the truth of it. Could her son be capable of murder? She couldn't bear not knowing.

Hannah pushed through the building's rear exit and stepped onto the grass. Her first glimpse across the long, green lawns quite literally took her breath away. She felt the sharp prickle of tears against her eyelids, blinked them back.

Before her Rievaulx Abbey lay cupped in a natural hollow at the foot of Rievaulx moor, held like a jewel between brilliant green grass in the foreground and the red-golds of the trees covering the slope of the moor. The morning's sun had given way to a soft, low overcast, and the moisture in the air seemed to saturate the colors with an elemental vividness.

She crossed the lawn slowly, her eyes on the soaring arches of the choir. Six hundred monks had lived here, eating, sleeping, praying, tending their sheep and their gardens. She could almost hear them singing as they worked, such was the timeless, dreamlike quality of the place. She knew for a fleeting instant how close they must have felt to their god, and a shaft of envy stabbed through her.

Patrick sat on a ruined sill with his back against one of the choir arches, his hair bright against the weathered stone. The nubby, brown wool of his Shetland sweater might almost have been the rough brown cloth of a monk's habit, but the smoke that curled from the cigarette he held between his fingers ruined the image. She'd never seen him smoke.

He showed no surprise at her presence, speaking only after she had stood there a moment, watching him. "I thought you might turn up. Magnificent, isn't it?" He indicated the choir around them with a tilt of his head. He dropped the cigarette and ground the butt with his toe. At her look he said, "I don't around Marta. I suppose I'd lose the advantage of my righteous superiority. Politicians," he smiled, his voice lightly self-mocking in a way she hadn't heard before, "never let go an advantage."

"Is that why you wanted to make sure no one found out about Cassie?" Hannah said, surprised to find her own voice steady. She hadn't meant to start that way, hadn't meant to accuse him outright, but the words tumbled from her mouth of their own accord. "What were you willing to do, Patrick, to make sure Marta didn't find out? To make sure you didn't lose Marta's parents' support and your election with it?" Hannah found her breath coming in little gasps and she began to shiver as if with a chill.

Patrick's brows lifted in surprise. He started to speak, then took a few steps toward the choir's center and stood with his back to her, hands in his pockets. After a moment he said, evenly, "I realize we're all suspect. Any fool would. But somehow I didn't expect an attack from you. How," he continued without turning, "did you come up with this . . . this fantasy?"

"Duncan Kincaid thinks Sebastian found out about you and Cassie and threatened to expose you—whether for money or just because he hated Cassie, I don't know."

He turned to face her now, still in that deliberately casual manner. "It won't wash, Hannah. Do you seriously think that Marta would leave me over a little bit of marital infidelity? That she'd go running back to her parents and her set in Sussex with her tail between her legs and admit she couldn't keep me? Or that her parents would publicly admit their daughter's humiliation? Not bloody likely. It's not only my ambition we're dealing with here, it's theirs as well and they'll not willingly let it go. Even confronted with irrefutable evidence they'd all turn a blind eye because that's what suits them. Oh, Marta would make catty little jabs at me and up her gin consumption, but that's as far as it would go."

"But what—"

"You think I'm callous, don't you?" Patrick's tone was surprisingly bitter. "You think that I chose Marta and her parents because of what they could do for me?" He stared at her challengingly for a long moment, but she didn't speak. "Well, they chose me, Hannah. I was the perfect vehicle to fulfill their social aspirations, the pet to be coddled and groomed like a prize cat, the charming son-in-law always willing to be sacrificed to garrulous old ladies. I'd say I've kept up my end of the bargain fairly well." The self-mockery touched his smile again.

It all sounded so smoothly, seductively plausible, thought Hannah. How could she not believe him as he stood before her, his shoulders hunched in an oddly vulnerable posture, the wind ruffling the straight, fair hair across his forehead?

"But Patrick," Hannah struggled to find the words to go on, "what did happen that night, the night Sebastian died? Duncan thinks Penny saw you."

Patrick came back to the choir arch and leaned against it, fishing a battered pack of Marlboros from his trouser pocket. He cupped the match against the wind and drew on the cigarette before he spoke. "I did go out that night. I told Marta I was going to the car for a book—whether she believed me or not I don't know. She was more sober than usual. We'd just arrived that morning and Cassie had been avoiding me all day, until I'd begun to think she didn't want to see me." He watched the wind fan the glowing end of the cigarette as he spoke and didn't raise his eyes to Hannah's. "I went to Cassie's cottage and knocked but she didn't answer. I'd left a notebook in my car so I tore a page from it and scribbled a note for Cassie's door."

"And then you went straight back to the suite?" Hannah tried to keep her voice level, tried not to betray how desperately she hoped it were true.

"Not exactly." Patrick dropped the match into the grass, still not meeting Hannah's eyes. "I thought she might be working late, an excuse to wait for me in her office. Stupid of me, I suppose. The office was dark, empty, as was the sitting room, but when I'd come back through the sitting room and started through the reception area I heard a sound behind me."

He seemed caught up now in his own tale, speaking more to himself than to Hannah, remembering detail by detail. "Someone's sharp intake of breath, almost a gasp. I turned, and after the second it took my eyes to adjust I made out a form standing by the sofa. Enough light came through the sitting-room windows that I thought I recognized Penny. I started to speak, but there was something about the way she stood there, not moving, not speaking. Furtive, almost frightened. Well, it occurred to me that I didn't really want to explain my movements either, so I just turned and left." He raised his eyes to hers for the first time. "I should have spoken up in the beginning. I didn't want to have to explain myself. Oh, I could have made some excuse, but excuses always sound like what they are. Then Penny didn't speak either and it got more and more awkward. It would almost have been funny, if the outcome hadn't been so tragic."

The roar of a lawnmower shattered the deep peace of the precinct. Hannah, startled, thought she'd never heard a more incongruous sound. Patrick sighed and rubbed his hand across his face. "I have no proof of anything, Hannah. No proof that I did nothing else that night but go to bed. But no one else has any proof that I did." He waited, looking at her now, expecting some response.

"What would you have done if things had gone the way Duncan said? If Sebastian had told Marta, and she had left you and taken her parents' money with her?" She spoke without heat, curiously.

"If I don't win this by-election, I'll win the next one, or the one after that, and I don't need their help to do it. I could be P.M. someday, Hannah, if I grab the right coat tails, and Marta is becoming more of a liability than an asset."

"Why," Hannah asked in the same flat voice, "after you married one woman who wanted to use you, would you pick another with the same thing in mind?"

He shrugged. "Bad judgment, I guess. I'd begun to see that, of course, but she's still very . . . attractive. I may know my strengths as a politician, but that doesn't make me infallible. Besides, I never meant to marry Cassie." His mouth quirked in that small, ironic smile and he straightened up, moving a step closer to her. "Now, let me ask something of you, Hannah. What gives you the right to accuse me? Or rather," he smiled again, "I should ask myself why I feel obligated to offer you a defense. Something . . . compels me to be honest with you. I don't understand it."

Hannah turned from him. She stood on the brink, the choice before her. To speak now required more courage than anything she had ever done in her life. He had placed the perfect opening in her hands, yet she stood mute, her mind frozen. She forced herself to breathe. After a long moment the halting words came, but they bore no resemblance to the ones she'd prepared.

"You should have seen me at sixteen, Patrick. Too tall, too bony, all arms and legs and awkward angles. No boy ever showed the least interest in me until I went home with a school friend for the long vac, and her older brother took pity on me. He must have been all of nineteen, and terribly sophisticated in my eyes. I was curious, and flattered, and he was very inept—but I didn't know that at the time, just that it was all rather disappointing." She half turned and risked a glance at his puzzled face before continuing.

"Of course, the consequences of such . . . such stupidity and naiveté were inevitable. You can't imagine what it was like to have to tell my parents I was pregnant. My parents . . . didn't make allowances for mistakes. I had already been accepted at university for the next year. To them it was unthinkable that I should keep the baby. And I . . . I didn't have the courage to withstand them. I could have managed—left school, found a job. I could have done something." Hannah's voice had risen. She found herself trembling again and clasped her arms tightly across her chest. After a moment she spoke again, more calmly. "It was all very discreetly arranged. I went to stay with an aunt. When the baby came my parents took him away, saying they had found a suitable home."

She turned now to face him, dropping her arms to her sides as if baring herself. "It wasn't until last March, when my father died and I had access to his personal files, that I found out what they had actually done. My father—he was a solicitor, did I say?—had among his clients a Major and Mrs. Rennie, desperate for a child of their own. Of course my father never told them it was his own grandchild he offered them. All neat. All so very tidy." Hannah strangled a sudden hysterical desire to laugh. "Do you know the worst thing of all? My father kept up with you all those years, and I never knew it. Your parents sent him school reports, photos of Patrick's first cricket match, Patrick's first pony—and I never saw them. To him you were a real person, but I . . . I never had that privilege." The words ran down, finally. She had no justification left to offer. For the first time since Hannah had begun she looked at him directly. Not until she saw the white stillness of his face did she realize just how unruffled he'd been when she had more or less accused him of murder.

Silence rang in Hannah's ears. She wondered when the lawnmower had stopped.

Patrick swallowed. "What . . . I don't believe it.

You? My mother?" His voice rose incredulously, for once out of control. "You can't be. You're too young—"

"I'm not, Patrick. I was practically a child."

He shook his head. "You can't—"

"Why would I lie to you? What possible reason could I have for telling you if it weren't true?"

He subsided for a moment. "But I knew him. Your father. He took Dad and me to lunch at his club sometimes when my father had business in London. I never connected the name. I never dreamed—"

"That he was your grandfather? No, he made sure you wouldn't." This final betrayal of her father's made her feel sick. She closed her eyes. The picture was quite clear in her mind. Her father, genial over cigars and brandy with the faceless Major Rennie, saying, "Don't tell the boy I arranged his adoption. It might make him feel uncomfortable." When she opened her eyes Patrick was staring at her in consternation.

"Why now, Hannah? You could have tackled your father long ago. You were an adult with an adult's rights. And why like this?" He sounded bewildered. "How did you find me? I mean here at Followdale House?"

"I hired a private detective." She flinched at his look of distaste.

"My god, I don't believe it. You had me followed? Spied on me—"

"I only had your parents' address. I couldn't just go to them and say I wanted to see you. And I wanted some time to know you on neutral ground, no judgments, no biases. I wasn't even sure I'd tell you."

"How nice and safe for you. Your choice, once again. What would you have done if I'd been unattractive? Or stupid? Walk away and pretend it never happened, just like you did nearly thirty years ago?" Patrick's expression was bleak, free of that overlying gloss of charm, and for the first time Hannah saw echoes of her own features. "Why did you decide to tell me, Hannah?"

"I found I had to, in the end. I couldn't live with not telling you."

"For the sake of your peace of mind, or mine?"

Hannah had no answer. She stood miserably before him, waiting for what would come next.

"What did you expect from me? Did you think you could just walk into my life after all these years and be welcomed with open arms?"

"Patrick, please—"

"It won't work, Hannah. There's nothing to build on. My parents have been *parents* to me, for Christ's sake. What have you ever given me, besides an uncelebrated entry into the world? Should I be glad you didn't abort me? I suppose you could have, even in those days." He gave a mirthless snort.

The words that had flooded from her had drained her utterly, leaving her without the strength to speak. How could she tell this suddenly harsh man how she had loved him all those months she'd carried him? How she had grieved when they had taken him from her? And how could she explain what had happened to her afterwards? It seemed ridiculous, absurd to even think of it. She drew in breath with an effort. "Patrick, I . . ." The tears she had managed to fight off until now tightened her throat. "You don't understand. I can't make you understand."

"No."

The silence lengthened until Hannah thought she must speak, must find some pebble to throw into this chasm that had opened between them. "I wanted . . ."

"You wanted," Patrick said, his tone more gentle now, "the impossible. How disappointing for you," he added ironically, "to find your long-lost son and think him capable of murder."

"No, Patrick, that's not true, I never thought that." Hannah's voice rose in agitation. "I was afraid for you, afraid things might be difficult for you. I didn't want you—"

"To spoil your image of the perfect son? Kept sleeping all these years like the fairy prince, to wake at Mother's kiss?"

Her tears spilled now, unheeded. "No, Patrick, please, that's unfair."

"I suppose it is," he said after a moment, "but so were your expectations. You should, as they say," his smile held no humor, "have left well enough alone." Patrick studied her, seemed to come to some decision. "I'm sorry, Hannah."

Hannah watched him lay his hand to the ruined sill, vault over it and walk away from her across the grass.

She sat on the toilet lid, a wet cloth pressed to her face. The tears had finally stopped and she felt drained, with that curious light-headedness that sometimes follows prolonged weeping. It had been years since she had cried like that, the sobs welling up from some place inside her she hadn't been aware existed. Now she felt oddly peaceful, almost purged.

Patrick had been right, of course. What had she expected? Acceptance? Even love? It had been a fantasy, fed on need. She had created an image of the perfect son to fill some undefined void within herself.

Hannah sighed and dipped the cloth into the basin of cold water. Well, it was finished now. She had done what she set out to do—there was no point in lingering to humiliate herself even further. If the police would let her go, that is. She bathed her face once more with the cloth and then patted it gently with a towel, afraid to look in the mirror. It would be hours before the swelling subsided and she had better tackle Inspector Nash now. Otherwise she might lose her resolve altogether.

Hannah tried Kincaid's suite first, hoping for moral support, but as she brushed her knuckles against the door, she found she couldn't face him and turned away. Better to see Nash alone.

The hall was empty, the house silent, and Hannah realized she had no idea of the time. Lunch? Early afternoon? Teatime? The divisions had become meaningless to her. She stood a moment at the top of the stairs, rehearsing what she would say to Nash. Her mentor ill? A rush to return to Oxford, some urgent project at work?

Guilt flooded through her. How could she have forgotten Miles' illness, these last few days. Not even a phone call to the clinic to check up on him, and after all he had done for her. It was high time she pulled herself together.

She heard no sound. Only the breath of air told her the door had opened behind her. Before she could turn, or speak, she felt a hard shove in the middle of her back.

As the stairs rushed up to meet her, her mind fastened on one small, inconsequential thing—the hand at her back had felt warm.

15

SUFFOLK TO SUSSEX to Wiltshire to Oxfordshire, ring around the roses. It made Gemma dizzy to think of the past two days. And tired.

Her clothes already looked as if they'd been slept in and this was only her second stop of the morning. Lavender Lane, Wildmeadow Estates. Ugh. What a horribly inappropriate name for this new housing estate on the outskirts of St. Albans. Boxlike clones of houses marched in neat rows across land that had been cleared of anything remotely resembling a wildflower. They didn't look cheap, though—Mr. Edward Lyle must not be doing too badly.

The house belonging to the Lyles was indistinguishable from its neighbors. Gemma stopped the car and carefully noted the mileage in her notebook. Kincaid never remembered to record his and it exasperated her no end. Maybe on a Superintendent's salary he could afford to be so careless. It must, she thought sardonically, be nice. Gemma sighed and wondered why she felt so out of sorts. She didn't like working alone, that was part of it. She'd grown accustomed to Kincaid's presence and found it oddly comforting—oddly because she remembered how nervous she'd been when first assigned to him.

And she felt so at sea with this case—if you could call it a case. How could she dig when she didn't know what she was digging for? The action lay in Yorkshire and she had no idea whether the disconnected bits of information she turned up were of any use at all.

Lavender Lane seemed deserted, as if all the inhabitants had suddenly packed up and gone to the moon. Not a pram in sight, no children's bikes or scooters left abandoned in the front gardens. Gemma tried the neighbors either side without success. Of course it must take two wage packets to pay the mortgages here—all the mums would be out working and the kiddies left with the sitter. She had turned back to the car in disgust when she caught the twitch of a net curtain in the house across the street.

The woman who answered Gemma's ring wore jeans and a tee-shirt, a sticky-faced toddler attached to her hip. "If you're looking for the Lyles," she said before Gemma could speak, her eyes alight with curiosity, "they've gone on holiday."

"I know. We're making some routine inquiries about some things that have happened where they're holidaying. Do you know them? Perhaps you could help me."

"Janet's all right, isn't she?" The child caught the note of alarm in his mother's voice and began to fret.

"Mrs. Lyle's fine, I'm sure, but there have been two unexplained deaths."

"Unexplained? You mean accidents?" The woman's arm tightened around the baby and he began to howl in earnest.

"Well, we're not sure." Gemma made an effort to pitch her voice over the baby's din. "That's why we're making inquiries. If I could just ask—"

"You'd better come in." The woman bounced the baby on her hip, saying, "Hush, Malcolm, hush," then stuck out her free hand to shake Gemma's. "I'm Helen North." She gestured toward the back of the house with her head. "Come back to the kitchen. Janet and I are friendly enough when *he's* not around," she said over her shoulder, "and I'd not like anything to happen to her. She's had a hard enough time as it is, poor dear."

Gemma followed her, thinking that Helen seemed rather an old-fashioned and elegant name for this rumpled young mother. Helen North seated Gemma at a small table in her bright kitchen, and set the baby down amidst a jumble of plastic blocks. "Here I am forgetting my manners. Would you like a cup of tea?"

"Please." Gemma usually thanked god for a strong bladder—her job required downing more cups of tea than a vicar's—but for once tea actually sounded appealing. Her early stop in Finchley had not even brought the offer.

"Fine," Helen said. "I'll just be putting the kettle on."

The faint sing-song in the woman's voice had grown more pronounced with her last words. "You're Irish," Gemma said, making it a statement.

"County Cork." Helen smiled. "I try not to sound fresh from the bog, but it has a way of slipping through on its own when I'm not paying attention. Would you believe," she tousled her son's ginger curls, "he gets his hair from his dad, and me Irish?"

"And my son," answered Gemma, "has hair as fair and straight as a Dane's." They laughed, common ground firmly established.

"Maybe that's why Eddie Lyle doesn't like me," Helen said as she set Gemma's cup before her and seated herself opposite. "Doesn't consider being Irish quite the thing. He's ex-service, though you wouldn't think it to look at him. Served in Northern Ireland and he lumps all the Irish together as a bad lot.

"Or maybe it's because my husband works for the builder." Her ringer made a quick circular gesture, indicating the housing estate. "I don't know where he gets off being such a snob. His parents owned an off-license in the old town. Perfectly respectable, but Janet says he doesn't like it mentioned. If you ask me, the man has a slate off and one sliding."

Under Helen North's chatter Gemma detected more than a spark of malice. Edward Lyle must have snubbed her pretty thoroughly. "How did you and Janet get to be friends?"

"We're the only two women on the street who stay at home. You get desperate for some adult conversation." She cocked her head and looked thoughtfully at Gemma. "Sometimes I envy women like you, out in the real world with the grownups."

"Probably not as much as I envy you," answered Gemma. She touched the wandering baby's hair and he gurgled at her.

"Well, it was my choice, after all, to stay at home

and make do with a bit less. I shouldn't grouse. But Janet, now, that was a different story. He wouldn't let her work, not even when her Chloe went to school. Didn't think it fitting, I ask you! And she trained as a nurse. God, what a waste."

Helen subsided, a look of disgust on her face. "Though I suppose," she continued thoughtfully after a moment, "her nursing came in handy when he moved his old mum in with them. Oh, yes," she went on as if Gemma had doubted her, "the old thing got to where she couldn't be trusted on her own, and who better than Janet to have the full-time job of looking after her? The old lady drank, you see. Started when her only sister died young, or so Janet thought. Overmedicated, too. She went to some old quack who insisted on filling her up with pills. It made Janet livid, but she couldn't do a thing about it."

"A dangerous combination," said Gemma.

"Oh yes," answered Helen, "it was."

"Was?"

"You don't know about the accident?" Gemma's blank expression answered her question. "Tragic." Helen clucked a little and shook her head. "The old woman took Janet's car one day when Janet had walked to the shops. Smashed herself to Kingdom Come. She was tanked up with booze and pills, they discovered afterwards."

"How terrible." Gemma leaned forward in her chair, ready sympathy in her voice. "Janet must have felt awful."

"She was sick with guilt. She should have done this, she should have done that. As if she could have watched the old woman every minute of the day. And didn't he carry on, the grief-stricken son. He never had the time of day for her when she was alive. I went to the funeral, for Janet's sake. He stood at the graveside, all dignified and proper with a little tear trickling down his cheek. Made me sick, I can tell you." Helen drew her brows together in consternation. "Why does she put up with him, can you tell me that?"

The question seemed rhetorical, but Gemma shook her head. "No. I wish I could. Has it been long since old Mrs. Lyle died?"

"Last winter. And it wasn't long after that he came up with this holiday scheme. Said it was to cheer Janet up, but she wasn't a bit keen. More likely he meant to impress his boss. Janet said he had to borrow the money to buy their week, and then he couldn't get a time when their Chloe was out of school and could come with them."

The little boy began to fuss and pull at his mother's shirt, having suffered inattention long enough. Gemma finished her tea and began to make leave-taking motions. "Thanks for the tea, and your time."

Helen North suddenly became embarrassed, the aftermath of too much confession. "I shouldn't have said . . . it's not really fair to Janet . . ."

Gemma reassured her. "You haven't said a thing I wouldn't have said myself. I have a neighbor who looks after her husband's mum—you wouldn't believe the things she puts up with from the old lady . . ." By the time she'd finished her anecdote Helen had recovered her equilibrium, and Gemma took her leave as smoothly as a surgeon removing a knife.

* * *

Kincaid stood on his balcony, as had become his habit when he needed to think. He turned up his shirt collar against the chill little wind that played around his ears. The weather, damp and formless, suited his mood.

He was finding it very difficult to accept the idea that Hannah could be Patrick's mother. He'd never have thought her old enough to have a grown son. And he had seen them together, seen some spark kindled, even felt a faint stirring of envy. Had Hannah seen it as well? No wonder she had been so distraught.

Dear god, what had he driven Hannah to do? He'd meant to shock her into giving him evidence she might be withholding, not to send her off into some rash confrontation with Patrick. For they were both gone, he'd made sure of that. Hannah had bundled him out of her suite with such urgency that he'd had no choice but to go. When he'd returned a few minutes later to try once more to persuade her to talk, he'd seen from the landing window the flash of tail lights as her car turned into the road.

Marta Rennie, sober and sullen, didn't know where Patrick had gone and didn't seem to care. "Sightseeing," she said with derision. "God, it makes me ill." She'd shut the door on anything else Kincaid might have asked her.

It seemed to Kincaid that everything he had done from the beginning of this affair had gone wrong. Every turn and feint he made came up blank, shadow boxing with an unseen enemy. He should have listened to Penny. He should have kept his ideas about Patrick Rennie to himself.

He should never have let Hannah out of his sight.

The burr of the telephone sounded through the French door, interrupting his recriminations. He dived to answer it, his life line to the outside world. Gemma's voice came over the line. "Just what sort of a wild goose chase have you sent me on?"

Kincaid laughed, cheered by the asperity in her voice. "I wish I knew. What's up?"

"My backside's welded to the car, that's what."

"Angling for sympathy again, are you? Well, you won't get it from me. At least you're doing something."

"True. I paid a call on Mrs. Marjorie Frazer at her office in Finchley, bright and early this morning. She was not pleased to see me, I can tell you. Very on-her-dignity solicitorish to begin with. Then she seemed to think about it and decide she didn't mind painting her ex-husband black. Says she had custody of the daughter, Angela, in the beginning, but got tired of playing the villain. Decided that if Angela had to live with Graham she might decide the sun didn't rise and set over him."

"I'd say it's certainly had that effect. I'm surprised Angela ever did feel that way."

"It seems Mrs. Frazer has changed her mind. Angela got herself expelled from her fancy boarding school last term. Drugs, I'd say, though Mrs. Frazer didn't specifically say so. Well, enough is enough, she says. She's determined now to get full custody, deny him access." Gemma paused a moment. "I didn't get the impression that Mrs. Frazer particularly cared for her daughter. More angry at him, and irritated with her." Gemma sounded both puzzled and incensed at such lack of maternal feeling.

"Poor Angela," said Kincaid. "So that's how it is. No wonder she's desperate for any kindness."

"He doesn't sound a very savory character. I've done some checking with some contacts in insurance. He's not well liked. A bit heavy-handed, I take it. And there are whispers—nothing concrete—about fraud, some deals that just skate the line." She paused for effect, and Kincaid waited patiently, having learned that it was best to let Gemma tell a story in her own way. "He also has a reputation for being pretty heavily into cocaine. Do you suppose Angela borrowed Daddy's stash?"

"Could be," Kincaid answered, running over the idea in his mind.

Gemma spoke hesitantly. "Do you think there could be sexual abuse involved as well?"

"I don't know. It's possible." It certainly was, considering the unhealthy nature of what he had seen of Graham and Angela's relationship. What if Angela had confided in Sebastian? That would account for Sebastian's venomous dislike of the man. What if Sebastian had threatened Graham with exposure, either to Cassie or his ex-wife? Gemma cleared her throat and he realized he'd left her hanging. "Sorry, Gemma. What else?"

Gemma recounted her interview with Helen North, then added, "I'd say that unless Mr. Lyle has an awfully good job, he might be a bit financially overextended—what with his mortgage and his wife not working and a daughter away at some posh boarding school. Sounds a right prig to me, besides," she finished.

"Another model husband and father?"

"And devoted son." Kincaid heard paper rustling as Gemma thumbed through her notebook.

"Where are you?"

"Call box in St. Albans. I haven't been able to get on to Miles Sterrett at Hannah Alcock's clinic. They say he's ill . . ."

"Hang on, Gemma. I thought I heard someone at the door." A ghost of a knock, so faint he thought he'd imagined it. When he opened the door there was no one in the hall. He returned to the phone. "Gemma? Must be hearing things. Listen, finish up what you can today and get up here as soon as possible. I feel uneasy about this whole business, melodramatic as it sounds."

They rang off and Kincaid stood for a moment, debating. He decided it was about time he had another little talk with Angela Frazer.

Kincaid was halfway down the first flight of stairs when he saw a foot, a woman's foot in a peach-colored sock, outstretched on the flight below him. A flat leather shoe lay overturned nearby. He skidded to a stop, then rounded the landing as his body began to function again.

Hannah Alcock lay crumpled beneath him.

16

Hannah lay sprawled head down, half on her back, her arms flung out as if she had tried to break her fall. While part of Kincaid's mind reeled with shock, another part noted details—her sweater, the same soft peach as her socks, had ridden up and exposed a wide, pale slice of skin. Her ribs, so ungracefully bared, rose and fell rhythmically.

Relief rushed through Kincaid in a sickening wave. He closed his eyes and breathed a moment, steadying himself, then maneuvered into a kneeling position beside her. Although her head seemed twisted at an awkward angle, her color looked healthy and he didn't think she was deeply unconscious. He touched her shoulder gently. "Hannah." She made a soft sound and her eyelids fluttered. He tried again, more urgently. "Hannah." Her eyes opened and she looked fuzzily at him, her expression blank. "Hannah. Hannah!"

A flicker of recognition moved in Hannah's eyes. She turned her head a little and winced. "What . . ." She shifted again, feeling and cognizance returning together. "My head. Oh, my god. What hap—" She tried to lift herself and pain shot through her face.

"Careful, careful. Take it easy. What hurts?"

"My head . . . the back of it."

"Not your neck?"

Tentatively, she rolled her head a little each way. "No. It seems okay."

"Good. Can you move your legs?" She flexed each leg and nodded. "Okay. That's good. No, wait," Kincaid said as she struggled to pull herself into a sitting position. "Let's do this a stage at a time." He slid his arm beneath her head and supported it level with her shoulders. "Better?"

"Yes. I think I'm all right, really. I can feel everything, and move everything." Hannah drew up her arms and legs again, demonstrating. "God, I feel like Humpty Dumpty." She gave a ghost of a smile.

"I'm just glad you don't look it," Kincaid said with feeling. He hesitated to move her, but after a few more minutes of Hannah complaining about the blood running to her head, he temporized. Slipping his arm under her shoulders, he lifted and turned her so that she sat across the step with her back against the wall.

Hannah moved her head fretfully. "I'm all right. Let me get—"

"Wait." Kincaid interrupted her. "Let's assess the damage first." He ran his fingers lightly over the back of her head. Near the crown a lump was already rising. "You're definitely going to have an egg, but the skin's not broken. What else?"

She clasped her right wrist in her left hand. "My wrist hurts like hell, but I can move it."

"Anything else?"

"I don't think so."

"Okay. I imagine you're going to have some bruising." As he straightened up he found his hands were trembling, and his fingertips seemed to retain an imprint of the texture of her hair and the swelling of the lump beneath it. The reaction would pass, he knew, and he pushed away that first image etched in his brain—Hannah lying still and broken beneath him.

"Now, tell me what happened."

For the first time Hannah looked afraid. "I was standing at the top of the stairs. The landing door opened—I remember wondering in a vague sort of way why I didn't hear footsteps or the normal jingly noises people make when they walk. Then I felt a hand at my back."

"Did you see—"

"No. There wasn't time. Just a hard shove and that's really all I remember." She felt her wrist gingerly. "I must have tried to stop myself falling."

Kincaid touched her arm. "Hannah, are you sure you don't know who it was? Not even an impression?"

She shook her head. "No. Why would—"

The front door slammed and they heard quick footsteps crossing the porch. Patrick Rennie came into the hall, his color high as if with anger or excitement. He stopped when he saw them and looked from one to the other, puzzled. "Hannah? Why . . . what happened?" His tone shifted from bewilderment to concern as he took in Kincaid's protective posture. "Are you all right?"

Kincaid, his hand still on Hannah's arm, felt her

stiffen. When she didn't speak he answered for her. "She's quite bruised and shaken." He paused, studying Rennie's face. "Someone pushed her down the stairs."

Rennie looked at them incredulously for a moment. When he managed to speak he stumbled and stammered like a schoolboy. "Wh— Pushed? Pushed, did you say? Why in hell's name would anyone want to push Hannah? She could have been . . ."

Kincaid thought nastily that for once Rennie's aplomb had deserted him. "I thought you might be able to—" he began, when Rennie interrupted him.

"Have you phoned for the doctor? What about the police? They've been hanging about all day and now when they could be doing something useful—"

"Calm down, man. I hadn't time to ring anyone. Perhaps—" Kincaid felt Hannah jerk beside him and she said softly, urgently, "Don't. Don't leave me."

"Perhaps," he continued to Rennie, without looking at her, "you could go and ring them now."

"You seem to be forever making me cups of tea." Hannah gave a wan attempt at a smile.

"My lot in life," answered Kincaid from the kitchen. "Born into the wrong era. I'm sure I would have made an excellent 'gentleman's gentleman.' "

"You as Jeeves? I don't think so." This time her smile was genuine, and it relieved Kincaid to see the lines in her face relax. With Rennie's help he'd walked her up the stairs and into her suite, where they'd settled her on the sofa.

Rennie hovered around Hannah, obviously wanting to speak to her without Kincaid's watchdog presence.

Hannah seemed to have relaxed since her earlier, almost instinctive recoil from her son, but she hadn't looked at or spoken to him directly. Kincaid had no intention of leaving as yet.

Rennie gave in, finally, with a return of some of his habitual grace. "Look, I can see I'm not wanted just now. But you will let me know if I can do anything?" He spoke to Hannah, not Kincaid, and when he reached the door he turned and addressed her once more. "I'm sorry, Hannah." Kincaid had the impression he had not been referring to her fall.

Kincaid returned from the kitchen bearing a tray with two cups of tea and a plate of digestive biscuits. "Teatime."

"Is it?" Hannah took a biscuit tentatively. "Do you know, I don't think I had any lunch. No wonder I feel so weak." Kincaid pulled the armchair across and sat near enough to hand her tea and biscuits. He searched her face as she accepted the cup.

When she had eaten and drunk a little, he spoke. "Hannah, tell me what happened today between you and Patrick. I think you must, you know," he added, softening the demand a bit.

She swallowed some tea and the cup rattled as she replaced it in the saucer. "I never meant it to go like that. I never meant—" Hannah turned her head away, her eyes, already red and swollen with earlier weeping, filling. "First I accused him of all these horrible things, all those things you told me. The words just came out. I couldn't seem to stop them. Then I told him . . ."

"That you were his mother?" Kincaid prompted.

She gave a little hiccuppy laugh. "What a prize I am.

Suspicious. Shrewish. No wonder he wasn't too thrilled with the prospect." Hannah hugged her arms against her chest and began to shiver in earnest.

"You're in shock." Kincaid leaned over her, contrite. "I shouldn't be pestering you—"

"No. No, I have to tell you. I want to tell you." Her voice rose and Kincaid watched her struggle to regain control. "I did everything wrong, you see," she continued, modulating carefully now. "From the very beginning. Successful. Independent. That's how I saw myself. Under no one's jurisdiction. I thought of marriage and family as a loss of autonomy." Hannah twisted the edge of the blanket in her fingers. "It was all such a sham. The truth was I had nothing to give, nothing to share." She raised her eyes to his. "And Patrick . . . I think what Patrick resented the most was my waiting—if knowing him was so important to me, why hadn't I found him years ago? And I could have, he was right about that. With all my illusions of strength and independence, I never faced my father. My father . . ."

Kincaid waited while she tried to find a more comfortable position. Exhaustion tugged at her facial muscles, her eyelids drooped involuntarily. "Hannah—"

"No. I must tell you, before it all slips away . . ."

Kincaid subsided, powerless against her compulsion to talk. He'd seen it often enough in victims of accidents, or shock, but Hannah was more coherent than most.

"Patrick . . . How could I explain what happened to me the last year? Biological clock's stupid, I know," her lips twisted in a faint smile, "but when I knew, finally, that I'd never have another child . . . something changed in me. Suddenly everything seemed so empty. Everything I'd done so pointless—"

Kincaid was startled into protest. "You're not going to trot out that old saw about women only finding fulfillment through marriage and children? I don't believe it of you."

She started to shake her head, then lightly touched her fingers to the back. "No . . ." She paused so long Kincaid began to think she'd drifted away altogether. Then she said quietly, "I don't think sex has much to do with it. It's the little lies, the accumulation of self-deception. Armor, all armor, hiding behind armor, like some soft-bodied sea creature. Afraid of . . ."

"Afraid of what, Hannah?" Kincaid didn't trust the delicacy of his touch.

Again came the almost imperceptible shake of the head. "Losing . . ." Her eyes skated away from his. She picked up her forgotten cup and drank the cold tea thirstily, retreating from whatever precipice she had approached.

Hannah blinked and then closed her eyes, the dark lashes fanning out against her cheeks. The empty teacup tilted in her hand. Kincaid had reached to take it from her when she spoke again, her eyes still shut. "One day I realized that if I didn't wake the next morning, no one would miss me. Except Miles.

"Miles and I were lovers once, in the beginning." Hannah smiled a little at the memory. "He lost interest when his health began to fail. Or maybe I hadn't enough to give, even then. Still, I'm all he has, except for some wretched nephew he doesn't care for, and

I've neglected him terribly since I became so . . . obsessed with Patrick."

She opened her eyes and looked at Kincaid, the late afternoon light shifting her irises from hazel to green, a green almost as clear as Patrick Rennie's. "Obsession . . . a selfish preoccupation," she said dreamily, then continued more forcefully. "What right had I to find Patrick and spy on him, passing judgement on his qualifications as a son? I could have gone to his office and told him the truth straight off, given him a chance to start on equal footing. Instead . . ." A desolate little shrug summarized the outcome.

"It seems to me," Kincaid said gently, "that you've castigated yourself pretty thoroughly for mistakes anyone could have made. We don't any of us have all the answers beforehand. Why is it too late for you and Patrick? Why can't you tell him what you told me? What have you to lose?"

"I . . . He doesn't want—"

"How do you know what Patrick wants or doesn't want? He didn't give me the impression just now of a man determined to sever all connection." Unless, of course, thought Kincaid, Patrick Rennie had seen an advantage in adopting a new role, that of the contrite son lovingly reunited with his mother.

"It's odd." Hannah interrupted his unpleasant speculation. "After everything that's happened today I feel terribly detached. It's like seeing things through the wrong end of a telescope. Clear and distant. I doubt it will last. I do see, though, that I can't go chasing after Patrick expecting him to plug the gaps in my life."

Hannah's voice had grown drowsier. Kincaid

cleared up the tea things and came back to her, finding that he could not let her rest quite yet. The unasked question hung on him like a weight. "Hannah, could it have been Patrick who pushed you down the stairs?"

She did not bridle, as she had before at any suggestion of Patrick's guilt, but answered him with sleepy thoughtfulness. "Of course I've wondered. I'd be an idiot not to, I suppose—but I don't think so." She paused, searching for the right words. "There was such . . . *malice* in that shove. I felt it." Her brow furrowed in concentration. "Today I saw a bit of the real Patrick, not my idealized version of him. There is some anger running under the surface, some bitterness, but also the ability to laugh at himself, to put his feelings in perspective. I just can't see him hating that viciously." She began to shiver again. "Why would anyone hate me that much?"

"What did he—"

A knock at the door interrupted his question, but Hannah put a hand out to stop him as he rose. "I won't tell you what he told me about Cassie and Penny. You'll have to ask him yourself. You do understand?" Kincaid hesitated, then nodded. There was no use bullying her—he'd begun to gauge her stubbornness. And besides, he did understand.

Anne Percy stood patiently at the door, doctor's bag in hand. Kincaid's heart gave an inexplicable leap and he cursed himself for a fool.

Kincaid met Chief Inspector Nash on the stairs. "I'm just on my way to take your Miss Alcock's statement." Nash spoke without preamble, in that sneering tone that made Kincaid bite back a childish retort.

"Dr. Percy's with her now. She doesn't seem too badly hurt."

"Is that so?" said Nash, dripping sarcasm. "Well, well. Now, isn't that surprising?"

"Just what are you insinuating?" Kincaid struggled to control the exasperation in his voice.

"Well now, laddie, has it not occurred to you that a fall is a very convenient thing? All alone, no witnesses, a little tumble down the stairs?"

"I found her myself. She was unconscious!"

"Very convenient, as I said, to be discovered by a sympathetic policeman." Nash clucked and said with great condescension, "And laddie, anyone can fake a faint." Nash fluttered his eyelids and moaned.

Kincaid closed his eyes and took a deep breath. "Have you any idea, Chief Inspector, why Miss Alcock would risk breaking her neck?"

"It seems to me that if you're bumping off people right and left it doesn't hurt to appear to be a victim yourself. It's an old ploy."

"What possible motive could she have for killing Sebastian or Penny?"

"What possible motive could any of them have? You tell me, laddie. You're the one's so chummy with her." Nash smiled at him impishly, and Kincaid felt the exchange slipping into utter farce.

"I'm sorry I can't help you, Inspector. You'll have to ask her yourself."

Kincaid plunged out the front door and shook his head as if the cold air would clear it. Even a small dose of Chief Inspector Nash made him feel like he'd wandered into a pea-soup fog. He had some questions to ask Patrick Rennie and he wasn't inclined to invite Nash along and allow him to make hash of the interview.

He paced around the darkening garden, wishing he had Gemma or Peter Raskin to use as a sounding board. The first floor of Followdale House was broken into sections by fire doors—one divided the area containing his suite and the balcony door from the area containing Hannah's suite and the main staircase. That area in turn was separated from the suites on the other side of the house by another door. As he had come through the door between his suite and the staircase he could have sworn he heard the far door closing.

He hadn't thought anything about it at the time, not until Patrick Rennie had come in the front door, flushed and breathing hard, minutes after he'd found Hannah. Kincaid had no way of knowing how long Hannah had lain there, but it might have been only minutes. Rennie could have run down the back staircase and around the building to the front, anxious to judge the results of his attempt on Hannah's life.

Kincaid returned to the house, hesitating for a moment in the front hall. Where was Peter Raskin? Had anyone tracked down the other guests and taken their statements?

He stood quite still, listening for some sound, some intimation of life or movement in the house. It amazed him that a house this size, with nearly a dozen people in it, could seem so utterly deserted. The noisy cocktail hour chatter of the first evening seemed almost unimaginable now—the guests had certainly lost their taste for one another's company.

He walked through the darkened reception area toward the sitting room, where a dim lamp cast a solitary pool of light. A slight sound from the bar drew Kincaid to the door.

Patrick Rennie sat alone at a table, morosely sliding a glass in its condensate puddle. "Just the man I wanted to see," Kincaid said, and Rennie's head shot up.

"How is she?"

"Dr. Percy's with her. I don't think she's badly hurt." Kincaid retrieved a beer from under the counter and sat down opposite Rennie. "Where is everyone?"

"Holed up in their rooms expecting fallout, I imagine. Chief Inspector Nash sent that constable around to take statements. I don't know if he's rounded everyone up yet. Listen," Rennie changed tack, not to be distracted from what was on his mind, "I behaved abominably toward Hannah today. And now this." Rennie waved his hand vaguely toward the stairs, then met Kincaid's eyes. "Did she tell you about me?"

"Yes."

"And did she tell you what an ass I made of myself this morning?"

"She said you resented her barging into your life," Kincaid answered drily.

Rennie rubbed long fingers across his forehead. "What she must have put herself through . . . and then I stomped all over her with all the sensitivity of an elephant." His eyebrows lifted in the self-mocking little smile Hannah must have seen. "It was the shock, I think. All those years of wondering who she was, what she was like, why she let me go—it all came back to me. Is it too late, do you think, to start again?"

Kincaid didn't relish the role of Miss Lonelyhearts under the best of circumstances, and particularly not when one party might have tried to hasten the other's demise. "I couldn't say." He sipped his beer, then added easily, "A great deal would depend on where were you today just before you came in."

Color flooded into Rennie's face. "God, I've been a bloody fool. You were right about Cassie, you know. It started last year. Marta knew something was going on but I badgered her into coming here anyway. I thought Cassie cared about me, that she was even worth risking my future." He shook his head as if bewildered by his own stupidity. "But nothing went right this visit. This afternoon I decided I had to pin her down, sort things out. I went across to the cottage and started to knock but the door wasn't quite shut. Well, it's the usual old story. Why should I have been so surprised?" He smiled, but his color was still high and his eyes didn't quite meet Kincaid's.

"Compromising?"

"Fairly."

"And who was the lucky chap?"

Rennie looked away. "Graham Frazer."

17

KINCAID PACED THE dimly lit reception area, listening, a little guiltily, for Anne Percy's light tread on the stairs. He'd left Patrick Rennie nursing a drink in the empty bar, and he felt less sure than ever whether the man was genuine or a most sincere and plausible liar.

If Cassie supported Patrick's story, would that give him a sufficient alibi? Hannah had told Kincaid she'd tapped on his door just before she started down the stairs. But it had been a very tentative knock, she'd said, as she'd thought better of it and decided to go on her own. Had that been the sound he'd heard while on the phone to Gemma? Or had he been on the balcony and heard nothing at all?

"Timing. All a matter of timing," he muttered. If Hannah had lain on the stairs only minutes, could Patrick prove he'd come straight from Cassie's into the hall? And for that matter, where did that leave Cassie and Graham? Safely locked in a lovers' alibi? Or colluding in a foolproof murder attempt? Assuming, of course, that Hannah hadn't been lying unconscious for half-an-hour or more—in which case it could have been any one of the three. But why would one of them, or anyone else, for that matter, want to kill Hannah?

And what had the rest of the cast been up to?

Kincaid smacked his fist into his open palm, grimacing in frustration. He might as well be tied up and blindfolded, for all he'd accomplished. He, who had so often complained of paperwork's drudgery, would have given anything for a stack of neatly detailed statements taken by his efficient sergeant. Chief Inspector Nash had gone from being deliberately obstructive to a kind of sly evasiveness, but both tactics produced the same end result—Kincaid had no facts.

Some movement in the shadowy room, a current of air perhaps, made Kincaid turn toward the sitting-room door. The light shifted and he had a brief second's vision of Sebastian Wade as he had first seen him in this room—propped nonchalantly with his shoulder against the doorjamb, hands in pockets, face split by an impish grin.

How the hell, Kincaid thought, did it all fit together?

Quick footsteps on the stairs drew him into the hall. Anne Percy met his questioning look with a smile as she descended the last few steps. "She's doing fine. A bit done in, of course. Wrist probably sprained, and a good-sized bump on the head. I told her that she had good bones." Anne's lips twitched with amusement. "No sign of creeping osteoporosis." She sighed and stretched, then said more seriously, "You will keep an eye on her, won't you, Duncan? I keep thinking . . ." Frowning, she paused for a moment. "Whoever pushed her . . . they might have stayed and finished the job."

"It's possible they heard me coming out of my suite. But then again, it's not that different from what happened to Penny or Sebastian. Opportunity seen—action taken, with little to lose. Bending over Hannah on the stairs would have been a much riskier proposition."

Anne shuddered. "What an awful thought."

"I know. I've told her to keep herself locked in and not to go anywhere without telling me. She says she doesn't want babysitting," he added in exasperation. "She was quite docile and agreeable until she began to recover a little."

"I've left her with Chief Inspector Nash. That's not exactly what I would call a tranquilizing experience."

"No. Best to get it over with so he'll leave her in peace." Kincaid studied Anne appreciatively. Under a bright yellow plastic slicker, she wore fuchsia leggings and a matching rugby-striped top, and looked to Kincaid as unlikely a doctor as he could imagine.

"What's so funny?" asked Anne, as the grin spread across his face.

"I was thinking of the crusty old country practitioner who looked after us when I was growing up."

She glanced down at herself, then met his smile. "Well, times change, don't they? Thank goodness." Her eyes strayed to her watch. "But some things never seem to. I'm late getting supper for my girls. I'm afraid I'll have to run."

He felt suddenly embarrassed, as if he'd been guilty of forgetting her obligations, but said equably enough, "Yes. I'll walk you out."

Her yellow slicker squeaked and rustled as she walked, and once her arm brushed lightly against his.

When they reached her car she opened the door and swung her bag in, then turned to face him. Kincaid stood close enough to notice that she smelled of lavender—a clean, comforting scent—and he searched for something to say that might detain her a moment longer. "Thank you. This has all been pretty beastly for you, I imagine."

Anne smiled. "Death's familiar enough. It's the circumstances that differ. Anyway, the police surgeon's back from holiday tomorrow, so I won't be officially on call anymore."

"I'm sorry," Kincaid said into the silence that stretched between them.

"I'm sorry, too," Anne Percy answered as she got into the car, and as Kincaid watched her drive away he wasn't sure what either of them had meant.

The evening drew in as Gemma drove north along the Banbury Road. Large, comfortable houses flanked the street on either side, their interiors looking warm and welcoming as only lamplit rooms seen in the dusk can. Trees filled the gardens, the fading light leaching the autumn colors from their leaves.

She'd never been in Oxford before—never had a case take her there, and it wasn't the sort of place her family would have chosen to go on holiday. Her mum and dad had gone to the same Cornish village for the same two weeks every year as far back as she could remember—an agreeable, dependable place, and not the least bit adventuresome.

Much to her surprise, Gemma found herself enchanted with the city. Once she'd arranged an evening appointment with Miles Sterrett through his housekeeper, she'd had several hours to kill, and had spent them exploring the city center. From Cornmarket down The High as far as Magdalen College and the river, the tranquil, green quads of the colleges beckoned.

She walked slowly, the collar of her navy cardigan turned up against the wind, and when she reached the bridge over the Cherwell she leaned her elbows on the parapet and watched the boat crews skimming the water as lightly as water-bugs.

A university education had been so far out of her reach that she'd never really envied others the privilege, but now she felt a fleeting longing for an opportunity missed. Kincaid had told her once, over an after-work pint, that he'd been eligible for a police scholarship to university, but hadn't applied. "A little late rebelliousness, I suppose," he'd said, lifting a quizzical eyebrow. "Too much what my parents expected of me. It seems a bit silly now, to have passed it up."

Gemma thought, as she slowed for the turning she had missed in the afternoon, that Oxford would have suited Kincaid very well.

The Julia Sterrett Clinic looked simply what it was, a large private house, set back on a side street near the Banbury Road. The only indication of its true function was a discreet plaque set into the brick near the front door. Gemma rang the bell and waited, and after a moment she heard the heavy shuffle of feet and the click of the bolts being drawn back.

"You're right on time, dear," the housekeeper said as she opened the door.

Gemma found the stout, little housekeeper a great improvement over the dragon of a secretary that had manned the clinic's desk that afternoon. "Hello, Mrs. Milton. Is he ready to see me?"

"I'll take you up straightaway."

Mrs. Milton toiled up the curving staircase, breath puffing, cheeks pink with exertion, while Gemma followed a little guiltily in her wake. Looking back, Gemma could see the reception room to the right of the front door, and she knew from her afternoon visit that the clinic proper occupied the ground and first floors of the house, while Miles Sterrett retained the top floor for his personal use.

Mrs. Milton tapped on a door in the upper corridor, motioned Gemma in and pulled the door closed smartly behind her. Gemma stood alone on the threshold, feeling a bit like Daniel thrown to the lions. From the receptionist's ferocious protectiveness, she had expected an elderly man, perhaps bedridden, perhaps in a chair with a rug over his knees, confined to a hospital-like room.

She found herself in a masculine study with book-lined walls, leather chairs, a glowing oriental rug under her feet and a fire burning brightly in the grate. Miles Sterrett sat at an ornate desk, head bent over some papers. He looked up and smiled, then rose and came across the room to greet her.

"Sergeant James."

"Mr. Sterrett. Thank you for seeing me." Gemma had to look up as she took his outstretched hand, for Miles Sterrett was tall and slender, with a thin face and fine hair that looked more primrose-yellow than gray in the firelight. He wore a pale yellow pullover jersey, and neatly creased dark trousers. Only the dark hollows under his eyes and a slight hesitation in his movements betrayed any illness.

"Come and sit down. Mrs. Milton's left us some coffee." He seated her in one of two chairs near the fire, and himself in the other. On a low table between them stood a tray with cups and a thermos. When he reached for her cup, Gemma saw the faint tremble in his hand.

"Shall I pour?"

Miles sat back, casually clasping the tell-tale hands on his knee. "Thank you." He accepted his cup, and when Gemma had hers, he spoke again. "Now tell me, Sergeant, just what this is about. Mrs. Milton assures me that Hannah is all right?"

His last statement ended on a faint interrogatory note, and Gemma thought that Miles Sterrett's natural good manners concealed a very real worry. "Miss Alcock's fine, sir. But there have been two suspicious deaths at Followdale House in the last week, and we're naturally very concerned for everyone's safety."

"You don't mean Hannah—"

"No, no, not specifically, but the sooner we get our inquiries cleared up, the happier we'll all be." Gemma took a sip of her coffee. Strong and rich, it bore little relation to instant or the marked-down tins in the corner grocer. "Do you know if Miss Alcock had any connection to either Sebastian Wade or Penny MacKenzie?"

He shook his head. "I don't recall her mentioning either of them."

"What about any other previous connection with the

timeshare? Did she give you any indication why she chose this particular place?"

Miles reached for his cup, and Gemma noticed that he held it only long enough to drink, then returned it to the table. "She didn't actually say much to me about it at all. It struck me as rather odd, because Hannah and I have been friends for more years than I like to count." He smiled, erasing the sternness from his thin face. "Hannah came to me almost fifteen years ago—highly recommended, of course—from a university research facility. I'm not a scientist, you know, and the success of our work here," he made an encircling gesture with his hand, "is entirely due to Hannah's brilliance and perseverance. Sergeant—" he stopped and stared at Gemma, his brow creasing. "I think that you are much too lovely to be addressed as 'Sergeant.' Could I call you 'Miss,' or 'Mrs.,' or perhaps the unpleasant and ubiquitous 'Ms.'?"

Gemma, who dealt with catcalls from yobs in the street without turning an eyelash, felt herself coloring at the courtly compliment. It was also rather chauvinistic, she had to admit, but she couldn't find it in herself to feel offended. "Well, 'Ms.' will do, if you like."

"All right, Ms. James. If you feel you need a character reference for Hannah, I know of nothing the least bit questionable in her past or present. I consider her as both friend and family, and would vouch for her behavior under any circumstances. Hannah is certainly not capable of killing anyone." His clasped hands moved convulsively as he spoke, and Gemma saw that the trembling had increased.

"Mr. Sterrett, I don't think the investigating officers

seriously consider that a possibility, but we must make these inquiries. You do understand?" Gemma searched for a change of subject to ease his obvious distress. "Is the clinic named for someone in your family, Mr. Sterrett?"

"My wife. She died from Creutz-Jakob disease almost thirty years ago. At the time, very little was known about it, and as I inherited my money, I thought it might as well be put to good use." He smiled at her again. "Don't look so unhappy, Ms. James. I'm not still grieving over my dead wife. It was a very long time ago. We had no children—which may have been just as well, considering the family genes. Her only sister was emotionally unstable and my nephew is a pipsqueak." Sobering, he added, "But I would not want anything to happen to Hannah. Not only for my sake, but this clinic depends on her, and what we do here is worthwhile."

Miles stared into the fire and finished his coffee, then said, with what seemed to Gemma an effort, "I'm surprised that Hannah hasn't called me. I suppose she thought it would worry me. It wouldn't have occurred to her I might be visited by the police, in however attractive a guise." Both smile and gallantry seemed forced this time, and Gemma thought she had outstayed her welcome.

She drank the last of her coffee, eyeing the thermos a little wistfully, and rose. "I've tired you, I'm afraid. Your receptionist would eat me alive."

Miles chuckled. "It's her way of staying even with Mrs. Milton. They've had a rivalry going for years." He stood, insisting on seeing her out. At the top of the stairs he took her hand again. "You won't mind if I don't come down? Mrs. Milton will unlock the door for you."

"Thank you, sir. I'm sorry to have troubled you." It was a stock phrase, but Gemma found she meant it.

She'd booked a room in a small hotel on the edge of the city, and once she'd checked in and unpacked, she spent the rest of the evening dialing Kincaid's empty suite.

Hannah slept curled on the sofa where Anne Percy had left her, head half buried beneath the cushion, blanket slipping haphazardly to the floor.

In her dream she walked the suburban streets of her childhood, under blossoming cherry trees. Familiar voices she couldn't quite place called from the gardens, and she increased her pace. Her house seemed always round the next corner—she felt sure she could find it if only the soft, insistent tapping would stop.

The sound nibbled at the edges of her dream, finally rousing her to a sluggish wakefulness. Her first instinctive movement brought a groan—her muscles were already stiffening and her head ached. The panes in the French door reflected her image. It was now fully dark and she couldn't tell whether she had been asleep hours or minutes. The knocking continued as she made her slow progress to the door, and she heard his imploring voice before she reached it. "Hannah, it's Patrick. Please, let me talk to you."

A moment's hesitation gripped her and then she flushed with shame. She would not doubt him, would not let fear rule her life. Humiliation had caused her withdrawal on the stairs, but since then she had thought much about prejudging. With unsteady fingers she pulled back the bolt on the door.

Patrick looked her over carefully before he spoke. "How are you feeling?"

"I imagine about as well as can be expected." Absently Hannah touched her taped wrist. "Dr. Percy said I'd feel about a hundred years old by tomorrow, and it's already begun."

He followed her into the sitting room and tucked her up under the blanket solicitously. After pulling up a chair so that he could sit facing her, he said with disarming frankness, "Duncan Kincaid thinks I might have pushed you down the stairs, although he very politely didn't quite say so." Patrick smiled. "Somehow I don't think good manners were his motivation. Hannah"—all traces of the smile vanished—"do you think I pushed you?"

She shook her head wearily. "No. Honestly. I would have told Duncan if I had." She met his eyes for the first time since he had come in. Patrick might have aged ten years in the course of a day. Fine lines that she hadn't noticed before crinkled around his eyes. It was as if he'd been stripped of a layer of veneer, thought Hannah, and he sat before her bare of his usual polish.

He sighed. "That's all right, then. But I'm worried about you, you know. When you don't understand why something's happening it's hard to put a stop to it."

Hannah didn't answer. She felt too exhausted to rehash her ignorance once again. After a moment Patrick continued. "And I was beastly to you this morning. I don't know why. Too many childhood fantasies came crashing down at once, I suppose." At her puzzled expression he tried to explain. "Oh, you know—the usual things. First it was my mother as Camille," he raised his hand to his brow and grinned, "dying in childbirth, blessing me with her last frail breath. Then later I imagined she'd be warm and soft and comforting—she'd find me and welcome me into the fold of another family. An only child's fantasy, that. Never"—he leaned forward and smiled at her again—"did I see her as successful, intelligent, stimulating, and attractive. It was quite a shock, I can tell you."

Hannah jabbed her fingers through her hair, suddenly aware of how she must look. "I'm sorry," she said, not knowing whether she meant she was sorry for springing her identity on him or for not fitting his mother image.

"You're sorry? I should have outgrown that emotional baggage long ago. And I never even asked about my father." Patrick's hands moved on his knees, and Hannah sensed a sudden vulnerability beneath his casual manner.

"I refused to tell my parents who he was, but I suppose you deserve to know something," she said reluctantly. "His name was Matthew Carnegie. A good family." Her mouth twisted. "As my father would have put it. I don't know what became of him, I didn't want to know. I never wanted to see him again." She cast her mind back through the barriers she had erected over the years, trying to remember what had attracted a sixteen-year-old Hannah to Matthew. "He was fair—that's where you get your coloring—and good-looking, in a lanky, unfinished way. He made me laugh." The memory surprised her. "And he was gentle."

Patrick digested this, and nodded. "It must have taken a lot of courage, not to have told your parents about him."

"Courage? No, it was pure stubbornness. That, and the knowledge that I couldn't bear the humiliation of his knowing, of his family knowing."

Patrick leaned forward, his gaze intense. "Hannah, do you think we could start again? Maybe not as either of us imagined it—we've both been pretty unrealistic—but just as . . . friends?"

Hannah closed her eyes, stilling her face against a sudden swell of longing. "I never thought I could replace your mother. Or be one, really. I only wanted some sense of belonging . . . of connection."

Patrick reached out and touched her shoulder a little awkwardly, as if unsure what gesture to make. "I'd better let you get some rest." He rose. "Hannah, you will be careful, won't you? I'd hate to lose you," his voice held a trace of irony, "now I've found you."

Kincaid discovered, as had Patrick Rennie before him, that Cassie's door stood slightly ajar. He tapped lightly. Hearing no answer, he slowly pushed open the door.

The only light in the cottage's sitting room came from a dim bulb in the hall behind it, so that it took him a minute to orient himself. Cassie's voice came from the direction of the armchair next to the fire, sullen and succinct. "Bugger off."

Kincaid fumbled for the switch on the table lamp, and blinked in the sudden bloom of yellow light. Cassie sat huddled in the chair, looking pale and disheveled, wrapped in a quilted dressing gown. Only her bare legs, stretched out before her, retained their elegance.

"You should learn to lock your door," said Kincaid, drawing his eyes, rather unwillingly, from her legs to her face.

"Not much point now, is there?"

Kincaid perched on the arm of the opposite chair, as he had before. "Looks like you've made a proper mess of things, doesn't it?" he said lightly.

Anger sparked in her flat, gold eyes. "Me? Jesus." She turned her face away and he saw the red weal along her cheekbone. "The bastard hit me."

"Who, Graham?"

"Of course, Graham! Patrick acted like offended bloody royalty and stalked out in a huff, but not until he'd made our situation quite clear to Graham. Who gave you the sordid details, anyway?" Cassie stared at him accusingly.

"Patrick."

"Oh, god." Tears filled her eyes and ran down the sides of her nose. She made no move to brush them away. "Everything's finished."

"No more Downing Street?"

"You—" Cassie began, then subsided, too despondent even to swear at him.

"Surely it was bound to happen," Kincaid said more kindly. "You were playing a risky game."

Cassie sat up a bit in her chair and tucked her legs beneath her, then wiped the backs of her hands across her cheeks. "I had no idea Graham would be so hard to put off." She sniffed. "It started as such a casual thing, before I ever met Patrick. But the more I tried to cool things off with Graham, the more persistent he got. Then I began to be afraid to break it off—afraid of what he'd do."

"Did he threaten you?"

Cassie shrugged. "Not in so many words. But he'd make these little comments—what if someone told the management I'd been sleeping with the owners? Would I lose my job? That sort of thing. I couldn't bear that, you see. For a while I was able to juggle them. Then Graham traded weeks—he didn't have to wait until term break because Angela wasn't in school, and he wanted to see me."

"I suppose," interrupted Kincaid, "that he was lucky to own a week during school holidays?"

"Lucky?" Cassie looked baffled. "He could have had pretty much anything he wanted. And he could have traded for just about any time, as well. There are always people willing to switch around. Why," she raised her eyes beseechingly, "did he have to choose this week?" The question seemed to be rhetorical.

It occurred to him that he liked her better this way, without that almost American sheen of perfect grooming, her oak-leaf hair rumpled, her slightly supercilious manner in abeyance. He supposed she lost that hard edge in bed as well, and it was that contrast that made her so appealing to Patrick and to Graham Frazer. Shoving his speculations aside, he asked, "So what happened today?"

Cassie swallowed and pushed her hair behind her ear. "Graham was furious. I've never seen him quite like that. He seemed to feel I'd made a fool of him—used him, he said." She raised her eyes to Kincaid's. "I wasn't exactly a willing participant today. But Patrick couldn't have known that."

"No. And then, after Patrick left?"

Cassie touched a finger to her cheek. "I was lucky to get off so easily. But it's finally over, I think."

"What time did all this happen this afternoon?"

"How the hell should I know?" Cassie flared at him. "My whole life is crumbling around me and you expect me to notice what time it is?"

"It could be very important, you know, just what the three of you were doing when someone decided to push Hannah down the stairs. Didn't anyone ask you?"

"That constable came around—the one who looks like a prize cow." Animosity sharpened her voice, and Kincaid remembered what a difficult time P.C. Trumble had with her the morning of Sebastian's death. "I told him I didn't remember."

Kincaid tried another tack. "Think back. What were you doing before Graham came?"

Cassie chewed her thumbnail meditatively. "I'd been working. The house was quiet as a tomb and I started to feel a little . . . uneasy. Then Angela came snooping around—"

"What did she want?" asked Kincaid, his curiosity piqued. He couldn't imagine Angela voluntarily visiting Cassie.

"I didn't say she spoke," snapped Cassie. "She just wandered around, fingering my things. That girl gives me the creeps, anyway, and she'd done herself up in full vampire regalia today. When I asked her what she wanted, she said 'nothing' and went out. Well, I'd had enough, after that. I came across to make myself a cup of coffee." She paused, concentrating. "It must have been after three—I'd been expecting a call by three and when it didn't come I switched on the answering machine."

"And Graham?" Kincaid waited, his attention sharpening. Gemma had called him about a quarter past three. He'd finished his conversation, gone downstairs, discovered Hannah, and had only thought to look at his watch after Patrick had come storming in the front door. It had been twenty minutes to four.

"Don't know. I'd made my coffee, gone to the loo."

"And how long had Graham been there when Patrick came?"

"Long enough," said Cassie with some asperity, "to start a slanging match and tear half my clothes off."

"And you wouldn't happen to know," Kincaid asked hopefully, "exactly what time Patrick left here?"

Cassie pulled herself up in the chair and glared at him. "Don't be bloody stupid."

As Kincaid left Cassie's cottage he saw Eddie Lyle scurrying across the car park toward the front door. "I'm late, I'm late, for a very important date," Kincaid said under his breath, and grinned. "Lyle!"

Eddie Lyle turned and waited until Kincaid caught up, his spectacles glinting in the light from the porch. "Did someone take a statement from you this afternoon?" Kincaid asked conversationally as they came abreast.

"Yes, yes, of course," answered Lyle, in his fussily aggrieved way. "I'd just come back from my walk when I heard all the commotion about poor Miss Alcock falling down the stairs." He shook his head, and Kincaid couldn't be sure whether he was deploring Hannah's accident or the disturbance of his afternoon.

"You'd been walking?" Kincaid rubbed the toe of his trainer across the gravel.

"Oh, yes. Lovely day up on the bank." Lyle waggled his hand in the direction of Sutton Bank. "Janet was having her rest after lunch, and I wanted to give her a bit of peace and quiet. She hasn't been feeling well, you know," he added confidentially. "Since Mother died, she's had these little tired spells. And now, with all these terrible things happening, she's quite exhausted."

"I'm sure." Kincaid nodded sympathetically, sure only that living with Edward would be exhausting enough for anyone.

"But I told Janet that we would stay until our time ran out on Saturday." Lyle jabbed his finger in the air for emphasis. "Not that Chief Inspector Nash would mind us going, of course, but I do like to get my money's worth. And speaking of going," he squinted at his watch, "the wife'll have my supper ready and I'd not like it to get cold." He gave a dismissive wave of his hand toward Kincaid and trotted up the steps.

Kincaid's stomach growled as if the word "supper" had activated internal alarm bells. He couldn't remember when he'd had a proper meal, and since he hadn't a generic wife to prepare it, he imagined he'd have to fend for himself. He grinned in the darkness. Eddie Lyle didn't know his own luck.

18

SHE COULDN'T BE gone.

Kincaid tried the door to Hannah's suite, the knob slipping in his suddenly sweaty palm. Locked. He stepped back and looked out the landing window at the car park. The phone-box red paintwork on his Midget gleamed cheerily back at him, but the space beside it where Hannah's green Citroën had stood was empty.

His stomach knotted as he told himself not to be an ass. No need to panic—she'd probably just gone down to the shops for some coffee or a newspaper. But no reasonable, rational explanation eased the dread that squeezed his chest.

He'd spent half the morning pacing the confines of his sitting room, waiting for word from Gemma, assuming Hannah was tucked up safely and obediently in her suite.

He should have known better. Hannah Alcock had lived by her own rules too long to do anyone else's bidding. Kincaid stared down at the car park, wondering what had sent her out this morning.

The door from the opposite wing swished open. Kincaid turned to see Angela Frazer slide through it and stop, watching him. Cassie had been right. All vestiges of a normal fifteen-year-old had disappeared, camouflaged by punk-vampire. Her face and lips were artfully chalky, her eyes dark-ringed as Cleopatra's, her hair mace-spiked.

As a defense mechanism he supposed it worked fairly well—she certainly *looked* unapproachable. What, Kincaid wondered, had driven Angela Frazer back undercover? He pushed his worry about Hannah aside for a moment and concentrated on Angela. The girl's stare made him feel like a fly under a microscope. Hitching his hip on the window sill and folding his arms, he fumbled for the thread of their earlier rapport. "Where've you been hiding yourself?"

No answer. That didn't surprise him. His opening sortie had sounded patronizingly cheerful even to his own ears. He tried a more combative tack. "What'd I do to deserve the silent treatment?"

The dark eyes disengaged as Angela ducked her head and moved around the wall toward him, running her finger along the molding top as if checking for dust. She halted just out of reach and her eyes flicked up at him again. "Nothing."

"Nothing? Come on, Angela, what's eating you? Nobody sees you for a couple of days and then you reappear looking like the Bride of Frankenstein. What's happened?"

Angela's eyes strayed toward her studded, black denim jacket and leather mini. Beneath the black skirt's hem her knees looked absurdly pale and chubby—a child's knees, even to the dimples.

Hug her or turn her over his knee and spank her—either option probably effective, neither available to him. Kincaid waited.

"You called me Angie before."

"So I did. I thought we were friends."

Her head jerked up at that and she said fiercely, "You didn't do anything. You promised you would. Now no one cares what happened to Sebastian. I don't mean," she added, suddenly tangled in her middle-class upbringing, "that I don't care about poor Miss MacKenzie and Miss Alcock. But Sebastian was . . ."

"I know. It's right that you should feel that way." Sebastian, whatever his faults, had deserved Angela's loyalty. Kincaid reached out, taking advantage of the thaw, and gripped her shoulder. "I've been trying, Angie. I'm still trying."

Angela's face crumpled and suddenly she was sobbing against his chest, her arms wrapped tightly around his waist. Kincaid made soothing noises and stroked the back of her head, where her untreated hair felt as soft as duck's down. He wished he could soak up her grief like a sponge.

Finally the sobs subsided to hiccups and she pushed herself away from him, wiping her hands across her eyes. Not possessing the snowy, white handkerchief the situation demanded, Kincaid dug a crumpled tissue from his pocket. "Here. I think it's relatively clean."

Angela turned her back to him and blew her nose, then said quietly, vindictively, "She made him do it."

Kincaid felt like he'd missed a cue. "Who made whom do what?"

"Don't be so stuffy." Angela sniffed. "You know."

"No, actually, I don't. Tell me." His pulse quickened but his voice reflected only mild, friendly interest—the wrong word or gesture could send Angela scuttling back to safe ground.

She hesitated now, pulling the zipper on her jacket back and forth. "That night Sebastian was . . . he said he didn't go out, but he did. I heard him."

"Your father?"

She nodded. "And the morning Miss MacKenzie died, I got up and he wasn't there. He said he was there all the time."

Kincaid pushed a little. "Angie, what do you think your father's done?"

"I don't know." Her voice rose in a wail. "But if he's done anything, she put him up to it."

"Cassie?" Kincaid asked, sure of the answer. Angela nodded.

"Why do you think so?"

"They're always meeting and whispering. They think I don't know." Kincaid heard the satisfaction beneath the censure. "They stop and move apart whenever I come in. With that look. You know."

"But you haven't heard anything specific?" Angela shook her head and moved back a few steps, the instinct to defend her father perhaps getting the better of her desire to accuse him. "It could be perfectly innocent, don't you think? Maybe you're blowing things out of proportion." Kincaid spoke lightly, a little derisively, goading her.

"I heard him tell her he was going to fix my mum," Angela snapped back at him, stung. "That she'd be sorry, and so would anybody else who tried to bugger things for him. What if . . ." Angela stopped, her eyes frightened. She had gone farther than she intended. "I have to go."

"Angie—"

"See you." She slipped out the far door and a second later he heard her soft tread on the main stairs.

Kincaid stared after her as the door sighed shut. Graham might have indulged in a little veiled bullying. On the other hand, what if . . . If only they could get a definite grip on the man, instead of a collection of rumors and second-hand accusations. Graham Frazer was as slippery as an ice cube and just as cold.

Kincaid met Maureen Hunsinger at the top of the stairs, her round face shining like a scrubbed apple, her hair frizzing damply as if she'd come straight from the bath. "I'd just come to find you," she said, beaming at him, then sobered. "I wanted to tell you goodbye."

"You're leaving, then?" Kincaid asked.

Maureen nodded. "Chief Inspector Nash gave us leave to go." She sounded almost apologetic. "It's been too difficult for the children. No point in prolonging it. Besides," she looked away, and Kincaid thought he detected embarrassment, "after what happened to Hannah yesterday, it could be . . . well, it could happen to anyone, couldn't it? We dare not let the children out of our sight. It's just too worrying." Maureen sighed and brushed a stray hair away from her face. Kincaid found he hated to see even a dent in her robust cheerfulness.

"I'm sure you're quite right," he consoled her. "I'd do the same."

"Would you? Maybe we'll sell our week here, or

trade it for somewhere else. I don't think I could ever feel the same about this place. Have you . . ."

"No. Nothing definite." Kincaid answered the question she hadn't formed and asked the one worrying him. "Have you seen Hannah this morning, Maureen?"

"Not to speak to."

"Wh—"

"We were taking the first loads to the car. Oh, it must have been at least an hour ago. You know how it is when you travel with a family—you can't imagine how you ever got all those things in the car to begin—"

"Maureen." Kincaid tried to nudge her back on track.

"Anyway, I was just coming out of the house as she pulled away. She waved at me and I tried to wave back, only I had my arms full of Legos." She smiled. "Emma helped me pick them up."

"Emma—"

"Was coming in as I was going out. Maybe she spoke to Hannah."

"Thanks, love. I'll see if I can find her." Kincaid grinned at her fondly. "Good luck to you, Maureen."

He had taken a step toward the stairs when Maureen stopped him with a hand on his shoulder. "Take care," she said quietly, then stretched up on her toes and kissed him, her lips exerting a warm pressure against his jaw, her heavy breasts grazing his chest.

He felt oddly comforted.

Emma found him before he found her. Everyone, thought Kincaid, seemed to be looking for him this morning except the one he most wanted to find.

They met in the entry hall, Emma nodding at him briskly, as if he had appeared on command. The nod, however, seemed a last remnant of her gruff strength. She looked exhausted, and somehow—Kincaid searched for the right adjective—unstarched. Her spine slumped in a way he didn't remember, and even her iron-gray hair clung limply to her head.

"Let's go out, shall we?" Her voice, he noted gratefully, had not lost its resonance. Emma led him out onto the porch and lifted her face for a moment to the sun. "Yorkshire's decided to give us one more day of glorious autumnal weather before we go. They're forecasting rain for tomorrow.

"Did you know," she turned to him, "that Sebastian's funeral is tomorrow? And I'm having Penny's body sent home, now that they've released it." Her shoulders sagged. "I'll be going home myself after the service tomorrow, to make what arrangements I can for Penny."

Kincaid thought that more than grief weighed on Emma—added to it was her need to do what she felt necessary and proper for Penny, to say a final goodbye. "I didn't know about Sebastian's service. I'll be there." And he would make sure that Angela Frazer came with him.

"Emma, Maureen said you might have spoken to Hannah this morning, as she was leaving."

"I did that."

"What did she say? I mean," he added impatiently, "did she say where she was going, or why?"

"I should think why would be rather obvious," Emma said tartly. "If someone had shoved me down the stairs, I'd get farther away than that."

"Than where?"

"She said she was going to see the falls, while the weather lasted. She was on holiday, after all, and the rest of you be damned. That's what she said, more or less," Emma finished with some satisfaction.

"What falls?" Kincaid kept his voice level.

"Aysgarth, I'd imagine. Up in Wensleydale. Only falls to speak of around here." Emma reached for the door, then turned back to him, adding, "She moved pretty well this morning, I'd say, considering the tumble she took. Didn't look a day over seventy." She gave him a ghost of her ferocious grin and went into the house.

Kincaid had started toward his car for a map when Janet Lyle stumped around the corner of the house, head down, hands shoved in the pockets of her lightweight anorak. She was scowling, the first expression of bad temper Kincaid had seen in her. Her face cleared when she saw him and she quickened her step, changing course to intercept him. "Say, you wouldn't be going into Thirsk, by any chance, would you?"

"Hadn't planned on it. Need a lift?"

"Oh, Eddie hared off in the car this morning." Exasperation animated her gestures, and for the first time Kincaid could imagine her nursing with the necessary take-charge, no-nonsense manner. "Something about sending a fax to the office. The thing is, I'd ordered some boots for Chloe—there's a marvelous bootmaker here. They were to be ready this morning, and the shop closes half-day on Friday. It's very annoying."

She did look put out, but without her usual mousy manner she looked quite chipper as well. "Your husband said you weren't feeling well."

"Oh, that." Janet shrugged it off. "It's just his way. When his mother died he made up his mind I was languishing and needed a regular holiday. Transference, isn't that what it's called?" She smiled at him, showing even white teeth against her olive skin. "If I'd been the one wanting a holiday, I'd have gone to Majorca."

Gemma nosed her car carefully through the gates of Followdale House and let it idle while she looked about her. She knew she had the right place because the first thing to meet her eye was Kincaid's Midget, angled jauntily on the gravel forecourt.

The next was the Super himself, standing beside it with a map spread on the bonnet. Cords and sea-green pullover, a tweedy jacket with elbow patches, toffee-colored hair artfully ruffled by the breeze—he made, Gemma thought, a pretty picture indeed. She pulled up beside him and climbed out of the car, slinging her bag over her shoulder. "My, we're looking the country gent today, aren't we? Planning your next hunt, or just posing for *Country Life*?"

He swung around. "Gemma!" The flash of pleasure on his face faded so quickly she thought she'd imagined it. "Where the hell have you been?"

"And greetings to you, too, ta very much. I've just busted my bum to get here and that's all you can say?" Gemma answered him good-naturedly but a little prickle of alarm ran up her spine. Although Kincaid didn't suffer fools gladly, it was unlike him to jump down her throat.

"Sorry, Gemma." The familiar smile returned, though with less than its usual wattage.

Gemma touched a fingertip to his chest. "Been changing a tire?"

Kincaid looked down at the dark, irregular smudges across the breast of his sweater. "No. It's mascara, I imagine." He shaded his eyes against the sun and searched her face. "Now, tell me where you've been."

She leaned back against the Escort, remembering too late that it needed a wash, and dug in her bag for her notebook. The pages fluttered as she flipped through it—they both knew she didn't need it, but the routine prop allowed them to make a smooth transition to business. "I finally managed to see Miles Sterrett. That dragon of a secretary at his clinic guards him like the Crown Jewels, so I tried his housekeeper and easy as kiss your hand, I'm in. 'A brief appointment after dinner,' she says, 'so as not to tire him.' " Gemma paused, closing the notebook over her fingers. "I did try to phone you last night. You didn't answer."

"Point accepted. Go on."

"He's had a slight stroke, but he's still sharper than a lot I could name who're supposed to be in full possession." Gemma paused, considering. "Younger than I expected, too—sixty, maybe—and still very attractive, in a gaunt and sober sort of way." Something in the angle of Kincaid's brows hurried her on. "He didn't know anything about what's happened here, and he was quite concerned about Hannah. I had the impression he thought this whole timeshare scheme a bit out of character for her, and it made him uneasy. Seems she runs that clinic practically single-handed and he hasn't got a bit of use for the rest of the staff. Without Hannah, he says, the relatives and the Inland Revenue would have to fight over the place, or maybe he'd just give it to the National Trust." Gemma smiled. "He's kept his sense of humor, considering his circumstances."

"Well, I've lost mine," Kincaid said. "Something *has* happened to Hannah—someone pushed her down the stairs yesterday."

"Is she—"

"She's all right. Or at least she was—she's disappeared this morning."

Gemma glanced at the map still spread on the bonnet. No wonder he'd been so uncommunicative. "You're going to look for her," she said, making it a statement. "Any idea where?"

"Hmm?" His gaze seemed fixed on a large garden urn. "A possibility," he answered vaguely. "Place called Aysgarth Falls."

"I'm coming with you. Don't argue," she added, although he gave no sign of having heard her. "Let me get my things from the car. You can fill me in on the way."

Gemma's case file had slid under the passenger seat and she was stretched half across the driver's seat digging it out when Kincaid said, "Oh, dear god."

The flat, utterly expressionless quality of his voice pulled her out of the car so fast that she banged her head on the roof and didn't feel it.

His mobile face was as blank and still as marble. Gemma's stomach contracted. "What is it?"

He focused on her with an effort and she saw his chest move as he drew a breath. "Hannah." His voice gained force. "Sebastian had nothing to do with it. He just got in the way, like Penny."

"Wh—"

"It wasn't what Hannah knew, or heard, about Sebastian's murder." Kincaid's hands came up to grip Gemma's shoulders. "Hannah was the target all along."

19

IT CAME TO Hannah, as she stood shivering in the cold seeping from the great stone slabs beneath her feet, that she had deceived herself. The feverish energy that had gripped her on waking had drained away and left her as light and hollow as an empty husk, and what seemed sensible enough then failed the test of logic now.

Bravado, that's what had sent her slamming out of the house this morning. She wouldn't let fear dictate her life, wouldn't be coddled and cosseted like some feeble old woman.

It had sounded convincing enough. But she might as well face it—she'd been running away as if all the hounds of hell were on her tail, away from the house and its faceless, hovering malice.

She pushed the thought away and looked downriver at the gentle valley of the Ure spread beneath her. A cloud blotted out the sun and Hannah hugged her cardigan closer. She might be alone in the world for all the signs of human habitation visible—not even sheep or drystone walls, only the falling slope of trees and a blue horizon, and on the opposite bank a shining carpet of russet leaves.

The sound of the water gurgling and murmuring across its stone bed should have been soothing, but it only increased her sense of isolation. Up toward the Middle Falls a family jumped about between the half-submerged stones, but she could only see their mouths moving, as if they were laughing and shouting in a silent film.

Hannah sighed, absently cradling her sore wrist against her chest. There was no comfort here. She might as well go back and face the music. Duncan would be furious, and Patrick—if Patrick saw her as a burden to be looked after, there was no help for it.

Hannah turned to the slope behind her, her tenuous resolve flagging at the thought of the steep climb back to the path. A figure appeared at the trail's head and slipped and slid down the incline toward her, tweed-jacketed, a Tyrolean hat set at a jaunty angle, walking stick swinging, round spectacles reflecting the light. With a start she recognized Eddie Lyle.

How odd, thought Hannah. He didn't strike her as the outdoors type. And how irritating—he was an irritating little man at the best of times, and just now she hadn't the energy to cope with him. She couldn't escape—he'd seen her and picked up his pace, waving cheerfully at her.

"How jolly to see a familiar face," Lyle said as he came abreast of her. "Thought I recognized your car in the car park." Hannah could think of no polite rejoinder, so she smiled at him rather weakly. He expanded his narrow chest with a deep breath and exhaled noisily. "Lovely, isn't it? Have you seen the Upper Falls as well? I must say I find these the most pleasant, whatever anyone else might say."

This last remark was uttered with that air of righteous superiority that she found so annoying, but she merely said, "Yes, quite," not willing to prolong the encounter by disagreeing. Hannah wondered how the man's wife tolerated him. She'd seemed pleasant enough, the few times they'd spoken. Maybe she escaped him whenever possible, thought Hannah, with a faint inward smile.

Lyle rattled on, pointing his stick about as he described the geographical features of the valley. Hannah made monosyllabic replies and glanced at him curiously. His manner seemed oddly agitated. He kept turning and scanning the banks behind them as he talked, as if watching for someone.

Hannah followed his gaze upstream and saw that the stone-jumping family were straggling toward the wooden steps that led from the Middle Falls up to the path. The last child vanished behind a screen of trees, its head hanging dejectedly.

"Look. Just here, in these stones." Lyle bent forward and aimed his stick at the river's edge. "Fossilized bracken, if I'm not mistaken."

Rather unwillingly, Hannah crossed to him and peered down. The fern shape in the white sheet of rock might have been a photograph, its clear outline as strong and delicate as ancient bones.

"Get Peter Raskin on the phone. Tell him—"

"Let me come with you," Gemma interrupted. "I'll phone from the car."

As Kincaid hesitated, Patrick Rennie came out the front door and walked toward them, his expression concerned. "Hullo!" he called to them. "Have you seen Hannah?"

Kincaid met Gemma's eyes. "There's no time. Find Peter Raskin, then bring Rennie with you. He'll insist on it, and I might need him if Peter doesn't make it." He grabbed the map from the bonnet and slid into the Midget, blessing the quick rumble of the engine.

"But what do I tell—" Gemma's fingers grasped the window's edge.

"Anything you like. Just come." Kincaid slipped the car into gear and pulled away, leaving Gemma to cope with Rennie's open-mouthed bewilderment. As Kincaid glanced back Gemma took Rennie's hand, saying, "He's going to look for Hannah. Come on . . ." Her voice faded as he turned into the road. Trust Gemma to have things well in hand.

The way Kincaid downshifted into the curves he might have been going for the cup at Monaco. The map lay open on the passenger seat, a snaky route marked quickly in ink so he wouldn't have to keep hunting for it. He left the main road at Thirsk, trusting to luck that the more direct B roads wouldn't slow him down. Looking down, Kincaid saw his knuckles bleached white and loosened his grip on the wheel. He drove on with methodical concentration, checking the map, scanning the road, but all the while the thoughts ran unbidden through his mind.

He should have seen it. All the bits and pieces had slotted into place as neatly as a shuffled deck and he'd held them in his hand. Could little things—contradictions, coincidences—add up to such a fatal sum? Eddie Lyle had apparently told his wife that he'd been unable to buy a week outside term-time. Yet when Kincaid, thinking about the Frazers, had suggested such a difficulty to Cassie, she'd been astonished. And Lyle had intimated more than once that the holiday had been Janet's idea, when according to both Janet and her neighbor, it had been entirely his. Gemma had described Lyle as overextended . . . with aspirations beyond his means . . . Kincaid's mind went back to the conversation he'd overheard that day in The Blue Plate—Janet worrying over Eddie's plans to send their daughter to a university she was sure they'd never be able to afford . . . Eddie's aunt dying young of a rare disease, as had Miles Sterrett's wife . . . Miles' despised nephew, and Hannah barring the way to Miles' estate.

Kincaid shook his head. Perhaps he was making it up out of whole cloth, his fear for Hannah distorting his logic. But then he thought of Eddie Lyle tearing off, shortly after Hannah's departure, on an unnecessary and unexplained errand, and his hands tightened again on the wheel.

The light shifted across the tops of the moors as Kincaid entered Wensleydale. He pushed his speed up on the straight stretches until the pastures ran into a green blur.

The ancient town of Middleham registered only as bright flags on the castle battlements and the steaming hindquarters of racehorses disappearing around a corner. Wensley and sleepy West Witton slowed him as old men and pram-pushing mothers turned to stare—then one last stretch of clear road to Aysgarth.

Just when he'd begun to breathe a little easier, a flock of sheep ambled across the road in front of him. He came to a dead stop and swore. There was no hurrying sheep. They milled about, a woolly, white, pulsating mass, marked with great splashes of red or blue dye. Kincaid leaned on his horn and nudged the stragglers with his bumper. The shepherd shook his crook at him, and the last sheep cleared the road with a scatter of stones.

The road made one last sharp turn and swooped down to cross the River Ure, and there on the left lay the car park for Aysgarth Falls. Kincaid left the Midget skewed across the first empty space and stood up to get his bearings. Hannah's green Citroën sat sedately in a corner by itself, empty.

Before him lay the path to the Upper Falls; behind him, across the road and down the valley, the path led to the Middle and Lower Falls.

Kincaid hesitated a moment, then sprinted down the Upper path, bumping sightseers and backpackers as he ran. The way grew dark with overhanging trees, mossy underfoot and filled with the sound of running water. Foreboding clutched him, but when he came into the open all he found were family picnics and booted hikers posing on the great stones. Of Hannah there was no sign.

The path across the road was as calm as a country lane. Open meadow lay on one side, and on the other the dense growth of the river bank. A family straggled into the path from a flight of wooden steps. The children looked damp and querulous, the parents harried.

"I want an ice cream now, Mummy. You promised!" The small boy's voice rose ominously.

"Hush, Trevor. I told you—"

Kincaid almost plowed into them. Between gasps for breath he said, "Anybody else down there?"

"Not with us." The man pointed. "Some folks a little further downstream, though."

"Two people?"

The man pursed his lips. "Think so. Wouldn't swear to it."

Kincaid left them staring after him, already forgotten.

He almost missed the signpost, and the body's-width opening in the tangled greenery of the bank. LOWER FALLS. EXIT ONLY. Ignoring the sign's discreet warning, he plunged down the track.

His feet slipped in the sand and loose stones, propelling him downward at breakneck speed. With a shower of gravel and a last grasp at a bramble, he slid out of the trees and onto the level surface of the bank.

Ten meters from him, Hannah Alcock bent over the river's edge. Behind her, Eddie Lyle stooped and Kincaid caught the white flash of a stone in his hand.

Kincaid shouted, afterwards he was never sure what. Memory gave it to him as a wordless, echoing yell, a soundtrack to the slow-motion scene playing before him.

Hannah straightened and turned, breaking into a smile as she recognized him. Lyle froze. An instant later his arm shot around Hannah's neck and he thrust his other hand into his coat pocket. Kincaid saw a dull gleam as Lyle pulled his hand out and lifted it to Hannah's temple.

A gun. The bastard had a gun. Hannah's brief struggle died as the pistol's blunt mouth pressed against her scalp.

Kincaid raised his hands and took a few careful steps forward.

"Don't come any nearer." Lyle's voice rose shrilly. His grip tightened on Hannah's neck and Kincaid saw her eyes roll.

"Can you hear me, Eddie?" Kincaid didn't shout, afraid that would make the situation even more volatile. "Listen to me, Eddie. It's no use. Let her go."

"No use?" Lyle laughed. "What's to stop me killing you both and no one the wiser?" The fussy mannerisms had been replaced by a kind a feverish excitement. He was enjoying it, Kincaid thought. Sebastian and Penny's murders may have been expedient, but Lyle had come to like killing. The knowledge froze Kincaid's bones.

Hannah must have made some sound, because Lyle forced her head back further. "I can do what I like, Superintendent." The words were contemptuous.

"Killing us won't stop it, Eddie. You left traces. The lab found latent prints on the handkerchief you hid, as well as Penny's blood."

A flicker of doubt crossed Lyle's face. Kincaid pressed his advantage. "You must have planned this for a long time, Eddie. You and your mother were Miles Sterrett's only relatives. How convenient of your mother to die just about the time you broke into Hannah's flat. Narrowing the field, were you, Eddie?"

"Copper's tricks, Kincaid. Going to keep me talking until the reinforcements arrive? Did you think I'd fall for that?" Beneath Lyle's light, almost bantering words, Kincaid heard the hostility that fueled him. "You've left out the flattery, Superintendent."

Kincaid swallowed to work some saliva into his dry mouth. "I was coming to that." Reinforcements were the last thing he wanted on Eddie Lyle's mind—he wanted him to think he had all the time in the world. But where the hell was Gemma?

And what argument could he use to sway this man who had nothing left to lose? Lyle would never see Miles Sterrett's money now, and he'd face life imprisonment whether he killed Hannah and Kincaid or not. "Satisfy my curiosity, Eddie. I know Penny must have seen you the night you killed Sebastian. Did she agree to meet you on the tennis court?" Kincaid's tone suggested they might be chatting over a pint. He weighed the possibility of reaching Lyle before he could fire the gun, then decided it was physically impossible. He'd have to rely on his tongue.

"A passing suggestion on my part." The smile came again. "It was as good a place as any."

"And Sebastian? What did Sebastian find out?"

"The bloody snoop." Lyle sounded peevish. "He saw me coming out of *her* room." His arm tightened on Hannah's neck, leaving no doubt whom he meant. "I'd been . . . checking on things. I couldn't have any connection made afterwards, could I?"

"No. No, I'm sure you couldn't," Kincaid answered as if it were the most reasonable question in the world. He thought he heard a faint scuffling from the path above, and he spoke quickly to stop Lyle hearing it as well. "Listen, Eddie—"

"I'm getting tired of this, Superintendent. Step over there." Lyle motioned with his head toward the riverbank. The sun caught the lenses of his glasses, giving him for an instant two round, opaque eyes, gleaming and metallic.

Kincaid heard a slither from behind him, then a thud. Patrick's voice came, rising on a note of panic. "Han—" It stopped abruptly, muffled, no doubt, by Gemma's hand. The sound of their rough breathing came clearly to Kincaid over the murmur of the river and the hammering of his own heart.

Lyle's head whipped back toward them and Kincaid saw the tension run through his body. "Get back. All of you." His grip on Hannah tightened.

"Give it up, Eddie. More police are on their way. Don't make it any worse for yourself."

"Worse?" Lyle's laughter edged toward hysteria. "Why shouldn't I have the satisfaction of taking you all with me? Especially her." He twisted the gun against Hannah's temple. "You make me sick, all of you."

"What about your wife?" Kincaid threw it out in last-ditch desperation. "And your daughter—what's it going to be like for her when you're plastered all over the papers? Oh, they'll have a field day with you, Eddie, you'd better believe it. And your Chloe'll never be free of it."

For the first time Lyle seemed to waver, his head twisting blindly. Suddenly Hannah crumpled at Lyle's feet.

Kincaid launched himself toward them. The still sunlight seemed to coalesce around him until he hung suspended in it, powerless.

Knocking his gold-rimmed glasses askew, Eddie Lyle pressed the muzzle of the gun to his temple and fired.

20

THE HUMPED UMBRELLAS, black and gray, gleamed like the wet backs of whales. The Thirsk church still listed like a sinking ship, and the rain fell in a fine, soaking drizzle—appropriate, Kincaid felt, to the occasion.

The ceremony marking Sebastian Wade's passing had been brief, as the vicar was forced to confine his personal remarks to Sebastian's school days. The crowd had been as sparse as the vicar's eulogy: Sebastian's mum, supported by two women introduced to Kincaid as cousins, a smattering of faces who might have been old school chums, and the small group from Followdale House. Sebastian's intense and often malicious interest in the personal affairs of others had apparently not earned him many friends.

Cassie, still sullen, declined to attend. "I'm sorry he's dead," she'd answered Kincaid, "but I despised him and I won't be such a hypocrite as to go and pretend I didn't." Case closed. Kincaid supposed one had to admire her honesty, if not her lack of compassion.

Emma came alone and left as soon as the service closed. Her farewells in the vestibule were even more brusque than usual, as if the foreshadowing of Penny's funeral had stretched her endurance to its limits.

Kincaid took her broad hand in his own for a moment. "I am sorry about Penny. If only I'd—"

"Don't take too much guilt on yourself, young man." Emma's clear gray eyes met his directly. "She should have told you what she saw that night. She had opportunity enough." Emma looked away and continued a little absently, "My sister wasn't a stupid woman, for all her fluttering. I sometimes wonder if she . . . well, never mind that. What's done is done." She gave Kincaid's hand a quick pump and thrust up her umbrella to meet the rain.

In silent accord, the four remaining moved out into the open. Patrick Rennie, who had left his wife behind, stood holding Hannah's arm possessively. The still-shocked gauntness of their faces emphasized their likeness, plane by plane. Patrick, Kincaid thought, was making up for yesterday's failures.

Yesterday it had been Kincaid who held Hannah and wiped the splattered blood from her face. "It's all right. You're going to be all right." The words he'd repeated came back to him, though he'd hardly been conscious of them at the time.

He remembered Gemma crouching next to him, rubbing Hannah's icy hands, the freckles splashed like stars against her white skin.

Patrick had stepped away and been violently sick.

Gemma had pleaded paperwork this morning and

stayed behind at Followdale House, but Kincaid thought that had merely been her way of letting him lay his own ghosts.

Kincaid did not, however, attend the funeral alone. He hadn't forgotten the promise he'd made himself regarding Angela Frazer. She rode with him in the Midget, silent, even her hair subdued without its violet spikes. It was only when he'd found a parking space near the church that she spoke, staring intently at the rivulets trickling down the windscreen. "It's not fair."

"No," he answered, and went round to help her from the car.

She stood next to him now, watching Graham's black Ford draw up to the curb. "I'll have to be going." Angela looked up at him gravely. "Thanks. I'm sorry about what I said . . . you know." Then, standing on tiptoe, she brushed her lips against his and ran down the walk.

"Do you think she'll be all right?" Hannah asked as they watched the car swallow her and draw away.

Kincaid grinned and brushed a finger against his lips. "I see some indications of resiliency. I'd say it's possible. If she can survive her parents another year or so. If she can leave them and their quarrels behind and make her own life. The question is," Kincaid turned to Hannah, "will you be all right?"

Hannah shuddered. "It still doesn't make sense. Sebastian and Penny needn't have died. They had no connection with me."

"That's what muddled things from the beginning. If we had started out looking for someone who might want you out of the way, we would have found him sooner. He wasn't quite as clever as he thought."

"Clever enough," said Patrick, "to have almost succeeded."

"He'd been planning for a long time, I think. The idea that Hannah stood between him and his uncle's money must have become an obsession with him."

"But Miles never intended to leave anything to me," Hannah protested, still bewildered.

"Not outright. But in Eddie's mind it made no difference whether the money went to you directly or to endow the clinic." Kincaid paused, marshalling his thoughts. "From what Janet said last night, it seems Eddie had little personal contact with his uncle—Janet didn't even remember his name, offhand—but his mother still corresponded with him occasionally. Some remark she passed on to Eddie must have given him the idea that you were essential to the clinic's continuation."

Hannah nodded. "That's probably true. It's very specialized work—it'd be difficult to find anyone else qualified to head the project. But still, Miles might have left his estate to someone else—"

"Not if he died intestate. Or Eddie might have had a plan for worming his way into his uncle's good graces. He was very resourceful. At any rate, I don't think Miles would have survived you by much."

Hannah drew a breath of dismay. "Not Miles, too?" Patrick's arm went round her shoulders.

"And why not?" Kincaid shrugged. He closed his umbrella and shook it. The drizzle had subsided to drips. "Our Eddie was a dab hand with a sedative as well as the blunt instrument. I imagine Eddie's old mum had a little help in crashing that car—"

"You'd never have proved it," said Patrick.

"No. Nor that he sedated Janet the night he murdered Sebastian."

"But what about Sebastian and Penny?"

"Victims of both circumstance and their own characters. Eddie said Sebastian saw him going into your room that night. Opportunist that he was, Eddie must have been looking for a way to kill you that would look accidental. It's my guess Sebastian couldn't resist needling him about what he'd seen, and Eddie couldn't take a chance on anyone connecting him with you after the fact."

"And Penny?"

Kincaid hesitated, a sense of his own culpability still strong. "We'll never be absolutely certain. I think Penny saw both Patrick and Eddie go into Cassie's office." Patrick nodded assent. "She wanted to be fair, to give both of you a chance to come forward before she spoke. Unfortunately, she picked the wrong man to confront first. Eddie Lyle didn't play by the rules."

"I still don't understand how he knew I'd be here this week—"

"Remember your burglary? You told me you'd felt violated."

"That long ago?" Hannah stared vacantly into the churchyard as she thought. "Yes. It was just after I'd signed the timeshare agreement. I remember I thought my papers had been gone through, but nothing was missing."

"And Eddie borrowed the money to buy into the timeshare just weeks afterwards," Kincaid said.

"Still, it was all circumstantial," said Patrick, his lawyer's instinct intact.

"But the prints on the handkerchief. You said—"

Kincaid answered Hannah gently. "The report still hasn't come back from the lab, but it's highly unlikely they found anything. It's a chancy technique."

Hannah closed her eyes, her face white. "A bluff? It was all a bluff?"

Kincaid nodded. "It seemed the thing to do."

Patrick shut Hannah's umbrella with a jerk and reached for Kincaid's hand. "I wouldn't like to play poker with you." He smiled, his charm reasserting itself. "I'll wait for you, Hannah." He turned away down the walk.

Hannah looked at Kincaid for a long moment. "I don't know what to say. I have to thank you. If you hadn't—"

"I'd rather you didn't. Gratitude isn't the best ingredient for a friendship. Do you think we might . . ." Kincaid trailed off, not quite sure what he wanted to suggest. Lunch when she came to town? A polite exchange of Christmas cards? Hannah had a lifetime's experience as a very private person—somehow he couldn't envision her feeling comfortable with him after their forced intimacy.

Hannah hesitated, her expression lacking the assurance that had seemed so natural to her. "I don't know. Not just yet, I think. Things are going to be difficult enough for a while."

"Yes." Kincaid looked toward Patrick, idling halfway down the walk.

Hannah followed his gaze. "I thought a lot about

what I wanted, what I needed, in those months I was looking for Patrick. Somehow," she smiled a little ruefully, "I managed to leave Patrick's needs out of the equation altogether, and it may be delicate going at first, finding the right balance. How we'll end up I can't say."

"You'll be all right." He smiled at her, then bent forward to kiss her cheek.

"Goodbye, Duncan." Hannah turned from him and caught Patrick up. They moved away down the walk, fair head bent over dark.

Kincaid made his way slowly toward the car park, absently avoiding the puddles standing in the cobbled street. He felt drained and somehow dissatisfied, as if all the tidying up of loose ends had left him dangling.

He turned the corner and looked up as someone bumped his shoulder. A woman in a bright yellow slicker hurried along in front of him. Her light brown hair curled damply about her head and she swung her handbag in rhythm with her stride.

Kincaid sprinted to catch up with her, his heart pounding. He touched her shoulder. "Anne?"

The woman turned to him, startled. Her face was unfamiliar.

Gemma stuck her head around the door of Kincaid's office. "Finished?"

"Now I am." He swept everything off his desk and shoved it in the drawer.

"Great filing system," Gemma said, eyeing the clear surface dubiously.

"At least it's out of the way." Kincaid stood up and

stretched. They had driven back to London separately, agreeing to face their accumulated avalanche of paper while still off duty.

Gemma came a few steps into the room and wrinkled her nose in distaste at the heavy odor of stale cigarettes. "Been having conferences in here while you were gone, have they?"

Kincaid grinned. "The evidence is irrefutable. Drink?"

Gemma considered. "Just a quick one."

They avoided the Yard canteen, with its unavoidable shop talk, and made for the pub down Wilfred Street. Kincaid elbowed his way to the bar and returned to their usual corner table with drinks, wine for himself and lager and lime for Gemma. "Ugh." He made a face. "Don't know how you drink that stuff." Kincaid always criticized, and Gemma never changed her order, probably, he thought, out of pure cantankerousness.

"Practice." Gemma took a good swallow of her drink and grinned. They sat quietly for a few minutes, the pub's Saturday night clamor eddying around them, until Gemma pushed her chair back a bit and sighed. "I do need to be getting home, though. Toby will be missing his mum."

"Yes." Kincaid imagined the welcome awaiting Gemma, and for an instant envy ran through him. He shook it off and forced a smile. "I wish . . ." What did he wish? That he hadn't gone to Followdale at all, in which case Hannah might have died, too?

Gemma thumped her glass down on the table and he raised his eyes to find an unexpected understanding in hers. The corner of her mouth twitched. "If wishes were horses, my old mum used to say—"

"Right." They smiled at each other companionably.

"Better luck next time?" Gemma suggested.

Kincaid raised his glass. "Cheers."

The adventure doesn't end for
Gemma James and Duncan Kincaid.
Join Gemma in the Scottish Highlands as she
learns that her oldest and dearest friend has hidden
a secret past—one that will lead to murder . . .

Turn the page to preview

Now May You Weep

The next new mystery from
award-winning author Deborah Crombie

1

Gemma James sat at a café table at the Chelsea Farmer's Market, finishing a lunch of plaice, chips and fresh peas. She supposed she should have chosen something slimming and fashionable, like rocket salad with Parmesan, but the warm, dreamy quality of the day had inspired comfort food. Now, for the first time in many months, she realized she was momentarily free of the nagging sense of loss that had become her constant companion. It would come back, she knew that, but for the moment she was content.

It was a perfectly glorious mid-May day with a clear aquamarine sky, a sun that tinged the newly-leafed trees with green fire and soaked into the skin of her bare arms and face like a benediction, and a sharp little breeze that blew fitfully from the northeast, providing a gentle reminder that such idylls do not last forever.

Signaling the waitress for the bill, Gemma gathered her packages a little nearer on the bench, like a mother duckling protecting her chicks. She had done odds and ends of Saturday shopping, but her prize lay concealed in a large pink and gold striped bag. She had bought, for the first time in her life, a hat. Stopping into the milliner's shop in Kensington Church Road on a whim, she had come out with a confection of cream straw, trimmed with burnt-cream ribbons and a lavender-colored rose.

Then, of course, she'd had to find a dress to do justice to the hat, a frock of lavender linen that set off her coppery hair. But where would she wear such things? Certainly not to work—the thought of turning up at Notting Hill Police Station in such an ensemble made her smile. Nor were the dress and hat suitable for the rough and tumble outings with boys and dogs that normally constituted her off-duty life.

As she sipped the last of her coffee and gazed at the hedges of California lilac bordering the café, a poster for the upcoming Chelsea Flower Show caught her eye. Even though she'd heard about the annual event since childhood, it had never occurred to her that she might actually attend. But why not? she thought suddenly. Sunshine, flowers, and an opportunity to dress up—what could be better? They could all go, she and Duncan and Toby and Kit. It had been months since she'd suggested a family outing, so they could hardly refuse her—and besides, if they were going to be householders, she had better learn something about gardening.

Pleased with her scheme, Gemma took the bus back to Notting Hill, feeling anew a rush of pride as she saw the brown and white house with it's cherry-red front door. The house on the corner of St. John's Gardens belonged to the sister of Duncan's boss at the Yard, Chief Superintendent Childs. When the owners had gone to Singapore for five years, Gemma and Duncan had taken the house on a long lease.

When Duncan and the boys came in, looking appealingly disheveled from their afternoon in the park, she told them her plan.

At least Duncan looked appealingly disheveled, she amended, with his thick chestnut hair falling over his brow, his gray eyes sparkling from the exercise and fresh air. On the other hand, twelve-year-old Kit looked damp and slightly sunburned, while Toby, her four-year-old, looked as if he'd rolled in a mud puddle. Before she could say "bath," Toby had disappeared from sight, leaving Kit, who grimaced at her proposal.

She'd thought Kit might roll his eyes and moan a bit, a flower show not being high on the list of activities considered exciting by a boy on the cusp of adolescence, but she had not expected Duncan's eyebrows to reach their vertical limit.

"Flowers?" he said. "You don't know anything about flowers."

With a last withering glance in her direction, Kit left the room in search of Toby and the two dogs, Geordie and Tess.

"I have to start somewhere, haven't I?" Gemma defended herself to Duncan. "If we're to have a garden. Besides," she added, "I have a hat." She lifted it carefully from the bag and peeled back the swaddling layers of tissue. Rotating the hat in her fingers until she found just the right angle, she placed it on her head.

His face was all the mirror she needed. "I thought you didn't like hats," she teased, laughing.

Closing his mouth, he said, "No. But I hadn't seen this particular hat, on this particular person. I suppose I'll have to take you to hobnob with the Chelsea set, after all. You do look impossibly fetching." He leaned forward to kiss her, muttering, "Awkward bloody things, though," then drew back, frowning. "But won't the show be sold out, love?"

"Oh." Gemma removed the hat and sat down, feeling deflated. "I suppose you're right. I didn't think of that."

"I'm sure we can manage," Duncan said, too quickly. Gemma knew how much he hated for her to be disappointed in even the smallest thing, as if her recent loss had rendered her so vulnerable she must be protected from the most trivial of blows.

"No, it's all right," she assured him. "We'll do something else. A picnic? We could—"

The doorbell rang, saving her from having to invent a suitable alternative.

"Expecting someone?" he queried.

"Not on a Saturday afternoon, unless it's Wesley. I'll just put the kettle on." She turned to the cooker as Duncan went to the door, but when he returned, he led not their young friend Wesley Howard, who sometimes helped out with the children, but Hazel Cavendish.

Hazel had been Gemma's landlady until the previous Christmas, when Gemma and Duncan had taken the enormous step of combining their households—and their children—and she was still Gemma's closet friend.

"Hazel!" Gemma exclaimed, hugging her. "What a surprise. Did you bring Holly with you?" Holly was Hazel's four-year-old daughter, and Toby's bosom friend.

"She's already gone to find the boys. Sorry to drop in like this, but I was in the neighborhood, and Holly's been missing Toby dreadfully."

"In the neighborhood?" Gemma repeated, as Duncan disappeared in the direction of the study. Notting Hill was a long way from Hazel's house in Islington.

"I thought I'd take Holly to the market," Hazel explained, meaning the Saturday market on Portobello Road. "And I wanted to go to *Books for Cooks.*" The tiny bookshop on Elgin Crescent was a haven for serious foodies.

"Why didn't you tell me what you had in mind? I'd have come with you." Gemma studied her friend, noticing the smudges beneath her dark eyes, the new hollows beneath the well-defined cheekbones. For a moment, Gemma wondered if Hazel could be ill, but she dismissed the thought as quickly as it had come. Hazel—therapist, perfect wife, mother and gourmet vegetarian cook—was the healthiest, most balanced person Gemma had ever known. "Sit," she ordered. "I'll bring you a cuppa."

As she busied herself with mugs and teabags, she thought of all the times Hazel had ministered to her in her Islington kitchen, dispensing tea and advice with equal generosity. Gemma had lived for almost two years in the garage flat belonging to Hazel and her husband, Tim Canvendish. As Holly was the same age as Toby, Hazel had cared for both children while Gemma was at work.

Then, the previous autumn, Gemma had been promoted to Detective Inspector with the Metropolitan Police, assigned to Notting Hill Police Station. The promotion, although a goal long set, had not come without cost. Not only had it brought long hours and increased responsibility, it had meant leaving Scotland Yard, ending her working partnership with Superintendent Duncan Kincaid.

But if their professional separation had proved unexpectedly painful, the new job had meant they no longer had to keep their personal relationship under wraps. It had been that, as well the pregnancy that had later ended so tragically, that had encouraged Gemma to leave the security of Hazel's little flat and move in with Duncan.

"I'm glad you came," she said to Hazel as she returned to the table with the tea things. "I've missed you. I thought I'd get to Islington more often than I have."

Hazel accepted a mug. "That's one of the reasons I came—and I have to admit I *did* have an ulterior motive." She glanced at Gemma, then fixed her gaze on her cup. "I thought it would be nice if we could spend some time together—some genuine uninterrupted-by-children time," she added, flashing Gemma a smile as the sound of shouting came from the garden.

"I know it's awfully short notice, but I've been invited to a cookery class in the Highlands next weekend, and I was hoping you might go with me."

"A cookery class?" Gemma asked, puzzled. "The Scottish Highlands?"

"It's a weekend course at a small guesthouse," Hazel

hastened to explain. "The owner is making quite a name for himself as a chef. His wife is an old school friend of mine, so I have a bit of an *in*."

"But—"

"It's only for four days. We'd go up on the Friday and come back on Monday. Could you get away from work, do you think? You haven't had a holiday in ages."

"Well, I suppose I could—but you know I'm not up to your standards," Gemma protested, thinking of some of her recent kitchen disasters. She had yet to master the oil-fired cooker in the new house, in spite of Hazel's helpful advice.

"The course is supposed to be very personalized," Hazel assured her. "And it's lovely country."

Gemma remembered Hazel telling her she'd spent part of her childhood in the Highlands. "Is this near where you grew up?"

"It's in Strathspey—that's the valley of the River Spey," Hazel explained, without really answering the question. "We'd take the train to Aviemore, and then it's not far by car. Say you'll come, Gemma, please."

"What about Tim, and Holly?"

"Tim's parents are coming up from Brighten for a few days. I'm sure they'll manage just fine without me. And Duncan wouldn't mind having the boys on his own for a bit, would he?"

"No." Gemma thought of the flower show, and of their proposed family outing. "But—" She was about to refuse, to tell Hazel they'd already made plans for the coming weekend, when she saw the look of tense expectation on her friend's usually serene face. How could she say no if it meant so much to Hazel, even though she found herself dreading even a brief separation from her family.

"I don't suppose," she said slowly, "that there will be an opportunity to wear a hat?"

Donald Brodie lifted one section of the wort vat's heavy wooden cover and breathed in the heady aroma of fermenting yeast and barley. He had been fascinated by this part of the distilling process even as a child, when his father had had to lift him up so that he could peer down into the bubbling depths of the vat. It still amazed him that the liquid produced by combining ground, dried barley with hot water could produce a final product as elegant as a malt whiskey—but perhaps that was why he had never lost his fierce love of the business.

Even today, when he had so much else at stake, he had gone round the premises after work finished, as was his habit. He closed the vat and crossed the steel mesh flooring to the stairs, his footsteps echoing in the building's cavernous space. Once down to ground level, he locked the door behind him and stepped out into the yard, stopping a moment to survey his domain.

Tomorrow he would entice Hazel into coming here—a not so subtle reminder of her heritage and of what he had to offer—but then, he had grown tired of subtlety. The phone calls, the notes, the whispered lunches in discreet London restaurants; all those things had served their purpose, but now it was time for Hazel to decide what she wanted from her life. His friends, John and Louise Innes, had done their part in getting

Hazel here by arranging the cookery weekend; now he must do his—and soon, he thought, his pulse quickening as he looked at his watch.

The mobile phone on his belt vibrated. Slipping it from its holder, he glanced at the caller ID. Allison. Damn and blast! He hesitated, then let the call ring through to voice mail. If there was one complication he didn't need this weekend, it was dealing with Allison. He'd told her he had a business meeting—true enough, with Heather, the distillery's manager, insisting on bringing Pascal Benoit, the Frenchman whose conglomerate was salivating over Benvulin. Not that he could put off Allison indefinitely, mind, but a few more days couldn't hurt, at least until he saw which way the land lay with Hazel. After all, he'd never been one to burn his bridges unnecessarily.

With that thought, he went to wash and change for the evening, whistling all the while.

"What if they don't eat meat?" Louise Innes stood at the kitchen sink, filling vases for the evening's flower arrangements. Although her back was turned to her husband, John knew her forehead would be puckered in the small frown that had begun to leave a permanent crease. "Did you not think to ask?"

"I assumed someone would have said, if there was a problem," John answered, keeping his voice even but whisking a little harder at the batter for the herb and mushroom crepes that would serve as that night's starter. Although the kitchen was his province, the house Louise's, she didn't mind questioning his menu choices.

"And venison, especially—"

"Och, it's a Highland specialty, Louise. And Hazel Cavendish is your old school friend— I should think ye'd know if she dinna eat meat."

"This weekend was a bad idea from start to finish," Louise said pettishly. Her English accent always grew more precise in proportion to her degree of irritation, as if to repudiate his Scottishness. "I haven't seen Hazel since the summer after university, and I don't approve of the whole business. She's married, for heaven's sake, with a child. You've always let Donald Brodie talk you into things you shouldn't." His wife pulled half a dozen roses from the pail of flowers John had brought from Inverness that morning, laid them across a cutting board and sliced off the bottom inch of stems with a sharp knife. The ruthlessness in the quick chop made him think of small creatures beheaded.

Louise had taken a flower-arranging course the previous year, attacking the project with the efficiency that marked all her endeavors. Although she could now produce picture-perfect bouquets that drew raves from the guests, he found that the arrangements lacked that certain creative touch—a last blossom out of place, perhaps—that would have made them truly lovely.

"If that's the case, perhaps ye should take some responsibility," he snapped at her. "It was you introduced me to Donald, ye ken." He knew he was being defensive, because he'd allowed Donald to wheedle him into taking Hazel and her friend without charge, and this meant they'd turned away paying guests on weekend at the beginning of their busiest season. But then, he had his reasons for keeping on Donald Brodie's good side, and the less Louise knew about that, the better.

Resting the heel of his hand on his knife, he quartered the mushrooms before chopping them finely. A glance told him Louise still had her back to him, her head bent over her flowers. He felt his temper ease as he watched her. She might not have approved of the arrangements for the weekend, but she would do her best to make sure everything went smoothly.

"You'll be glad to see Hazel again, will ye not?" he asked, in an attempt to placate.

Louise's shoulders relaxed and she tilted her head, her neat blond hair falling to one side like a lifted bird's wing. "It's been a long time," she answered. "I'm not sure I'll know what to say."

"I'm sure Donald will fill in the gaps," he said lightly, then cursed himself for a fool. Louise would never be able to resist such an opening.

"That's the problem, isn't it?" She turned towards him, a spray of sweet peas in her hand. "Donald always fills in the gaps, and never mind the consequences. He's as reckless as his father, if not more so. Heather's livid, and we have to get on with her once this weekend is over."

"I don't see why it should make any difference to Heather," he said stubbornly. "Hazel's her cousin, after all. Ye'd think she'd be glad to—"

"You don't see anything!" Spots of color appeared high on Louise's cheekbones. "How can you be so dense, John? You know how precarious things are at the distillery just now—"

"I still don't see what that has to do with your friend

Hazel coming for a weekend." He added a clove of garlic to his board and chopped it with unnecessary force.

She turned, and he saw from her expression that it was too late to salvage the argument, or the evening. "What's got into you, John?" she spat at him. "How could you possibly have thought I'd approve of your conspiring to sabotage another woman's marriage?"